Cork on

Cork on the Water

Macdonald Hastings

Greycliff Publishing Company
Helena

©1951 by Macdonald Hasting
This edition published 1999 by Greycliff Publishing Company

Cover illustration by Philomena O'Neill, Seattle, Washington
Cover design by Geoffrey Wyatt, Helena, Montana
Printed by Advanced Litho Printing, Great Falls, Montana

10 09 08 07 06 05 04 03 02 01 00   10 9 8 7 6 5 4 3 2 1

Library of Congress Cataloging-in-Publication Data

Hastings, Macdonald.
      Cork on the water / Macdonald Hastings.
            p.   cm.
      ISBN 1-890373-06-0
      I. Title.
   PR6058.A79C67   1999
   823'.914—dc21   99-36890
                                                             CIP

To the memory of my friend
CLAUDE WILSON

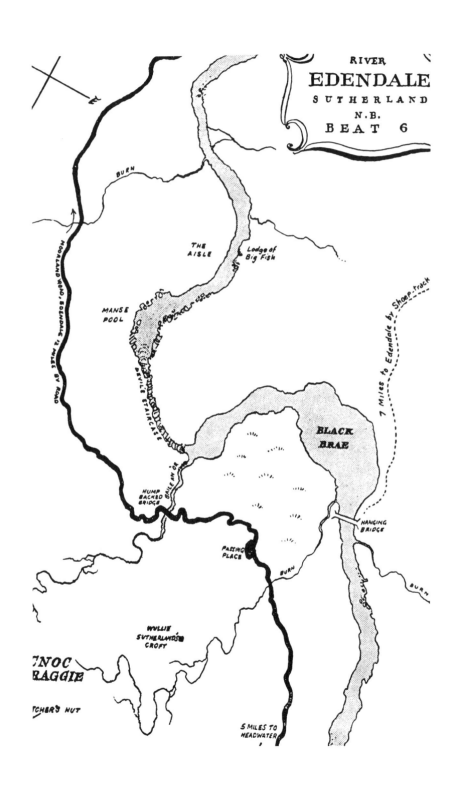

One

THE day, the unforgettable day, was July 4th, 1949. The time was about seven in the evening. Six hundred and sixty-seven road miles from London, on a Highland stream whose peaty waters winked blood-red in the sunlight, a solitary angler was battling with the biggest salmon he had hooked in his life.

Lt.-Colonel Adrian de Crecy Johnson was fishing the River Edendale for the twenty-ninth summer in succession. On the first Sunday of April each year, immediately after settling the affairs of the Bagnor Foxhounds, in Shropshire, of which he was honorary secretary, he travelled north to Sutherland to fish salmon until the last day in July. On July 31st, or the nearest Sunday, he returned to Shropshire in time for the opening of cub-hunting and the revival of the ever-open conflict as to how much the hunt should pay for the excellent sport which the foxes enjoyed slaughtering the local chickens. But, to Colonel Johnson, the most serious business of the year was his annual engagement with the salmon that came up from the sea at Edendale. Every day of the week, except Sunday, when he was forbidden to fish by the laws of Scotland and actually prevented from fishing by the watchful eyes of the Wee Frees—the native Sabbatarians whom he detested even more than the fowls of the tenant farmers in Shropshire, and only slightly less than the Government, whom he deemed wholly responsible for the steadily declining income from his investments—Colonel Johnson kept his fly on the water, as long as the water was fishable, from April to July, from 9.30 a.m. until double whisky time.

Mr. Mackenzie, who kept the Estuary Hotel at the mouth of the river where Colonel Johnson made his summer quarters, always advised the occasional visitors, up for a few weeks fishing, not to put up their rods without having a word, which meant buying a double whisky, with the Colonel first.

'He knows the river like his own countenance,' said Mr. Mackenzie, rolling the words round his mouth. 'He knows every trick of it and every stone, and sometimes I truly believe that he can recognize the verra fish running up the river to spawn that he watched go down to the sea as wee smolts.'

Admittedly, Mr. Mackenzie had a vested interest in boosting Colonel Johnson's reputation. In return, the Colonel, on being approached for his opinion, saw to it that all the expensive flies and casts which the visitors brought from London were discarded in favour of the local tackle which Mr. Mackenzie thoughtfully provided in the hotel store. Nevertheless, Mr. Mackenzie's appraisal of Colonel Johnson's skill as an angler was well founded. He did know every pool, every stickle, every rock and every bed of weeds on the River Edendale as other people know the road from home to the office and back again. For twenty-nine years, he had kept a daily record in his leather-bound fishing diary of the height of the river, its colour, its temperature; the state of the weather; the physical details of every fish that had come to his fly; the size and pattern of the fly he used; and the exact spots, on the six beats of the river, from the headwater loch to the sea pool, where he had hooked each of the two thousand nine hundred and seventy-two salmon which, up to July 4th, 1949, he had so far credited to his own rod.

Indeed, Colonel Johnson had applied himself to salmon-fishing with such single-minded purpose for so long that, with advancing years, he had acquired a noticeable resemblance to a salmon himself. His, though, was not the vigorous beauty of a fresh-run salmon, silver from the sea. Colonel Johnson, after years up the river, was a spent fish. He was lean and spindly-shanked. His chin reached up to his nose and his nose reached down to his chin in the pincer-shape of the jaws of an old cock salmon working his way down the river, back to the sea, after the exhaustion of spawning. In salmon-fishers' parlance, Colonel Johnson was an old kelt; discoloured, hungry-looking and, to all practical purpose, worthless.

When the great salmon took his fly on July 4th, 1949, Colonel Johnson, perched on his matchstick legs on the edge of a granite rock, was nearly jerked into the river. Another man would have been broken in the fish's first rush for freedom. A lesser angler, under the driving pressure on the tackle, would have lost control immediately in the snag-strewn broken water. Even Colonel Johnson, unprepared for the fish's cannon-ball strike, nearly botched it. For a breathtaking moment, in the salmon's first upstream rush, his rod point was dipping in the river. But he gave him line in time. The rod went into an arc and sensitively handling his reel, he began to play his fish.

In spite of his apparent calmness now that he was on

9

something like fighting terms with the salmon, Colonel Johnson was trembling with excitement. He was madly, ecstatically excited. He knew for a certainty that he was well-hooked into the fish of a lifetime. Forty pounds, fifty pounds, even sixty pounds, of fighting fresh-run salmon. It would be the biggest fish, spring fish included, ever caught on the River Edendale. It might even be the biggest fish taken by fair angling on a rod in the whole of the British Isles. There would be an article about it, probably a photograph too, in *Country Life*. Marston would want all the technical particulars—size and pattern of fly, temperature and condition of the water etc. etc.—for *The Fishing Gazette*. The editor of *The Field* would almost certainly invite him to call for a personal interview when he was passing through town at the end of the month on his way back to Shropshire. For, in spite of the fish's size, Colonel Johnson never doubted that he would land him. But it was going to be a tough fight. Even at that unforgettable moment in his career, he found time to curse the Government which had so impoverished him that he couldn't afford a ghillie to gaff his fish. By God, he could use a ghillie now.

For a moment, as the fish paused after another headlong rush which ran out the thirty-five yards of silk line to the hemp backing, Colonel Johnson glanced half-hopefully over his shoulder at the hill behind. But he knew that it was hopeless to expect to see anybody on the black slopes of Cnoc Craggie. The people fishing the other beats—each of them with a ghillie, blast them—were all down stream of him to-day; even if they hadn't gone home already. Here at the top of the strath, in this cup-shaped wasteland of heather-clad hills and outcroppings of granite rock, it was unlikely that there was a living soul within miles. The only evidence of human life was the deserted croft on the hill-face where Wully Sutherland had lived and died; the outline of his own battered motor-car parked in one of the passing places on the single track moorland road up the brae behind him; and the idiot-faced hill sheep sitting in the middle of the way in the certain knowledge that nothing would disturb them until another man came up to fish the top beat at 9.30 a.m. the next morning. He was alone with his fish in the most deserted stretch in the winding eighteen miles of the Edendale's course to the sea.

After that, he had no more time to look about him. The great fish, which had temporarily allowed himself to be led quietly down the stream, spun on his spade tail and raced up-river. Colonel Johnson knew at once that there was no turning him; he knew the river too. The salmon was running out of the glide of easy water where he had been hooked—a calm stretch between low grass banks which the ghillies called The Aisle—and he was driving straight through the Manse Pool into the turmoil of the Devil's Staircase above.

The Devil's Staircase was aptly named. It was a flight of rocks where the river-bed narrowed into a steep triangular gully between broken walls of red granite. In spate, the river stampeded through it, in clouds of mist, like a charge of white horses. Even in low water, as this was, the Devil's Staircase was a series of boiling cauldrons which spilt over from one shelf of rock to another; a ladder easy enough for a salmon to climb, but a place that any angler might dread. There was nothing to do except pray for luck and try to follow the fish.

For all his sixty-seven years and unprepossessing physique, Colonel Johnson was a fit man. Tearing line off his reel by hand to give the salmon all the slack he could to play about with, he leapt like an old goat along the rocky ledges of the river bank. He saw the black back of his fish twist in the white water as the salmon negotiated the fall at the top of the Manse Pool. And, as the fish drove on upstream, he noted that between his quarry and himself there were enough rocks sticking out of the river to break him half-a-dozen times over.

He clambered along the bank holding his rod point high above his head to keep the line clear of disaster. At the same time, he wondered what on earth to do next. It was obvious that the fish was travelling straight through the Devil's Staircase. He guessed correctly that he would make for the deep runnel in the roughs above. But, between himself and the roughs, on his own bank, lay a major obstacle. As he followed his fish, he was stopped short by a deep cutting in the rocks, too wide to jump, where a burn joined the river.

The burn, called Baile an Or, was one of the places where, in the old days, they used to pan for gold. And Colonel Johnson would have given a gold nugget to be free of it that fatal day. He wasn't wearing waders and the drop into the river was precipitous. But, to his credit, he never hesitated. Holding tightly on to his rod, he slid straight into the rough water.

Searching for a footing in the treacherous boulder-lined river-bed, he struggled on until, waist deep in the river, leaning forward on the current to support himself against it, he reached the edge of the deep run where the fish was lying. Where he hoped and prayed the fish was lying with the fly still firmly fixed in the back of its jaw.

When he tore off slack line to give the salmon a free run through the Devil's Staircase Colonel Johnson was sure that the fish hadn't broken him. What he couldn't know was whether the salmon had now got the line snagged round a rock; whether the fish had had the chance to break the frail gut cast, as he could do so easily if he could bring his great tail to bear; or whether he was lying there quietly at the bottom of the river believing that he had freed himself from the unexpected pressures which had imposed themselves so lately upon his liberty of movement.

Steadying himself in the water, Colonel Johnson carefully wound in line. He wound until the angle of the line from the rod stretched straight down into the water. Then, delicately tightening the pressure on the top joint, he felt for a movement.

The impossible had happened. The gamble had come off. The fish was still firmly hooked. As he increased the pressure of the rod, the salmon moved sluggishly in the stream. But Colonel Johnson wasn't deceived. He knew that this fish had plenty of fight in him yet. He reeled in gently and felt the salmon swimming towards him. A few yards more, and he might even see the fish. But the salmon would see him too. The game would be on again.

He watched his rod point and watched the water. Then he actually saw the salmon, deep in the clear water but not more than a rod's length from his feet. Sixty pounds, if he was an ounce, of magnificent fighting silver fish. He was so close that Colonel Johnson, with his experienced eye, could even spot a scar, obviously the mark of a seal-bite, in the salmon's shoulder. He held him as lightly as a sea trout in readiness for the next rush. But he didn't fear the fish this time. Above was the deep dark pool of the Black Brae. At the head of it was a leap which even a fish as big as this fish couldn't clear after the effort of fighting for twenty minutes, forty minutes—for the first time in his life, Colonel Johnson had omitted to look at his watch when he hooked the fish and he realized that he'd lost all count of time since—no fish could stand what this one had stood from a split-cane salmon rod in the hands of a master and then leap the Black Brae at the end of it.

The salmon made his next rush just as Colonel Johnson had anticipated; straight up the deep runnel in the middle of the rough water, into the glassy tail above, and then deep down into the heart of the Black Brae below the fall. With seventy yards of line stripped off the reel, the fish stopped.

Colonel Johnson, arms aching with the strain of handling the taut rod, breathing heavily from his efforts to hold his ground in the fast current of the river, felt confident that he could now take his time.

Keeping an even pressure on the fish, digging the butt of his rod comfortably into the pit of his stomach so that he could control it with one hand, he cautiously manœuvred himself out of the stream and on to the bank again. Back on dry land, in his own element, he advanced slowly upstream towards the fish, recovering line as he walked and considering the next move in the battle.

The Black Brae was notably one of the best pools on the river to play a fish, but it was a difficult pool to gaff one in; hopeless without a ghillie and impossible in a meeting with a great fish like this one.

In the huge bowl of the glen, the Black Brae was like a plughole cut into the solid rock at the bottom. The water that overflowed from the loch about five miles upstream funnelled into the Black Brae like white suds down a sink. Two burns that scarred a passage down the steep slopes of the hills joined the river there. Even when the river was low, the Black Brae was full of oily water which surged and whirlpooled and moved in strange cross currents about its rocky bed. The pool was enclosed in a rough circle of high rocks, high enough to unnerve many people who looked down from the brink into the water, but not too precipitous to deny an agile person a footing on the sharp ledges of the rock strata. It was a tempting place to fish because the salmon lay all along it waiting their turn to leap the fall. And it was a good place, as Colonel Johnson remembered with satisfaction, to tire a fish out when you had hooked him.

As he climbed along one of the rocky shelves on the bank above the pool, holding his fish, he made up his mind to play out the fight where he stood. When the salmon was dead beat, and only then, he would lead him downstream to a gap in the bank below, where he could gaff him in easy water. But he realized that he had no hope of gaffing the fish for some time yet. Mackenzie at the hotel would be wondering why he hadn't come back to dinner. They might even send out Jock, the hotel porter, with the cab to see what happened to him. All the better if Jock arrived in time to help him gaff the fish. Colonel Johnson was beginning to feel very tired. He was cold from his soaking in the water; and, although he had never had such a thought when he was fishing before, he felt lonely and a little apprehensive.

The salmon was now sulking on the bottom. Colonel Johnson gave him pressure with sideways pulls of the rod. But the salmon never moved. He had his nose down in the bed of the river and he was using his tail to try and shake himself free. The danger was that, after this long fight, the hold of the tiny hook in the fish's jaw might loosen. It was essential to get him on the move again.

Colonel Johnson twanged the line with his fingers to

send the vibrations down to the salmon, with a view to irritating him into action. He slipped an angler's lead on to the line and let it slip down to tap the salmon on his nose. But there was no movement. The sun was falling, it was becoming colder and Colonel Johnson heard the cry of a barn owl starting the night's hunting.

From his position near the crown of the rocky bank of the Black Brae, he looked behind him once more in the wild hope that there might be another human being abroad in the glen. And there, on the slopes of Cnoc Craggie, standing beside the shuttered croft where Wully Sutherland used to live, he saw the figure of a man watching him. Colonel Johnson gave a wild shout. He whistled, he cooeed, he waved his handkerchief; but the man on the hill made no movement. Colonel Johnson started to climb higher up the bank but, as he did so, his tired and trembling arms played him false. He gave the rod a dangerous jolt. The hold on the fish appeared to slip but, mercifully, as he raised the rod point, he felt it tighten. The pressure eased, the bend on the rod changed, and the line started to move again in the water. The feel of the salmon, he thought, was somehow different, but he was moving; at last, sluggishly and heavily, he was moving again. Colonel Johnson gritted himself for the final effort.

He leant back on the bank and, labouring his strength, pulled the rod towards him. There was a slow swirl in the dark waters. A chain of gaseous bubbles burst on the surface. With a retch of horror, he saw that he was now fast hooked, not in the salmon of a lifetime, but in the decomposed corpse of a man.

The corpse, bobbing head down on the surface, floated obscenely down the pool. Caught in the edge of a whirlpool, it revolved slowly into a bay of slack water under the bank. Then it stopped.

White with exhaustion, ruled by habit, Colonel Johnson held up his rod-point and judged the pressure on his line as if he was still playing a salmon fresh-run from the sea. For a few moments, he stared at his catch. Then, as the horror of the thing took hold of him, he threw aside his rod. He turned his back on the Black Brae and he ran, stumbling through the bracken, shouting and screaming for help till the seagulls and the oyster-catchers screamed and whistled in astonishment too.

As he fumbled with the door of his car, he was reminded of the figure he had seen standing on the hill. He looked for him, but he was gone. The man had disappeared in that desolate waste of moorland like a creature of the Highland mists.

Two

THE date, on the silver mounted desk calendar, was Friday, July 15th; eleven days after Colonel Johnson's unlucky adventure on the River Edendale.

Mr. Montague Cork, general manager of the Anchor Accident Insurance Co., was sitting in his oak panelled room, in the company's head offices in the City of London, listening to the friendly tick of the Queen Anne clock on the shelf over the fireplace and wondering what on earth he was going to do with himself for the remainder of the day. Mr. Cork had cleared up all his outstanding work preparatory to going on his summer holidays. And like most men who lead busy and useful lives, Mr. Cork, released from the discipline of labour, felt as restless as a town-bred dog in a world without lamp-posts.

To tell the truth, Mr. Cork resembled a wise old dog himself. His deeply-lined face, big nose and sad gentle eyes, with dewlaps underneath them, gave him the appearance of an old hound; a kindly old bloodhound wearing half-glasses and a wing collar, and dressed in a black suit with pin-striped trousers. Mr. Cork, although he was personally quite unaware of it, was a formidable-looking person, but then Mr. Cork was a formidable man. If he had been a barrister, as he might have been quite easily because he had the brains as well as the face for a wig, he would have been a public figure. As it was, in that honeycomb of offices round the Royal Exchange, in the world-wide financial network which has its centre in the City of London, Montague Cork's was a name to magic with. It was axiomatic that, when London was called upon to take an insurance risk, Montague Cork's initials were the first that the brokers sought to get. If Montague Cork wrote his line at the top of the list to cover a film star's legs, a Turkish battleship, a tame giraffe or a sky-scraper in New York, the rest of the underwriters followed him. Mr. Cork's judgment, like his signature, was legendary. But Mr. Cork no more thought about that than he did about his appearance.

Like many another successful man, Mr. Cork was cursed with the nagging habit of self-criticism. Just at the moment he was quite ridiculously ashamed to find himself in the position of having nothing to do. He was wondering what any of the juniors might think if they came into his office and discovered him, theoretically speaking, twiddling his thumbs. He was checking over in his mind, for the hundredth time, whether in the excitement of going for his holidays, he had incalculably overlooked something important.

As he always did when he was unsettled in his thoughts, Mr. Cork felt in his hip pocket for his gold cigarette case: a rather ostentatious case he always felt, but Phoebe had given it to him on their twenty-fifth wedding anniversary. What a long time ago that seemed now. It was a long time ago too. Mr. Cork reminded himself that he was now sixty-one.

He picked out a Passing Cloud, the brand of cigarette he had smoked ever since he saved his first thousand pounds, tapped the ends with a nervous gesture on the back of his case, and, in his mind, started checking over the work again. The Board meeting, thank heaven, was over; not that the other directors had anything to worry about. The company was flourishing and, although more people were trying to kill themselves on the roads than ever, even the Anchor's profit on motor risks was well up. Mr. Cork put that down to his unswerving policy not to accept risks from anybody with an accident record, or professions with a proclivity to motor-smashes. No bookmakers, for example. Bookmakers, by the nature of their jobs, were always driving in the accident-prone areas of race-meetings. Further, it was Mr. Cork's experience that bookmakers generally drove cars which were too big and too fast, too recklessly. No, no commission agents for Mr. Cork. And, if a commission agent pretended to be something else, like that fellow who described himself as a dealer, it could go to arbitration as far as he was concerned. The Anchor wouldn't pay.

Mr. Cork suddenly wondered whether his ruling on this matter was clear to all heads of departments. It would be maddening if they slipped up on a little thing like that while he was away on his holidays. His finger was already on the switch of the house telephone before he checked himself. No, he mustn't do that. He must get out of the habit of not trusting other people. Baker knew what his instructions were, and it would be most unlike Baker if he fell down on them. Mr. Cork rebuked himself for a bad habit he had got into when the whole show depended on him, and him alone. After all, he would be retiring in a few years; and then the company would have to worry along without him. In fact, he was probably only fooling himself, he reflected, that he mattered even now. The whole business these days ran on tram lines. It wasn't once a year now that *his* instinct, his long experience of the game, was really needed. His instinct. All his life, he had worked on instinct. It was the secret, he supposed, of such success that he had had, the success that the company had had. But it was hardly ever needed now.

Thinking back, Mr. Cork remembered with a grim smile the day when he cancelled that accident insurance for £100,000 on a rich American. Twenty-nine, that was the year of the depression, wasn't it, when they all went bust in America? Mr. Cork had looked over his accident risks one day, when they came up for renewal, and found this one on the life of a New York financier.

' If I was him,' Mr. Cork had said to Baker, his assistant, 'and I had a wife and children and saw all my investments going to blazes, I'd arrange an accident on the strength of a policy like this.'

He had instructed Baker to tell the brokers that the Anchor would not renew and, within a week of the policy running out, the fellow had stepped accidentally on a live electric rail. Somebody else had to pay.

But things like that happened so rarely. These days, Mr. Cork reflected, he might just as well not come to the office at all; probably better for the new generation if he didn't. He ought to buy Phoebe a nice house in the country and spend the rest of his life doing his tapestry, going fishing and playing a little golf. Good sport fishing; it lasted a man right up to the time when he dropped off the hooks.

Thoughts of fishing reminded Mr. Cork of his holiday and that he had some flies to collect which Hardy was tying for him. He half wondered whether he would leave the office at once, waste some time looking at the tackle in Hardy's shop on the way home and surprise Phoebe by arriving in time for tea. But no. After all, it was the last day at the office. Somebody might want to see him and it would create a very bad impression if it was discovered that Mr. Cork had left before the proper time. Miss Scott, his secretary, might even have some letters for him to attend to. Mr. Cork listened, half-hopefully, for the sound of typing in Miss Scott's office next door. But there was none. He looked at the blank page in his diary: no appointments either. Of course not. Miss Scott, with her usual efficiency, had drawn a blue line through the pages of the appointment book for the next three weeks.

Three weeks in Scotland, salmon-fishing. That was the one recreation in which Mr. Cork could put work entirely out of his mind. With a rod in his hand, and the chance of a fish, Mr. Cork was a completely contented human being, even if, as he believed, he was such a bad fisherman. It was a pity that Phoebe couldn't come this year. Mr. Cork never enjoyed himself quite so much without his wife. But still, Phoebe needed a rest from the responsibility of looking after him. And Mr. Cork could be sure that she would see to it that everything was beautifully arranged for his own holiday. She would send all the right clothes. The car would be properly packed under her instructions and everything, from waders to whisky flask, would be provided. There was nothing to worry about in Phoebe's department. Mr. Cork realized that, in his wife, he was an extremely fortunate man.

Indeed, Mr. Cork thought to himself that he was fortunate all round. He had good health, apart from an occasional bout of fibrositis; he had all the money that any reasonable man could want; he had a home he loved; he was proud of his business; and he was satisfied that his own was the most beautifully fitted office in the City of

London. All Mr. Cork wished for at the moment, as he tapped another Passing Cloud on the back of his case, was that he could think out some way of passing the time.

When someone knocked at the door, Mr. Cork almost rose from his chair with pleasure. For a moment, he was conscious of a temptation to scatter some papers in front of him and look busy; but he immediately rejected the idea as dishonest. If Mr. Cork wasn't working, then Mr. Cork had better admit it.

In answer to his call, Mr. Smithson, the claims manager, came into the office. At once, Mr. Cork caught himself calculating what had brought Smithson to see him. Was it something that he had carelessly omitted to discuss with Smithson? Was Smithson reluctant to take responsibility for a decision which, in the future, he must learn to carry on his own shoulders? In spite of himself, Mr. Cork snapped out: 'What do you want, Smithson?' for all the world as if he resented the intrusion. It was a habit he always regretted and constantly tried to check in himself. But he couldn't help it. And the result he supposed was that all the staff thought he was an old bear. Hastily trying to put things right, he offered Smithson a chair.

'I thought I'd done with work for a few weeks,' he said.

'It's nothing that we need to trouble you about, Mr. Cork,' said Mr. Smithson, 'but before you leave for your holidays we thought you might be interested in a rather unusual claim we've had to-day.'

Mr. Smithson settled himself in the chair on the opposite side of Mr. Cork's desk, and turned the leaves of a file of papers.

'It's for £25,000 on the life of a man named Gabriel Daggers, who insured with us only five months ago. To be

23

precise,' said Mr. Smithson, Mr. Smithson was always precise, 'we accepted him on February 16th of this year.'

'An expensive risk,' said Mr. Cork philosophically. 'No queries, I suppose? We've got to pay?'

'There's no question about that,' said Mr. Smithson.

Mr. Cork felt like remarking: then why on earth do you bother me just as I'm going on my holidays? But, recalling his weakness, he restrained himself, and, peering over the top of his half-glasses, waited for Smithson to give his own explanation.

'What I thought you'd be interested to know, sir,' said Mr. Smithson, wilting a little under the embarrassing stare of his general manager, 'I thought you might like to be informed of the circumstances in which the insured met his death.'

'Well?' said Mr. Cork.

'He was accidentally drowned when he was out salmon-fishing in Sutherland and, seeing that you're such a keen fisherman yourself, Mr. Cork, I thought that may be . . .'

Mr. Smithson started to dry up. As he was talking, the doubt had grown in his mind whether the idea of telling Mr. Cork about the claim, which seemed such a good idea when he was discussing it with the people in his own department, was really wise after all. Mr. Cork detested being bothered unnecessarily, and Mr. Smithson could never be quite sure how the G.M. would react.

'What I was thinking, Mr. Cork,' Mr. Smithson went on lamely, 'was that, since you are just leaving on a salmon-fishing holiday, and, since you happened to mention to me that Mrs. Cork was not accompanying you this year . . .'

'You thought you'd better warn me to be careful, eh,

Smithson? Or perhaps you were thinking of suggesting that in view of my own predilections for fishing, I ought to increase my personal insurances?'

Mr. Cork gave one of his grim smiles. It was decent of little Smithson to think of it. Still, for Smithson to bring this claim to him to hear about, especially as there was no query, was obviously a lot of nonsense. From time to time, it was well known that people get drowned in rivers; bad luck that, in this case, the Anchor carried a heavy accident risk insurance on the man concerned; but, for all that, death while fishing was an unlikely occurrence and the chances were that the Anchor would never get another claim like it again. Surely Smithson realized that.

Mr. Smithson was cursing himself for ever mentioning the matter to Mr. Cork at all. After all, he was only telling the old boy something which, as a fisherman, he thought he would be interested to hear. Instead of that, the whole business had somehow got twisted up into a suggestion that the G.M. ought to increase his own insurance.

But Mr. Cork, with one of those sudden changes of manner which always puzzled his employees, was offering Mr. Smithson a Passing Cloud. Mr. Smithson preferred a Player's, but he realized the significance of the gesture.

'I appreciate your sentiments, Smithson,' said Mr. Cork, 'but, personally, I'm far too nervous, and too old, to take any unnecessary risks nowadays while I'm fishing. When I was young, it might have been different. At sixty-one, I hold on tight to a ghillie. Did our man have a ghillie?'

'He did sometimes, but, on this particular occasion, he apparently went out alone.'

'The river was high, I suppose,' reflected Mr. Cork. 'Our fisherman wasn't as young as he used to be. He waded too deep, lost his footing and the current swept him away. A woman was drowned like that last year with a ghillie only two hundred yards away from her. And the ghillie nearly drowned himself trying to get her out. Personally,' went on Mr. Cork, 'I won't put my fly over those pools where you can't cover a fish without floundering about in treacherous water. No salmon is worth it. Leave it to the younger men, that's my view.'

'Apparently the young men aren't so safe either,' said Mr. Smithson, going through the file in his hand. 'Our man was only thirty-seven; thirty-seven, to be precise, on October 5th this year.'

'Could he swim?' asked Mr. Cork.

'We don't know that. But he was in the services during the war and, although he had been wounded, our medical report, when we accepted him, gave him high marks for physique and general health, so he ought to have been able to look after himself.'

'What did they say at the inquest?'

'There wasn't an inquest.'

'No inquest?' demanded Mr. Cork, sharply.

'Scotland, sir,' said Mr. Smithson complacently. 'In Scotland, we don't have inquests; not, anyhow, in the English sense.'

Mr. Cork grinned. Mr. Smithson, in spite of his name, was of Scottish origin. And self-effacing as Mr. Smithson was in most matters, on the question of Scotland, he was a bigot.

'I'd forgotten, said Mr. Cork, apologetically. 'But they have something like an inquest, don't they?'

'There are considerable differences,' said Mr. Smithson pontifically. 'Scottish law provides for what is known as a Fatal Accident Enquiry. But the enquiry is conducted in

26

private by the procurators-fiscal in the various areas and, if there's no suggestion of foul play, that's the end of the matter.'

'But they publish the findings of the enquiry?'

'Not unless there's evidence of foul play. In a case like this, of accidental drowning, the schedule is simply deposited with the registrar who records the cause of death. Personally, I venture to think that it's a much better law, Mr. Cork, than the English one because, under the Scottish system, the relations of the dead man are spared all the unnecessary suffering of a public enquiry. English coroners, you know, often nose about into questions which are really quite irrelevant . . .'

Mr. Cork cut him short.

'All I really want to know, Smithson, is that we're quite satisfied that we know how this man died.'

'I think there's no doubt about that, Mr. Cork. We know that the procurator-fiscal has completed his enquiries. The death certificate has been granted. And, as a matter of fact, the local papers published quite a detailed report of the case which the solicitors of the deceased have passed on to us.'

'Who are the solicitors?' asked Mr. Cork.

'Swainson and Lester, sir.'

'Good firm,' said Mr. Cork. 'What do they say?'

'Well, the claim has come direct from them as the executors of Gabriel Dagger's estate. As a matter of fact, they only heard of the accident themselves through the police several days after the body was found. Gabriel Daggers seems to have been a funny sort of bird. He had no relations, apart from a married sister in Canada, and he only came to Swainson and Lester when his mother died during the war. Swainson's were the mother's solicitors and Daggers became a client of theirs as a result of the business of his mother's estate.'

'No relations?' said Mr. Cork. 'Then why did he take out an accident risk for £25,000? Has he left a will?'

'Yes, I asked Swainson's about that. But they say all his affairs are in order. Of course, we won't know, officially, who gets the money until the will is filed for probate.'

'Do we know unofficially?'

'Very unofficially . . . well, yes, we do, sir.'

Mr. Cork smiled. There were occasions when Smithson was brighter than he looked. Mr. Smithson himself gave a nervous cough.

'It happens,' he went on, 'that the managing clerk of Swainson's is a friend of mine. We're fellow members of the Burns Society and we occasionally get talking over a hand of dominoes during the lunch hour.'

'I've no doubt that a lot of reputations get shuffled up with the dominoes, eh, Smithson? Well, very unofficially, who gets our money?'

'A young lady, Mr. Cork.'

'What sort of a young lady?'

'One of those, I think, sir.'

Mr. Smithson raised his eyebrows significantly.

'What do you mean by 'one of those', Smithson? Is that your damned Calvanistic way of saying she's a prostitute?'

'Not exactly that, Mr. Cork. She's actually a dancer on the stage. Quite a well-known young person, so I'm told.'

'What's her name?'

'Anna Pryde, if that conveys anything to you.'

Mr. Cork pressed down a switch on the office inter-communication system.

'Miss Scott?'

'Yes, Mr. Cork?'

'You're a theatregoer, aren't you?'

'Yes, Mr. Cork.'

'Who is Anna Pryde?'

'You mean Anna Pryde, the ballerina?'

'Ballerina, is she?'

'She's one of the principals at the Opera House. Would you like to see her picture?'

'No, don't bother, Miss Scott.'

'She's very lovely.'

'I'm sure she is. Do you know anything about her personally?'

'I've seen her often on the stage.'

'Would you describe Miss Pryde as a respectable young woman?'

Mr. Cork gave a sideways look at Mr. Smithson. Miss Scott's voice, distorted by the instrument, came back with indignant emphasis.

'Why, of course, Mr. Cork. Only the other day she was received by royalty.'

'Then I suppose that settles it,' replied Mr. Cork. 'Thank you, Miss Scott.'

Mr. Cork took his hand off the switch.

'Apparently, Smithson, Anna Pryde is not "one of those."'

'People may think differently,' said Mr. Smithson dourly, 'when the news is published in the papers that she has inherited a fortune under this man's will.'

'I suppose so,' said Mr. Cork, absently. He was reading the report of the drowning in the clipping from the *Northern Times*. Mr. Smithson waited for him to speak again.

'Funny business,' said Mr. Cork at last. 'Funny in all sorts of ways.' He pursed his lower lip together with his fingers, a mannerism which he had when he was puzzled.

'It seems that the body wasn't discovered, or the man missed, until about six or seven days after the accident.'

'The theory,' Mr. Smithson explained, 'is that the body got caught up on the grappling hooks at the bottom of the river which they put in to foul the poachers' nets if they try to get the salmon out of the pools.'

'So I see,' said Mr. Cork. 'Nasty experience for that poor old fellow Johnson dragging out the body after it had been a week in the water. Difficult to identify too, after a period like that. I wonder what happened to him exactly. The evidence is entirely circumstantial, Smithson. This Colonel Johnson, playing a big fish, loses it and, as the hook comes away from the fish's jaw, it gets snagged in a man's body. The man is identified as Mr. Gabriel Daggers, a well-known and experienced angler on the Edendale, who was known to have been alive and well, and fishing this particular beat of the river, on June 28th. In fact, he was conveyed to the river on the morning he disappeared by the hotel cab.

'On arrival at his beat, he gave instructions to Jock, the hall porter, not to collect him in the evening as he was going to walk over the moors to spend a few days with friends. Who the friends were is not revealed. But, as a consequence of the message, nobody at the hotel missed him. Neither were they surprised that he went off without baggage. He had done the same thing on many occasions before.'

Mr. Cork looked up from the press cutting.

'He was certainly a funny bird, as you say, Smithson. However, the hotel didn't miss him. And, in due course, Colonel Johnson had the nastiest surprise of his life.

'It seems that, later, Daggers's fishing rod, broken, was also recovered, with all the line stripped off the reel. The theory is that he must have got into a big salmon—perhaps this same fish that Colonel Johnson, lying in his bed with a chill and nervous prostration, talks about with such fervour to the local reporter—and, in the excitement, Daggers slipped and fell into the river, possibly knocking himself unconscious on the rocks as he did so.

'Well, there it is. There's no suspicion of foul play. Your procurator-fiscal, Smithson, is satisfied. And the Anchor, I suppose, has got to pay. But I'm glad you told me about it. It's certainly a strange accident.'

Mr. Cork rose from his desk and, going to the open fireplace, picked up the tongs and clamped the press report of the accident in the jaws. Then, holding the fire-tongs at arms length, with the press clipping dangling on the end, he solemnly offered it back to Mr. Smithson.

'You don't seriously believe . . . ?' said Mr. Smithson.

'Believe what?' said Mr. Cork, blandly.

'That it wasn't an accident?'

'Who are we,' said Mr. Cork, 'to doubt the findings of the procurator-fiscal?'

He replaced the tongs in the grate and went to his desk. Mr. Smithson hovered uncertainly between his boss and the door.

'Is that all, Mr. Cork?'

'If you say so, Smithson.'

'Then it only remains for me to wish you a happy holiday, sir—and tight lines.'

Mr. Smithson held out his hand. Mr. Cork paid no attention.

'You can save that for to-morrow, Smithson,' he said.

31

'But to-morrow's Saturday,' said Mr. Smithson, in tones of obvious alarm.

'So I believe,' said Mr. Cork.

'But I thought you were going away to-night, Mr. Cork?'

'So I was, Smithson. So I was. But you've changed my mind for me.'

Mr. Cork pressed the switch to talk again to Miss Scott.

'Yes, Mr. Cork?'

'I want to speak to Swainson and Lester, Mr. Lester senior, on the phone. I also want Shirt to come up here and wait in the outer office until I'm ready for him. Oh, and by the way, Miss Scott, call up Mrs. Cork, tell her that I shall be late for dinner to-night, and find out what time the curtain goes up at the ballet; unofficially, of course.'

Mr. Cork looked at Mr. Smithson, and grinned.

Three

'WAS she expectin' you?'

The stage doorkeeper, caged like an old parrot in a shabby glass box littered with cracked tea-cups, rows of keys and grubby bits of paper, cocked his head on one side and examined Mr. Cork with pin-eyed hostility.

'I have already explained that I haven't got an appointment,' said Mr. Cork testily. 'But, if you will be good enough to send up my card, I am sure that Miss Pryde will see me.'

'Sorry. We don't send up cards 'ere. We've only got one pair of 'ands, you know.'

As if that determined the matter, the stage doorkeeper gathered up the evening paper and, lowering his nickel-rimmed spectacles from his greasy forehead to his red beak of a nose, gave all his attention to the labour of reading. Seeing that Mr. Cork was disinclined to remove himself, a pimply-faced individual, who was also inside the glass box, where he was engaged in coaxing an ancient paraffin stove into smelly activity, volunteered a comment.

'Miss Pryde don't usually see nobody, not even her regular boy friend, till after the show,' he said over his shoulder. ' 'Sright, ain't it, Bill?'

Bill, perched on his stool, ruffled himself and nodded disinterestedly.

'This is a business matter,' said Mr. Cork firmly.

The pimply person turned away from the stove and studied Mr. Cork's appearance, from his bowler hat to his Briggs umbrella, with sly interest.

'You aren't, by any chance, a bum, are you?' he enquired suddenly.

'I am neither a bum nor a boy friend, young man,' said Mr. Cork, glaring over the top of his glasses. 'I am the general manager of the Anchor Accident Insurance Company. I wish to see Miss Pryde on an urgent business matter. Now, will you have the courtesy to direct me to this young woman's dressing-room; or must I send for the manager?'

Mr. Cork's authoritative manner made an impression even inside the glass box. The stage doorkeeper and his tea-brewing associate looked at each other in mild surprise. This was not the way that visitors to the stage door usually talked.

'Why not call 'er up on the blower, Bill?'

'Blower's out of order,' said Bill, obstructively.

'Can't do any 'arm letting 'im in, can it?'

'Orl depends,' said Bill.

While the stage doorkeeper ruminated, Mr. Cork impatiently tapped the ferrule of his umbrella on the stone-flagged floor. The gesture had the desired effect.

'Orl right,' said the stage doorkeeper grudgingly, 'you can go up. But I 'ave to warn you,' he added, 'that all visitors must be out of the dressin'-rooms ten minutes before the rise of the curtain. Them's the management's orders.'

'Where is Miss Pryde's dressing-room?'

Breathing heavily, the stage doorkeeper pushed his head through a pigeon-hole in the glass box and pointed.

'Down those steps, turn right, then along the passage, and it's up on the first floor. Room 5. And, remember. Out of 'ere at ten to seven sharp.'

As Mr. Cork departed on his way, the stage doorkeeper gave a valedictory sniff.

'Thinks an 'elluva lot of 'isself, don't 'e? Be'aves like a bloomin' prima donna.'

'Don't worry, Bill. Anna'll give 'im a flea in 'is ear, if I knows 'er.'

'Probably give me a flea in m'ear for lettin' 'im in. Oh, well . . .' Bill settled down again fatalistically to his paper. 'Thank God for a good murder to read about.'

It was the second time in his life that Mr. Cork had been behind the scenes of a theatre. Once before, he recalled, he had been back-stage when the Anchor was investigating the circumstances of a highly-suspicious fire, a fire which was purported to have started with a short-circuit in Cinderella's illuminated coach during the performance of a pantomime. As a consequence of that enquiry, the Ugly Sisters, who were also the lessees of the theatre, went to gaol for arson and the Anchor, which had covered the risk, saved about £50,000. But, on the occasion of that first visit, the theatre was gutted, and Mr. Cork was accompanied by a solid phalanx of experts from his own fire department. It was a different cup-of-tea venturing, as he was now, into the mysterious world behind the footlights at a time when an actual performance was about to begin. A mildly embarrassing business too.

Mr. Cork wondered if all stage doorkeepers were as insolent to visitors as the people at this theatre. Was it possible that Harris, his own commissionaire, was equally rude to people he didn't recognize? Mr. Cork made a mental note to make sure that that sort of thing didn't go on at the company's head offices. After all, you could never be quite sure how these petty officials behaved behind your back.

From a personal viewpoint, Mr. Cork would infinitely have preferred to have met Anna Pryde by appointment: or, better still, seen her in the calm and stable atmosphere of his own office. Heavens, when he arrived at her dressing-room, he might find that the woman had no clothes on. Theatrical people were always said to be unusually lax in matters of that kind. Still, that was a risk to be faced. Instinctively—with that sure instinct, which he always trusted in himself—he felt that he must catch Anna Pryde by surprise: face her before she had time to compose herself, if she had anything to hide, with a glib answer.

Mr. Cork, wandering through dreary stone passages, painted in mud brown and stagnant green, became aware that he had lost his way. An iron fire curtain barred further progress. As he looked hopefully for a way out, a young girl, obviously one of the artists, pattered on flat shoes down the passage. In her white ballet dress and pink tights she reminded Mr. Cork irresistibly of a fairy queen at the top of the Christmas tree. Grasping his umbrella firmly, and feeling singularly overdressed, Mr. Cork raised his bowler hat. The girl, equally surprised by Mr. Cork's appearance, greeted him with an amused smile.

'I'm looking for Miss Anna Pryde's dressing-room,' said Mr. Cork.

'You've passed it, darling,' said the fairy queen, cheerfully. 'You'll see the stairs at the end of the passage.'

With an embarrassed word of thanks, Mr. Cork hurried on. The fairy queen called after him.

'By the way,' she said. 'Is Anna expecting you?'

Mr. Cork, unwilling to be subjected to another cross-examination, said firmly over his shoulder, 'Yes.'

'I just wondered, that's all,' said the fairy queen. She watched Mr. Cork disappear up the stairs to the dressing-rooms with a look of detached curiosity.

A nest of doors, each one marked with a number, opened out from a sort of hall at the top of the stairway. Mr. Cork went to the door marked five, and knocked. There was no answer. He knocked again, more sharply.

'You can't come in,' a girl's voice called out petulantly.

Mr. Cork coughed, and knocked again. This time, the door opened and a pink ballet shoe, thrown from inside the room, hit him full in the chest. Carefully picking up the shoe, Mr. Cork removed his hat and walked in boldly, closing the door behind him.

'Who the hell are you?'

A young girl stood by the dressing-table staring at him in amazement. With the trained eye of the insurance expert, Mr. Cork calculated that she was not more than twenty-three or twenty-four years of age; as a matter of fact, Anna Pryde was twenty-four and any insurance company would have willingly accepted her on sight as a first class life without the evidence of a medical report. She was small in figure, as a ballerina must be; she was five feet four inches in height and she weighed exactly eight stone. She had dark hair, large dark eyes and an oval face. Her face was framed in a head-dress of white swan's feathers, fitted closely to her head, and topped by a silver diamanté crown. She was wearing pink tights and she had an old silk wrap thrown round her shoulders. Mr. Cork had obviously disturbed her in the middle of making-up. The lower lid of one eye was outlined with a long black pencil line with a bright red spot of paint next to the tear duct; the other eye was still as nature left it. But, in spite of her odd appearance, Mr. Cork could see through the grease-paint that Anna Pryde had the bone-structure which distinguishes the great beauty. Although he did not admit it to himself, Mr. Cork was strangely disturbed by the sight of her.

Dressing-room was a polite term for the untidy rabbit-hutch that she occupied. Mr. Cork had a notion that the dressing-rooms of lovely prima ballerinas were gilded boudoirs, waist deep in flowers, with Recamier couches and ornate mirrors, and certainly a marble bath and several seductively arranged screens. Tidied up, Anna Pryde's dressing-room would have served as a cell for a nun. The mirror was a cracked glass stained with rusty patches. The dressing-table was a board, littered with dirty little stubs of make-up paint, bits of cotton wool, caked-up powder puffs and soiled face tissues. A single chair, with a broken cane bottom, was placed in front of the board. The bare wood floor was lined with dozens of pairs of ballet shoes, ready to hand, thought Mr. Cork ruefully, to greet unwelcome visitors. On a hook on the wall hung a tu-tu, a stiff white ballet skirt with two leg holes, like spectacles, in the underpart.

Anna Pryde, with legs astraddle and fists on her hips, looked at Mr. Cork appraisingly; and Mr. Cork, in spite of himself, looked at her. She stood there, with the wrap hanging loosely on her back behind her arms, watching Mr. Cork take in the outline of her figure. Mr. Cork caught himself noticing the prominent lumps of her thigh muscles, her absurdly slim hips and the concave curve of her stomach. She looked a pugnacious little thing; and Mr. Cork felt in his bones that Anna Pryde not only looked pugnacious, but was.

'Your shoe, I think,' said Mr. Cork, gravely handing her the pink silk slipper with its hard flat nose and trailing ribbons.

'Thanks. They're wretchedly expensive.'

She took the shoe and tossed it among the others on the floor.

'I'm sorry I threw it at you,' she said casually. 'I thought you were David. He's my partner, in case you don't know. He's quite a darling really, as pansies go, but I'm in a lousy mood to-night and, if he'd come in here preening himself, I think I should have screamed.'

'What are you in a temper about?'

'Things, that's all. By the way, what do you want? You don't look like a wolf. Are you one of the types that collects autographs?'

Young as she was, Anna Pryde talked with the easy authority of someone who had made a success in the world; a prima ballerina who was accustomed to command a stage and a woman who expected to exercise the privileges of her beauty off-stage too. Mr. Cork glowed with an approval which he nicely misinterpreted as paternal feeling. But he was glad that Phoebe wasn't with him.

'You must forgive the intrusion, Miss Pryde,' he said, balancing his bowler on the hook with the tu-tu. 'What I want to see you about is an important business matter. May I take off my coat?'

'I hope you can find somewhere to put it.'

Anna looked wonderingly at her elderly visitor. Her eyebrows lifted when he removed his blue Melton coat and revealed the wing collar, black suit, and striped trousers. She covered her face with her hand to hide her smirks.

'You're not a gynæcologist, you're not a lawyer and

you're not a bank manager,' she said. 'No, don't tell me, I'm guessing. I know what you are. You're an angel.'

'An angel, Miss Pryde?'

'Yes, a backer. Somebody who puts up the money for shows. That's what you are, isn't it?'

'Since I arrived in this asylum ten minutes ago,' said Mr. Cork solemnly, 'I have been mistaken for a bum and a boy friend; I have been addressed as "darling" by a young woman I don't know, and who doesn't know me; and, in our short acquaintance, Miss Pryde, you have already suggested that I may be either a wolf or an angel.'

'At any rate, nobody could mistake you for a pansy,' said Anna, giggling.

Mr. Cork, blushing a little, felt that he was losing his grip on the situation. He cleared his throat by way of a warning signal. Anna took the hint.

'I'm sorry I haven't a spare chair,' she said. 'These dressing-rooms are rather squalid, I'm afraid. But perhaps you can talk to me sitting on that property box. You'll have to hurry though. I've got a show in half-an-hour.'

As if in answer to her, there was a knock at the dressing-room door as an adenoidal voice sang out: 'Half-an-hour, please.'

'That's the call boy,' Anna explained. 'I hope you don't mind me getting on with my make-up. Don't worry if I don't seem to be listening. I promise that really I shall be listening carefully all the time. Now, what do you want to tell me?'

She started pencilling in her other eye.

'I want to talk to you,' said Mr. Cork, deliberately, 'about a man named Gabriel Daggers.'

Anna Pryde dropped the slim stick of make-up and looked at Mr. Cork's reflection in the glass.

40

'Who are you?' she said coldly.

'I'm sorry,' said Mr. Cork. 'I ought to have introduced myself. But I'm afraid I was somewhat disconcerted by your welcome.'

'That was a misunderstanding. Forget it. Go on. Tell me who you are.'

'My name is Montague Cork. I am the general manager of the Anchor Accident Insurance Company.'

'So what?'

'A man named Gabriel Daggers took out an accident insurance with us early this year for a considerable sum of money. Gabriel Daggers has since been found drowned. A claim has been made through his solicitors, who are the trustees of his estate, for payment of the insurance. We understand, in confidence, that you, Miss Pryde, are the chief beneficiary under Gabriel Daggers' will.'

'Surely that's no concern of an insurance company?'

Anna resumed putting on her make-up. Mr. Cork discerned a new tone in her voice, but she was completely in charge of herself. Temperamental she might be but, clearly, she could be cool enough if the situation demanded it.

'You are quite right, Miss Pryde. It is no business of an insurance company what happens to the money paid out under a policy. All we want to do is to satisfy ourselves that the terms of the policy are covered and that the claim is proved. Ordinarily, we should have no interest in a matter of this kind. But this is not an ordinary case.'

'Why not?'

'That's a matter in which we believe that you yourself may be able to help us.'

'Me? How?'

'There are circumstances connected with Gabriel Daggers' death which, to say the least of it, are unusual.

I'm afraid that this must be a painful subject for you, Miss Pryde. But, if I may . . .'

'Go on. There's nothing painful about it. It's rather sordid, that's all.'

'You surprise me, Miss Pryde. I imagined that your relationship with the dead man must have been an intimate one.'

'For God's sake,' said Anna violently, 'don't talk in that mealy-mouthed way. Gabriel meant nothing to me at all.'

'Yet you speak of him by his Christian name and you inherit a not inconsiderable fortune under his will.'

'I don't want the bloody money,' Anna shouted.

'Don't talk nonsense, young woman,' said Mr. Cork, firmly. 'Everybody wants money. What you mean, if you mean anything at all, is that you don't want money from this particular source. Perhaps you think it's tainted in some way. Tell me, Miss Pryde, what was your relationship with this man?'

Anna laughed.

'Forgive me,' she said, 'but you talk like an old judge.'

'I am an old judge, Miss Pryde.'

'Suppose I refuse to answer your questions. What then?'

'You would be quite within your rights.'

'What the hell are you getting at, Mister . . . ?'

'Cork. Montague Cork.'

'What do you really want, Mr. Cork?'

'I want you to tell me about Gabriel Daggers.'

'Is there any reason why you should want to pry into my private life?'

'A very good reason. I have reason to believe that the claim made under this insurance policy, in which you are interested, may be a fraudulent one. I suspect that Gabriel Daggers is still alive.'

Anna stared at Mr. Cork. Watching her features, he thought he saw something very like alarm in the girl's brown eyes.

'What are you talking about?' she said quietly. 'Gabriel is dead. I've had a letter from the solicitors confirming it. I didn't know, until I got the letter, that he'd left me any money; I repeat that I don't want Gabriel's money. It's true that I used to see a lot of him. But that was all over and done with. Done with completely.'

'But you're upset by the news that he's been drowned?'

'Of course I'm upset. Somehow it isn't the sort of thing I expected to happen to Gabriel. You can't help being upset when beastly things like that happen to anyone. That's why my nerves have been so bad lately. My dancing's gone absolutely to hell. But now you say he's not dead; that he's still alive.'

'I didn't say anything so definite as that. I said we suspect that he may be alive. We think it necessary to make further enquiries. That's why I've come to see you.'

'How do you suppose I can help you?'

'You can tell me more about Gabriel Daggers. He appears to have been a very strange man.'

'He was a strange man.'

Anna pressed her forehead nervously.

'I still don't understand what makes you think he's alive. There was the finding of the body, the Fatal Accident Enquiry, the confirmation from the lawyers . . .'

'You appear to be very well informed about the case.'

'Of course, I've found out all about it. I've told you I was in love with him, or thought I was once.'

'You hadn't mentioned it.'

'Well, I've blurted it out now. Not that there's any reason why I shouldn't. It's not a crime, falling in love, is it?'

'Not a crime, Miss Pryde, but, as we say in insurance, a risk. In your case, it seems that it was a bad risk.'

'What are you getting at now?'

'Surely you told me that the affair between yourself and Daggers was over?'

'Completely.'

'Then why did he leave you this money?'

'I don't know. That's just what I don't know.'

There was an unmistakable note of hysteria in Anna's voice. Mr. Cork went on more gently.

'Was the break on your side, or on his?'

'On my side. Entirely on my side.'

'Was he in love with you?'

'In his own queer way, yes.'

'Why queer?'

'How can I tell you that, or anybody who didn't know Gabriel? He just wasn't an ordinary person.'

'When did you first meet him?'

'I don't know why I should tell you but, really, there's nothing particularly shaming about it. The first time I saw the name Gabriel Daggers was in a bouquet of flowers handed up from the orchestra pit after I'd danced the lead in a new ballet. "Pompadour" I think it was. In my dressing-room afterwards I noticed the card with the name "Gabriel Daggers." I guessed he was some enthusiastic fan and thought no more about it.'

'When did this happen?' asked Mr. Cork.

'Three years ago. Exactly three years ago when we were doing the summer season.'

'You were then about twenty?'

'Twenty-one actually.'

'How long was it before you met Daggers personally?'

'A few months later. He kept on sending me flowers,

44

so much so that the other girls in the company started to tease me. But we were just leaving to do a season on the Continent and I hoped that would be the end of it. We opened in Amsterdam and, that very night, there was a bouquet and a card from Gabriel saying that he was in front. It happened again in Brussels, in Paris, and then in Monte Carlo. I met him for the first time in Monte Carlo.'

'He asked to see you?'

'He sent a message to the hotel asking me to have an apéritif with him at one of the cafés after class in the morning.'

'And, although he was a stranger to you, you accepted his invitation?'

'It wasn't quite like that. In his note to me, he said he was a friend of my brother, Bobs, who was killed in the war.'

'And was he?'

'Yes. They were in the Normandy landings together. They crossed the Channel in the same assault boat. My brother showed Gabriel my picture, and talked to him about me while they were making the crossing. Bobs was killed on the beaches a few hours later.'

'You were fond of your brother?'

'Very. Mother died when we were quite young and I . . . well, I used to look after him. He was only nineteen when he was killed.'

'So it's very understandable that you should have wanted to meet Gabriel Daggers. Understandable too that he should have wanted to meet you. You had something in common and you were immediately attracted to each other.'

'Don't you think it's high time we brought this unpleasant interview to a close?'

'You'd prefer me to report my suspicions at once to the police?'

It was a cruel suggestion, and Mr. Cork regretted it as soon as he had made it. But the effect on Anna was instantaneous. She wavered.

'You're not seriously thinking of doing that, are you?'

'Not if you're ready to assist me with my own enquiries.'

'What else do you want to know?'

'I want to know what made you fall in love with Daggers; more important still, what made you fall out of love with him; and why, when you had agreed to part, he left you a fortune in his will.'

'We never agreed to part. Gabriel was always determined to marry me.'

'But, for some reason, you wouldn't marry him?'

'No.'

'When did he first propose to you?'

'The first time I met him, in the café at Monte Carlo.'

'As suddenly as that. What did you say?'

'I said that I'd only just met him, that my career anyhow was in the ballet and I hoped he wouldn't make such a foolish proposal again.'

'Well?'

'He just looked at me with those burning black eyes of his and asked coldly if there was any other man in my life. I said there wasn't. And he said "There'd better not be."'

'He promised me in Monte Carlo that he wouldn't try to see me again for a month. He told me he was going to Scotland to fish. He was mad keen on salmon-fishing. But he made me agree to lunch with him in London when he returned. Perhaps I hoped that he wouldn't turn up. But, of course, he came. And it was odd but in some funny way, I was almost glad.'

'Perhaps he reminded you of your brother?'

'Gabriel? No, Gabriel was nothing like Bobs.'

'What was he like?'

'He wasn't like Bobs.'

'Yet you were extremely attracted to him?'

'How can I answer this stream of questions? Who can tell you why they fall in love, or out of love? It's just one of those things, that's all. As you get to know people better, find out more about them, your attitude changes. You can't explain things like that.'

Mr. Cork smiled at her comfortingly.

'You're quite right, Miss Pryde. As you were talking, I was asking myself exactly what made me fall in love with my own wife. You know I'm bound to tell you that, after all these years, I can't remember. But then, unlike you, I've never fallen out of love.'

'You're lucky.'

'How does it feel, Miss Pryde; falling out of love?'

'Miserable.'

'I thought so.'

'Is there anything else you want to know?'

'Had Gabriel Daggers any friends?'

'Not that I know of. He seemed to have no friends, and no outside interests, except his business and, of course, me.'

'What was his business?'

'I don't know. It was something connected with jewellery, I think. He seemed to know a lot about stones. He gave me this.'

From her dressing-table, Anna picked up a diamond brooch and flashed it casually at Mr. Cork. It was modelled in the shape of a leaping salmon.

'I told you that Gabriel was mad keen on fishing,' she said.

'You mentioned that. But I still feel, Miss Pryde, that I

47

know little more about Gabriel Daggers than I did when I entered this room. What are you holding back?'

'Nothing.'

'You say he had no friends. You must have gone about with him a lot. Did you never meet anyone he knew?'

'Once, yes. It was in a hotel cocktail bar. A cheery sort of man came up to Gabriel, slapped him on the back and addressed him, I remember, as "The Black Bastard"; "if it isn't the Black Bastard himself," he said. He pressed us both to have a drink but Gabriel said we had an urgent appointment and dragged me away. When I asked him who the man was, he said he was a fellow who was in the Commandos with him in the war. He was angry that I even mentioned the matter.'

'From the way you talk, it seems that he wasn't a particularly likeable sort of man.'

'He wasn't easy to understand.'

'What did you do with yourselves when you were together?'

'We went for drives in the car. We went swimming. I'm very fond of swimming—I'm a good swimmer as a matter of fact—but Gabriel was marvellous. We talked about my work. Gabriel knew a lot about the ballet. And, sometimes, he told me about his fishing.'

'Did you ever go fishing with him?'

'Oh, no. Generally, I was working. But apart from that, I don't think Gabriel would have wanted me. Fishing was his great private sport.'

'Did you see him again after you finally refused to marry him?'

'I saw him sometimes.'

'Was he as solicitous as ever?'

'Quite.'

48

'Had he any relations?'

'He had a married sister whom he hadn't seen for twelve years. His mother, he told me, had been killed in the blitz during the war. I think he was fond of his mother because he was very bitter about the way she died. He lived in her old flat in Kensington, 32A Addison Road. I went there once or twice. It was looked after by a daily woman. Gabriel wasn't interested in it except as a place to sleep when he was in London. He had a work-bench there where he played about with bits of jewellery and there was a room he used as an office.'

'You never met any of his business associates?'

'Nobody except that one acquaintance from army days. And I don't remember what his name was, even if I heard it at the time. In appearance, he was short and dark; much the same type as Gabriel himself; if you could call Gabriel a type.'

'You say that Daggers used the flat when he was in London. Did he go abroad a lot?'

'Yes, often for short visits to the Continent. And, of course, he went up every year to Sutherland for a month to fish.'

Mr. Cork, who had been chain-smoking throughout the interview, lit another Passing Cloud on the butt of the last.

'That's all I know,' said Anna.

'Are you sure?'

'I think so.'

'When did you get the news of Daggers' death?'

'At the beginning of this week.'

'From the lawyers?'

'Yes. They wrote to me saying that I was to inherit this money, and enclosed Gabriel's letter.'

'Letter? What letter?'

49

'Gabriel had left a letter for me with the lawyers which he told them to pass on in the event of his death.'

'Did the letter say anything important?'

Anna hesitated.

'I don't know why I should tell you all this,' she went on, 'except I suppose it's a good thing to get it off my chest instead of bottling it all up inside. I've had a helluva week, I can tell you that, and so can everybody else in the company.'

'May I read this letter?'

'I suppose so. If I don't show it to you now, you'll find some way of seeing it in the end.'

Anna reached for her handbag and, pulling out the letter from the top, passed it to Mr. Cork.

'The first part isn't important. It's typical of hundreds of love letters that Gabriel sent me. It's the last page that matters.'

Mr. Cork scanned the first page of the letter quickly, then turned it over. His brow wrinkled as he read it through. Then he looked at Anna and read it again.

'So the will has a special provision. You are to have the income from the money but the capital doesn't become yours for three years and then only providing that you don't get married in the meantime.'

With a worried expression, pursing his lips together with his fingers, Mr. Cork studied Daggers' letter again.

'He says here that, whatever happens to him, you can be sure that he will always be near you.'

He quizzed Anna over the top of his glasses.

'He seems to have had a premonition of his own end.'

'Yes. Are you satisfied now?'

'More dissatisfied than ever, Miss Pryde.'

He rose to his feet and reached for his hat and coat.

'What are you going to do next?' Anna said.

'I'm going fishing,' said Mr. Cork, 'on the dangerous River Edendale.'

There was a flurry at the door. A fat female dresser burst into the room.

'Anna, dear, you ought to be ready. And you,' she added, looking accusingly at Mr. Cork, 'you ought to be out of the theatre. You'll get Anna into awful trouble.'

The call boy's nasal sing-song sounded the words 'Beginners, please' in the passage. An electric bell rang insistently.

'There goes the bar bell,' sighed the agitated dresser.

Mr. Cork didn't say good-bye to Anna. She was throwing off her dressing-gown and thrusting her legs into the stiff shape of the tu-tu. But the two of them exchanged a look. And the look in Anna's eyes was a look of fear.

As Mr. Cork hooked his umbrella on to his arm, anchoring himself solidly to sanity in a tinsel Bedlam, amplifiers in the passage outside the dressing-room broadcast the suffering groans and squeals of the instruments in the orchestra being tuned up for the overture. He could hear the murmur of the audience as they moved into their seats. Girls, decked in white ballet frocks and masked in grease paint, gambolled past him through an iron door which presumably led to the stage. A dreamy young man in tights wet his fingers on his tongue and groomed his eyebrows with spittle before he too wafted on with a backward glance at the odd creature in the passage wearing a bowler hat and hugging a rolled umbrella.

When Mr. Cork arrived at the stage door, Bill's head was squeezed through the hole of his glass cage looking for him.

'I was just comin' upstairs after you. You can tell the bloomin' time, can't yer? You'll get me the sack, that's what you'll do.'

Mr. Cork, without comment, pressed a folded five pound note into Bill's hand. He realized that it was something he should have thought of sooner. Bill glanced at the note under the cover of his palm. His voice changed to genuine respect.

'Blimey, you're a toff, sir; and no mistake. Just like the old days when the nobility thought nothin' of givin' you a sovereign just for the chance to pinch a girl's bottom. But we don't often see it to-day, sir. This 'ere Government 'as bitched all that up. But never you mind. If ever you wants to slip in again, just give me the nod. My name's Bill. I'll fix it, see. I'll be like Nelson. You know?'

Bill gave a laboured wink.

'I think it unlikely that I shall come here again, Bill,' said Mr. Cork. 'But perhaps, with your knowledge of the world, you can tell me something I want to know. Have you come across a gentleman called Mr. Daggers, Gabriel Daggers?'

'I thought you might want to ask me that,' said Bill leeringly. 'Do I know Mr. Daggers? You might just as well ask me if I know a bad smell when I meet one. 'Im and me is just like that.'

He held up his fingers in the form of a cross.

'If you don't mind my givin' you a little bit of private advice, sir,' he went on, lowering his voice confidentially, 'you want to be careful with this 'ere Daggers. If 'e knew you'd been 'ere in Anna's dressin'-room to-night, 'e'd set fire to the bloomin' theatre. 'E would, yer know. 'E's a proper basket.'

'I can see you don't like him.'

'Like 'im? If 'e fell under a bus, I'd get be'ind and push.'

'What does he look like?'

'Looks as if 'e's been under a bus already.'

Bill gave a drainy sniff.

' 'E's ruined 'er, you know. Anna, I mean. She used to be the nicest little thing you ever met. "Morning, Bill," "Evenin', Bill." " 'Ow's your corns, Bill?" she used to say. "Got any nice letters for me, Bill?" " 'Ave a chocolate, Bill." And all the rest of it. But now . . . ever since 'is lordship popped up on the scene, she's become a real tartar. A proper little cat, that's what 'e's turned 'er into, beggin' yer pardon, sir.'

'Have you seen Daggers lately?'

'Not for a month or two. But 'e'll turn up again. You see. 'E'll block up my place 'ere with flowers—Cor, the flowers—and then 'e'll turn up 'isself; lookin' about as 'appy as a man with a butcher's knife in 'is belly, and workin' on Anna till you'd think she'd swallowed a rotten oyster.'

'You don't think you might have seen the last of him?'

'The last of 'im. Don't make me laugh. 'E's permanent, like colds in the 'ead and all the other 'orrid ailments of society.'

Mr. Cork put his hand into his hip-pocket and took out his cigarette case. Then, with a nod to Bill, he left the theatre.

'Good night, sir.'

Shaking his head wisely, Bill dipped his beak into an enamel mug of cold tea.

Taking mirror, powder-puff, comb and face tissue with her, Anna ran out of her dressing-room down to the stage just as the orchestra played the opening bars of the overture. She arrived in the prompt corner—where Harry, the stage manager, presided—like an excited white moth. David, her partner, was already there, tapping his toe on the ground and waiting impatiently.

'You're late, Anna,' said Harry cheerfully.

'Sorry, Harry.'

'O.K. But watch yourself, darling.'

'What on earth's the matter?' said David, edging up to her. 'You look absolutely ghastly, Anna dear.'

Anna stuck out her tongue at him. David shrugged his shoulders and flexed his legs in a plié. Julia rubbed her feet in the rosin box.

Somehow, she must concentrate on the job. She was dancing Odette in Lac to-night, and that was a rôle you had to keep your mind on; as if she could keep her mind on anything at the moment. Thank heaven she wasn't doubling Odile's part as well. Her dancing had suffered already; she knew that. Lizette, the ballet mistress, had raised her eyebrows after the performance last night. But that was before Anna had met Mr. Cork, that funny old boy who looked like a wise old dog. She wondered whether she was right to talk to him as she had. But she had to say something. After all, it was only a suspicion she had, an intuition if you like, that Gabriel was still alive. When the old boy in his wing collar had suddenly echoed her own secret fears, she had thought at first she was going to be sick. A mad notion had entered her head that Mr. Cork must be a messenger from Gabriel himself. But she'd carried it off. Carrying off the lead in the thirty minute ballet to-night couldn't be worse than that.

'Come on, Anna,' said David petulantly. 'If you don't limber up, it'll be more like dancing with an old boot than a swan.'

'I'll be all right,' said Anna.

Resting her hands on the wall, she went through the routine of pliés, grand battements and échappés. She rose on her points and moved her arms. Then, with David standing behind her to hold her waist, she practised supported pirouettes. As the overture ended, and the curtain went up, she looked quickly in her mirror and tidied her hair and face.

Two minutes to go. Standing in the wings, waiting for the music cue, Anna fidgeted with her tights, smoothing and pulling them to make them more comfortable. The classic ballet of *Lac des Cygnes* had opened. The Huntsmen made their entrance and carried out the first short mime scene with the Prince. The Prince took the crossbow to shoot. The music cue was coming up.

'Take it easy, Anna,' she heard Harry say.

Then she ran to the centre of the stage, into the blinding white lights, and executed the first pas-de-chat of the traditional dance. The rhythm of the music and the excitement of the movements gripped her now. She carried out the conventional mime with the Prince. 'Who are you?' 'I am the Queen of the Swans'. 'I honour you. I protect you.' And she was back again in the wings waiting for the Pas-de-Deux.

That was the passage she dreaded. The Pas-de-Deux in Lac was notoriously one of the most exacting in all ballet, demanding complete concentration and harmony to get it across. Anna made up her mind to put every other thought aside. It would be too dreadful if she tottered or fell backwards on David in the pirouettes. Thank heaven, he had safe hands, even though he was liable to be catty afterwards if anything went wrong.

Anna made her entrance. They were coming to the

fourth pirouette when some gremlin inside Anna's mind tempted her to look towards the seat on the prompt side of the stalls circle where Gabriel used to sit when he came to the theatre. He chose that side seat because it was one of the few places in the darkened auditorium, apart from the boxes, where you could recognize a face from the stage.

As Anna looked, her eyes misted. Sitting there in his usual place was Gabriel Daggers, boring into her with his eyes. She was sure of it. Then she felt David's hands steadying her round the hips.

'Relax, Anna, relax,' he was saying.

Somehow, she recovered herself. Somehow, by sheer force of habit, she mechanically completed the routine and took her bow. The audience applauded rapturously, as they always did. Perhaps it didn't look quite as terrible from the front as Anna feared. But she could see Lizette peering down at her from the management's box. She'd know.

As Anna went into the wings, she forced herself to look again into the corner. But Gabriel Daggers' seat was vacant. And David was pressing behind her.

'What in heaven's name happened to you, darling? You fluffed that fourth pirouette completely. And, afterwards, you carried on like an absolute robot.'

'Oh, go to hell,' said Anna.

'That's no way for a Swan Queen to talk,' said David. Tossing his head, he went into a corner to sulk.

Anna went across to Harry, the stage manager, sitting in his compartment in the prompt corner. Harry, amongst all the make-believe, was a pal, a real-life person.

'Not feeling too good, old girl?' said Harry.

'Lousy,' said Anna.

56

'I thought so. I know I shouldn't say it, Anna, but why don't you play up you've slipped a muscle, and give yourself a rest?'

'What'll Lizette say?'

'What does that matter? It's yourself you've got to think of. Get out of this madhouse, and have a holiday.'

'I want to. Between ourselves, Harry, I need to go somewhere very badly.'

'Where's that?'

'It's a place right away in the Highlands of Scotland.'

'Another man?' said Harry. 'I should have thought you'd had enough by this time. Go on. Here comes your cue.'

Anna went on to dance the solo.

Four

'YOU can call off your enquiries,' said Anna.

In the solid and solemn atmosphere of Mr. Montague Cork's office, she looked as out of place as a piece of Dresden china on a deed-box and as fresh as a carnation in the button-hole of an over-ripe company director. Mr. Cork could well imagine the stir which the arrival of this young woman must have created in the underwriters' room downstairs. Miss Scott, his dim and faithful secretary, was almost indecently excited by Anna's unexpected visitation. When she showed her into the office, Miss Scott stood there goggling like a besotted schoolgirl. Even old Smithson had to be shoo-ed out of the room, shifting his feet and touching his tie with self-conscious interest. But Anna, accustomed to being gaped at, was unembarrassed.

After the interview she had had with the waspish Lizette, following last night's performance, even the experience of her first contact with the world of big business seemed, by comparison, unalarming. True, when the taxi crawled out of the West End into the bewildering maze of narrow lanes and oddly-named streets east of St. Paul's, Anna felt like a migrant swallow heading in the wrong direction. When the cab-driver put her down at the head offices of the Anchor Accident Insurance Co., and she looked at the vast block of Portland stone and the marbled magnificence of the reception hall, she made her entrance with the same sinking feeling inside which she associated with a first night. And, when she asked the beribboned commissionaire if she could see Mr. Montague Cork, she realized the enormity of the request that she was making.

'Have you an appointment, Miss?' said the commissionaire, loftily.

She shook her head and the commissionaire looked at her with Olympian remoteness.

'I'll see if Mr. Cork is in,' he said.

He rang through on the telephone to somebody who rang through to somebody else. Anna waited self-effacingly. Inside the theatre last night, Mr. Cork was a nice old gentleman. But here, in his own world, he was a star; a 'prima insurina assoluta,' she thought to herself, translating Mr. Cork into her own language.

As she stood there, she peered over a partition into a huge office, crowded with people bending under green table lamps. The underwriters' room. In the reception hall, she watched the comings-and-goings of top-hatted messengers from the banks; of boys collecting and delivering cables; of men in dark suits and bowler hats with important-looking dispatch cases; of clerks bustling to-and-fro with files of papers and ponderous leather-bound ledgers.

'Mr. Cork will see you immediately, Miss,' said the commissionaire. Anna noticed that his attitude towards her was now distinctly respectful.

'You,' said the commissionaire to the first of a row of office boys waiting on a bench behind him. 'Escort the young lady to the G.M.'s office.'

The boy led her to a lift with gates worked in elaborate

brass filigree. When they reached the first floor, a secretary nearly tumbled over herself guiding Anna along a thickly-carpeted passage to an office separated from the outer world by heavy double doors.

Mr. Montague Cork, looking twice as formidable as he seemed yesterday, welcomed her gravely. Anna, feeling half her ordinary size, sat down uncomfortably on a leather chair.

'I've been thinking things over,' she said. 'It's quite obvious that, if I withdraw my claim for the money under Gabriel's insurance, the matter, so far as you're concerned, is closed. You can tear up the policy, save yourself trouble and also your wretched £25,000. That's what you're worried about, isn't it? The money. If you save your money, everything's all right.'

Mr. Cork, gazing over the top of his half-glasses and, sucking in Passing Clouds, listened intently until Anna had finished.

'Well?' she asked anxiously.

'First of all, Miss Pryde, you are clearly under a misapprehension regarding my company's interest in this claim. We are not concerned about the payment of £25,000. To you and me, £25,000 is a great deal of money. The Anchor Insurance Company deals in millions.'

'Then what are you concerned about?'

'Integrity, Miss Pryde. Business integrity. This great City of London you're in now has become what it is for many reasons, but the first of them is honest dealing. That is what we are so anxious to preserve.'

'So you won't help me?'

'Of course, we'll help you.'

'By uncovering all sorts of unhappy things that are best left undisturbed? Surely there are human considerations which are more important than your so-called business integrity.'

'You're surely exaggerating this matter out of all perspective, Miss Pryde. I've told you, unofficially, that it's our intention to make further enquiries into the circumstances of Gabriel Daggers' death. Officially, we know nothing yet to justify us in withholding the claim.'

'But suppose there's no claim?'

'There is a claim, submitted to us by the insured's lawyers.'

'Damn the lawyers.'

'Swainson and Lester are a very reputable and old-established firm. I fancy they'd be shocked by your remark and even more shocked by the proposition you're making to me now.'

'They were Gabriel's lawyers, not mine.'

'Precisely. You are the beneficiary under the will, not the claimant. The claimants are Swainson and Lester, the executors of Daggers' estate. You couldn't withdraw this claim, even if you wished to. You must realize, Miss Pryde that what you're suggesting is quite unethical.'

'Isn't it unethical to have me followed by one of your snoopers?'

Mr. Cork looked at Anna searchingly.

'Followed, Miss Pryde?'

'You needn't look so innocent about it. You've had me shadowed from the moment you left the theatre last night. The fellow even tailed me to this office to-day.'

'I can assure you that, whoever it is, the Anchor Insurance Company is not involved.'

Mr. Cork cleared his throat to ease his conscience.

'It's true that we occasionally make use of the services of our Enquiry Superintendent.'

'Was it him then?'

'Certainly not,' said Mr. Cork, reaching for his cigarette case.

'You expect me to believe that?'

'Where have you been followed?'

'The man was waiting outside the stage door last night and to-day. He saw me call a taxi this morning. Then, when I arrived here, I noticed him getting out of another taxi behind me.'

'An admirer, perhaps.'

'Funny sort of way for a fan to behave.'

'Have you seen this man before?'

'Of course not.'

'Would you know him if you saw him again?'

'I'd know him anywhere. He's a big man, six foot or more; he's got a cast in his left eye and he looks as if he's permanently smiling. He's also wearing the foulest electric blue tweeds I've ever seen.'

'Whoever he is, we know nothing about him. You must take my word for that.'

'Then who is he then?'

'We shall try to find out. If what you say is correct, it might be as well if we did keep an eye on you.'

'I can do without it,' said Anna firmly.

Mr. Cork tapped his fingers thoughtfully on the desk. Then he took a piece of notepaper out of the desk drawer, scribbled a message and pressed the bell for Miss Scott.

'Give this message,' he said, when Miss Scott appeared, 'to Mr. Shirt immediately.'

'Is that your Enquiry Superintendent?' said Anna, as Miss Scott went out of the office.

In answer to her cheeky smile, Mr. Cork looked serious. Getting to his feet, he held out his hand.

'We shall let you know the result of our enquiries, Miss Pryde, in due course.'

'In due course,' repeated Anna angrily. 'And what am I supposed to do in the meantime? Knit socks?'

'Your behaviour is very unorthodox,' said Mr. Cork.

'How do you describe your own behaviour, breaking into my dressing-room last night?'

'I admit,' said Mr. Cork, with confusion, 'that I don't ordinarily . . .'

'Then why did you do it this time?'

'If you must know, Miss Pryde, it was an instinctive decision; an intuition, if you like, that you might be able to help me.'

'Then I have an intuition, too, an intuition that you would be well-advised, Mr. Cork, to call off this trip of yours to Scotland.'

'Why?'

'I can't tell you why. I can only warn you that you might regret it.'

'I'm grateful for the warning.'

'You still mean to go?'

'Unless you have new evidence, Miss Pryde, to persuade me that Gabriel Daggers met his death in natural circumstances, I intend to continue with my enquiries.'

'But you've already got the evidence. The identification of the body, the findings of the Fatal Accident Enquiry . . .'

'You're a very persistent young woman.'

'You're a very persistent man.'

'Then we ought to get on well together,' said Mr. Cork, smiling.

'I hope I shall never meet you again.'

Anna made ready to go.

'I'm sorry you feel that way,' said Mr. Cork, opening

the door for her, 'because I think we're going to see a lot of each other in the near future.'

'What are you suggesting now?' asked Anna suspiciously.

'As we're obviously journeying to the same place,' replied Mr. Cork, 'I was wondering whether you would care to have a lift in my car?'

Anna brushed past him out of the office without answering.

'Look out,' shouted Mr. Cork in an agonized voice. The young man at the wheel of Mr. Cork's silver Bentley reduced the speed from forty to twenty miles an hour.

'I promise you it's quite all right, sir,' said the young man wearily. 'These roads may be narrow but forty miles an hour in a car like this is actually quite a safe speed.'

'I wasn't thinking of the speed or the road,' said Mr. Cork. 'What I was looking at were those sheep.

'You know, Shipley, on these Highland roads, you can't be too careful. Every sheep sitting on the grass verge is a potential accident risk. Every year, we have to pay claims amounting to thousands of pounds caused entirely by sheep running out into the road. There they are. They're doing it now. Go on, Shipley, blow your horn.'

With a wry grin, Robert Shipley obeyed the instructions of his boss. It really had been an appalling journey. In the three days run from London to Inverness, Mr. Cork had been reminded of every motor crash he had ever paid a claim on. At Doncaster, he had wasted half-an-hour phoning the office to find out if the Anchor covered a particular fleet of trucks on the sole grounds that he had observed one of the fleet on the road taking what Mr. Cork considered an unnecessary risk. At Penrith, he had insisted on stopping the car because a bee had flown in through a side-window; bees inside cars, Mr. Cork declared, were a fertile source of serious accidents. Outside Dunkeld, when Mr. Cork himself was taking a grim turn at the wheel, Robert Shipley happened to sneeze. Mr. Cork, with a startled exclamation, jerked the Bentley to a stop and had to be persuaded that a tyre had not burst and that the luggage was still safely lodged on the grid.

When Mr. Cork was driving, their speed on the six hundred and fifty mile journey to Sutherland never exceeded thirty-five anxious miles an hour. When Mr. Cork was a passenger, he leaned forward over the speedometer, with one arm round the back of the driver's seat and both feet working feverishly at an imaginary clutch and brake pedal. Under Mr. Cork's driving and, even worse, under Mr. Cork's directions, the Bentley, built for a hundred miles an hour plus, idled resentfully at a maximum speed of forty.

To Robert Shipley, who was accustomed to taking his corners with a racing change at sixty, the experience of driving with Mr. Cork moved him to silent blasphemy. As they pottered along at thirty miles an hour, he day-dreamed to himself of driving this heavenly Bentley all out, with the G.M. safely locked up in the boot. But then, as Mr. Cork never ceased reminding him, Robert Shipley was not insurance-minded. Indeed, it was for that very reason that Mr. Cork had chosen him as his companion on this strange mission to the Highlands. Mr. Cork scented danger. And he needed a fellow like Shipley, with no personal sense of danger himself, to come with him.

Four days had passed since Anna Pryde had come to Mr. Cork's city office. Even now, Mr. Cork realized that he had no solid evidence to support his instinct to postpone his own carefully arranged holiday and to set off on a madcap journey to Sutherland on the thin chance of finding out for certain whether this fellow Gabriel Daggers was dead, or not. If Daggers lived, it was self-evident that he must be a murderer, because there could be no doubt that somebody's corpse had been hooked out of the Edendale.

True, the body had been officially identified as that of Gabriel Daggers; but that was after a week's immersion at summer temperatures in the water. And who had identified it? The proprietor of the hotel where the man stayed, the hotel's hall porter and a fellow angler, Colonel Johnson. None of them would have cared to look at the thing particularly closely. They would have recognized the general build, perhaps the clothes, and anyhow they would have had no reason to suspect that the body could be any other than that of Gabriel Daggers, the angler who was known to have been fishing on the particular beat of the river where his corpse was recovered; who was last seen there, and who, as it turned out, hadn't been seen by anyone else since that morning. The doctor's evidence would confirm that the body had been immersed for approximately the expected period. And the procurator-fiscal would quite properly accept all the evidence at its face value.

And yet, right from the moment when he read that press cutting that Smithson showed him, Montague Cork had been puzzled. After all, there were at least two unusual coincidences in the circumstances of the accident; first, that if Gabriel Daggers had wished to arrange his disappearance so that no one would miss him at his hotel, he could not have planned it better; second, that in the process of getting drowned, he had contrived to get his body caught up in the grapnels, put there to foul the poachers' nets in the bed of the river, with the consequence

66

that his body wasn't discovered until decomposition must have made it practically unrecognizable. And, apart from those two considerations, it was surely strange that a man of Daggers' physique, an ex-Commando, an experienced angler, and a first class swimmer, so Anna said, should have had such an accident at all.

Then there was Anna herself, with the extraordinary story of her own personal relationship with Daggers. It was too easy to explain that affair by arguing to oneself, as old Lester, the lawyer, argued, that she was a young and hysterical girl. Heaven knows, Anna had shown no lack of poise in her dealings with Mr. Cork. And, although she was young, and probably impressionable, it seemed hardly likely that a successful young woman, and a reigning beauty too, would fall for the wiles of any odd man who made a pass at her. No, there must have been something quite exceptional about this fellow Gabriel Daggers to hold this girl, to hypnotize her, as he did.

Of course, there was the possibility, as Mr. Cork had considered, that Anna, for some obscure reason—and, after all, this was an obscure enough business—might be lying. That was why he had put Shirt, the Anchor's Enquiry Superintendent, on to the job. Little did Anna realize how Mr. Cork's heart sank when she came into his office and blandly informed him that she was being followed. He immediately assumed that it was Shirt. When Anna's description of the man showed that it wasn't Shirt, but somebody else, he didn't know whether to feel relieved or otherwise. If it had been Shirt falling down on his job, there would at least have been no further mystery. As it was, who on earth was this fellow whom Anna described? When he sent Shirt a note to check up on the man, he had disappeared. Anna's story had to be accepted.

But, on Anna's side, it was only fair to admit that everything that Shirt had been able to ferret out over the week-end without, on Mr. Cork's express instructions, revealing the origin of the enquiry, confirmed what the girl had told him in her dressing-room, and made the mystery of this menacing figure of Gabriel Daggers more intriguing.

It was true that he was a sort of dealer in precious stones and metals; he was known in Hatton Garden and it seemed highly probable that he did business on the Continent as well. Shirt had been clever enough to trace the daily woman who had looked after Daggers' flat in Addison Road. Characteristically, in these days when nobody can keep a servant, this woman had only 'done' for Daggers for a few weeks; but it was interesting to note that she was on the point of handing in her notice because Mr. Daggers was such 'a terrible man.' It was evident that even the daily cleaner was frightened of him.

Altogether, Shirt had done a good job. Mr. Cork was especially pleased with some expert information about Gabriel Daggers as an angler which Shirt had talked out of one of the assistants at Hardy's tackle shop. It was a pity that he had been unable to pick up the trail of the man who had been following Anna. But it was pleasing to have confirmation that his instinct had not misled him as to her personal intentions. That same evening after she had called at the offices of the Anchor, she had taken the night sleeper to Inverness. Obviously she, too, was on her way to Edendale.

True, as it turned out, the check on Anna's movements was unnecessary because, the following morning, all the Sunday papers carried the story that Anna Pryde, the famous ballerina, had sprained a muscle and would be unable to dance again for several weeks; the news, too, that she was taking a well-earned holiday in her native Scotland. Daggers, if he was alive, would see that; indeed, it almost seemed as if Anna intended he should. And, if Daggers was the man he was described to be, Mr. Cork was convinced that he would be incapable of leaving Anna alone, especially if he suspected that she was on her way to the fateful river Edendale.

Nevertheless, Mr. Cork was only too conscious that he was setting out to make his own investigations with one hand tied behind his back. Whatever his personal suspicions, he realized that, at this stage, he could not commit his company to any action at all. He had been most careful to warn Shirt to keep clear of the police. He had told Smithson specifically that there must be no hint of a query yet awhile about payment of the Daggers' claim; anyhow, the business would be held up automatically for several weeks while they were waiting for the will to be filed for probate. And finally, in his telephone conversation with old Lester, of Swainson and Lester, he said no more than it was his bare duty to report: that Anna Pryde had been to see him and that he had advised her to act on the instructions of her lawyers. Perhaps a little dishonest of him, Mr. Cork reflected; but better that than to risk the good name of the Anchor by disclosing suspicions which he was unable to support; suspicions, nevertheless, which even old Lester, in his innocence, tended to confirm.

Mr. Cork had not asked for the information but old Lester had burbled out the story; how Gabriel Daggers had come to him over the business of his mother's estate and, in consequence, become a client of Swainson and Lester himself.

'He was an impossible fellow, Cork, an impossible

69

fellow. We never really knew anything about him. Had a good war record in the Commandos; when I first saw him, he was wearing the ribbon of the D.C.M. But he wouldn't talk about it; just scowled when I mentioned the matter. Afterwards, he came in here once or twice but we never got friendly; he wasn't the sort of chap you could get friendly with, you know. I don't know what he did for a living but he seemed to have plenty of money; his bank manager gave him good references and all that. And the result was that when he asked us to draw up his will for him, leaving all his money to this young girl and so on, I didn't feel encouraged to discuss the matter, as we usually do, with our clients. We just drew it up, and he signed it, in the same way that we acted for him when he asked for this heavy accident insurance at the beginning of the year. There didn't seem any objection to it and we just went ahead. I'm afraid it's turned out a bad risk for you, old boy. I'm really very sorry about it.'

Mr. Lester's loquacity encouraged Mr. Cork to ask how he had come to hear that Daggers was drowned.

'We didn't hear anything about it for nearly a week. He hadn't got any relations, you know, except a sister, whom he didn't seem to get on with, in Canada or some place. The news came to us through Daggers' bank. Apparently, the police found his cheque book in his pocket and called them up. The bank passed on the news to us.'

'Was Daggers well-to-do?'

'Yes, as I told you, he always seemed to have plenty of money. And, frankly, I was rather surprised when the manager told me that he had no securities at the bank, only a comparatively small account. And he'd drawn on that pretty heavily before he went on this fishing holiday when he got drowned. Weird man,' concluded Mr. Lester. 'Sad case, Cork.'

Mr. Cork, as he put down the telephone, had reflected that sad was an inadequate adjective to describe it. Macabre was the word that suggested itself. The whole business was macabre and, in some way, threatening. Mr. Cork thought again about the will. The will provided what was really the most significant clue of all. Without that qualifying clause in Daggers' will that Anna must not marry for three years, you might be forced to discount altogether all the other suspicious circumstances of the case. After all, why three years?

If Gabriel Daggers was dead, the three years ban on marriage was a meaningless provision. But, if Gabriel Daggers was alive; if Gabriel Daggers, for some reason, had deemed it necessary to disappear, to pretend to be dead, what more ingenious and diabolical trick could he devise to keep his girl for himself during his enforced disappearance than to leave her such a fortune that, by comparison, to remain single for three years, would seem a trifling sacrifice? If you accepted that premise, and it fitted exactly into the possessive and twisted character of the man that built up with every new fact that Mr. Cork uncovered about him, then all the rest made sense: the two coincidences that delayed the discovery, and impeded the identification, of the drowned man's body; the letter, charged with double meaning, that Daggers deposited with his lawyers to be given to Anna after his supposed death; the withdrawal of an appreciable sum of money from the bank when he left for Scotland to fake the accident; and the unlikelihood of a fit man and a fine swimmer losing his life in a Highland stream.

But, if that was the solution, why did Daggers decide

to disappear? What set of circumstances made it essential for him to be crossed off officially as dead? Who was chosen as the wretched understudy for Daggers' own body at the bottom of the river? If Daggers was still alive, what was he planning for the future? He took out the accident insurance at the start of the year; so, presumably, his intention to disappear formed itself in his mind quite a few months before he carried out his decision. But what determined him to do as he did? Was it possible that the man who, according to Anna, followed her from the theatre to the offices of the Anchor, was concerned with this weird business?

Mr. Cork felt satisfied, in his own mind, that this was very far from a simple case of shamming death to collect the insurance money. The possibility, and he recognized that it was a possibility, that Anna was Daggers' accomplice, he couldn't regard seriously; somehow, it wouldn't wash.

Nevertheless, there was no doubt that Anna believed herself that Daggers was alive. He was satisfied that the voicing of his own suspicions had only confirmed her own. It was evident, too, that she was ready to go to unusual lengths to cover Daggers from the consequences of his actions, whatever they might be; else, why had she come to the Anchor's offices with that cock-and-bull suggestion of withdrawing the claim, and done her damnedest to dissuade Mr. Cork from going to Edendale? Indeed, why had she gone to Edendale herself unless it was her purpose to contact Daggers, if she could; and warn him of his own imminent peril?

But that Anna herself shared Daggers' guilty secret, that she was forewarned of his intentions, didn't fit into the pattern of her behaviour. If she had been his accomplice, she would surely have comported herself with more self-control in the interview in her dressing-room: she wouldn't have come blundering into Mr. Cork's office; least of all would she have pointed the way on the road to Edendale.

No, Anna's behaviour could be explained much more simply by discounting only one statement in her own story of her relationship with Daggers; the statement, which she probably believed herself, that she had fallen out of love with him. What she surely meant was that she had quarrelled with Daggers as only a woman who is deeply in love can. It was possible that the bitterness had come about as a result of Anna discovering for the first time that Daggers was engaged, as he must have been, in some nefarious activity. Alternatively, it might be that there was no more to it than a clash between two violent and unusual personalities.

Anna was miserable about the break; 'miserable' was the word she used herself. When she got the news that Daggers was dead, or she had the suspicion that he wasn't dead, this otherwise self-possessed and competent young woman was thrown into an emotional turmoil. She felt that what had happened was, in some way, her own terrible responsibility.

Daggers was obviously a 'no gooder.' He might have loved Anna 'in his own queer way' but Anna certainly loved him, loved him in spite of herself. Perhaps she identified him in some way with that brother who was killed. Perhaps there was something in her own make-up which drew her to this friendless, eccentric and presumably unhappy creature. One thing was certain: her heart was irrevocably, unquestionably and hopelessly committed to Gabriel Daggers.

She was also in danger. Mr. Cork was sure of that. Daggers, if he lived, was now a desperate murderer. Further, there was something uncomfortably sinister in Anna's story of the man with a permanent smile, a cast in his eye and wearing electric blue tweeds, who had been following her round London. That was what had finally decided Mr. Cork to bring that good-for-nothing-else young Shipley with him as a bulldog. Nevertheless, Mr. Cork, as always, was full of self-criticism. In his position as general manager of the Anchor Accident Insurance Co., he felt that he had no case yet to take to the police. Yet, as a private citizen, he believed that Anna needed protection.

It was a puzzling dilemma. If he left Anna to her own devices, the chances were that she would lead him to Gabriel Daggers. If he called in the police, it would probably ruin his own hopes of getting to the bottom of the business.

He discussed it with Phoebe—he told Phoebe everything—but she was adamant.

'Your first duty,' she said, 'is to the Company. Take young Shipley to look after the two of you and, if you're as clever as you usually are, it'll all come right in the end.'

So that was that. Mr. Cork thought what a pity it was that Phoebe couldn't have engineered a meeting herself with Anna before the girl went off to Scotland. They'd have got along like a house on fire—everybody liked Phoebe—and a nice womanly talk, as she called it, might have made all the difference. Still, that was out of the question now.

At the memory of Phoebe, Mr. Cork smiled to himself happily; what a wonderful woman she was. Lost in his thoughts, he relaxed his grip on the back of the driver's seat. He leant back comfortably, took his eye off the winding moorland road, and quite omitted to notice that the needle of the speedometer had crept up to a steady fifty-five.

Robert Shipley, at the wheel of the car, didn't notice it either. The engine was quietly purring, the brakes answered as smoothly as a kiss, and the great car swept up and down the heather-clad hills as effortlessly as a daydream. Robert Shipley was thinking too.

His mind went back to last Saturday morning—it was only Wednesday now but it seemed like a lifetime ago—when he got the summons to go at once to Mr. Cork's room. He'd slipped over the road from the underwriters' room to have a cup of coffee at Lyons when somebody came panting up to the table with the shattering news. The old man had not gone for his holidays. He had turned up on a Saturday morning for the first time within the memory of the oldest inhabitant. And he was storming round the place, pressing bells and calling everybody up on the telephone as if he'd got a claim on every blasted policy on the books. And then he'd demanded to see Shipley.

Robert was in no doubt that the news boded ill for him. He had only been called to the old man's office twice in the three years he'd worked at the Anchor. And, every time, it was a landmine. The first time he had lost a policy. The next time he'd come back an hour late from lunch— she was worth it too—on the one day when old Cork took it into his head to ask him how he was getting along. This was the third summons. Robert, as he rushed madly across the road, through the front office and up the marble stairs, buttoned up his coat and at the same time realized with horror that he was wearing a country suit. Who the hell could guess that any of the bosses, let alone old Cork himself, who was supposed to have gone on his holidays, would come to the city on a Saturday morning? It was the rocket all right. And, after the interview with old Cork, he would have to break the news to his own old man too.

Outside Mr. Cork's impressive double-door, carved with pictures of great events in the commercial life of the City of London, Robert stopped for a moment, took a deep breath, and knocked. No answer. Instead, the door was opened by old Smithson, the claims manager who, as he walked out, said severely: 'Mr. Cork will see you now.' Robert gulped and walked in.

Mr. Cork was sitting there, glowering across the desk at him, with a Passing Cloud smoking gently between his fingers.

'Don't stand there gaping, Shipley. Come in and sit down. And what the devil do you mean by coming to this office dressed like a commission agent?'

Robert started to murmur apologies.

'All right, you needn't apologize. If I hadn't thought you were quite hopeless in an insurance office, I wouldn't have sent for you now. I told your father you hadn't the temperament for a serious profession like this. . . . How is your father by the way? I haven't seen him in the Club lately. Is his arthritis any better?'

Robert made some foolish comment.

'You tell your father from me to have his teeth out. That's the real cause of the trouble. Teeth. Phoebe, my wife, was just the same. We had the whole lot out. And, now, she's a new woman. You haven't met my wife, have you, Shipley?'

More and more bewildered, Robert said that he hadn't had that pleasure.

'Pity. She was enquiring about you the other day. She's an old friend of your father's, you know; plays golf with him down at Walton Heath. But I haven't sent for you this morning to talk about that.

'I've got a job for you, Shipley, rather an unusual job; a job, unlike insurance, which I have hopes you may be some good at. You were in the Chindits or something during the war, weren't you? Put up a good show, got a D.S.O. and bar?'

'Nice of you to say so, sir.'

'So I presume you know how to look after yourself in a tight corner, and other people. All right, don't mumble. Can you drive a car?'

'I've done a bit of racing driving, sir.'

'I don't mean do you know how to kill yourself in a car. Can you drive safely? Have you got a clean licence?'

'Yes, sir.'

'Can you shoot?'

'Men or game, sir?'

'Both.'

'Yes, sir.'

Robert grinned. This really began to look like something.

'All right, I'll take you. Report to Mr. Smithson that I'm transferring you to one of our branch offices for a special job which may last about three weeks. And the rest of your instructions you can keep under your own hat.

'Pack your bags and your salmon fishing tackle. Don't bring too much—I don't want to overload the car—and report at my flat at 7 a.m. on Monday morning. You're coming with me to Sutherland. I'll tell you more about the purpose of the trip on the way up. That's all, except . . . you'd better bring a stalking rifle with you and, if you've got it properly licensed, a pistol too. If you haven't got a police licence, don't bring it because I can't permit any employee of this company to commit an illegality.'

And that was that. Robert left old Cork's office in a haze, a haze which hadn't really cleared from his mind even now. On the first night out from London, when they stayed at Scotch Corner, Mr. Cork had bought champagne and behaved as amiably as a sentimental old uncle. Afterwards, he put Robert more or less in the picture, obscure as it was. Still, his job was clear enough: to play the knight-errant with Anna Pryde (and who wouldn't?) and to carry out Mrs. Cork's instructions about her husband; no hanging over heights which upset his nerves, no wading unless Robert stood within reach of him, and no road speeds faster than forty-five miles an hour.

'You're driving too fast, Shipley,' said Mr. Cork suddenly.

'I'm only going at . . . oh, sorry, sir, I didn't notice the speedometer.'

'Another twenty miles an hour won't save us more than a few minutes,' said Mr. Cork, 'and we shall both arrive at the hotel with our nerves in good order.'

As he spoke, there was a squeal of brakes behind them. Another car, following them at high speed round a blind corner in the winding road, was skidding uncontrollably into their stern. Robert, with a glance at the driving mirror, touched the accelerator and swung the Bentley on to the verge. The car gave a violent lurch and, for a few seconds, rocked crazily among the outcrop stones, the bracken and the heather of the moor.

Mr. Cork, with a cry of 'Look out' was thrown out of his seat. The veins stood up blue on Robert's hand as, his muscles tensed to control the writhing steering column, he brought the Bentley to a halt.

The car behind them skidded past and stopped, broadside across the road, twenty yards ahead of him. Robert, leaning on the wheel of the Bentley, gave a low whistle of relief.

'I'm very sorry, sir,' he said to Mr. Cork, 'I had no choice.'

White-faced, Mr. Cork gathered himself together. Then he opened the door of the car and got out.

'You needn't apologize, Shipley,' he said. 'You're doing the job I brought you here to do. You can leave the rest to me.'

He walked towards the second car. Out of the passenger's seat came a tall man. At the sight of him, Mr. Cork stopped suddenly in the road and plunged his hand into his hip-pocket for his cigarette case. The man came up and, with a cool smile, gave a little bow.

'I'm afraid I owe you an apology,' he said. 'My friend was driving too fast, definite too fast.'

Still smiling, he waited for a reply.

'What you have to say can be said in court,' growled Mr. Cork. 'You are a menace to the road. I must trouble you for your name and address.'

'So,' smiled the man. 'You are angry?'

'And why the devil not?'

'But it was such a trifling incident, so trifling.'

He shrugged disparagingly.

'Trifling, man? You might have killed us.'

'Come, come. You are exaggerating, sir.'

Still the man smiled.

'The magistrate can decide that,' said Mr. Cork grimly. 'Now will you kindly give me your name and address.'

'Very well. If you insist.'

The man took out his wallet and, withdrawing a card, offered it with another mocking bow to Mr. Cork.

'I am Kurt. Kurt, the photographer. You have possibly heard of me. No? But then, in this country, people never look at photographer's names. They only admire the work.'

'Maybe.'

'May I ask you for your own card, sir?'

Mr. Cork obliged.

'Ah,' said the man, smiling more than ever as he looked at the card. 'Now I have the great understanding. You are the man who pays out the accident money.'

Mr. Cork ignored him.

'What's your address?' he said. 'There's no address on this card of yours.'

'A thousand pardons. You are absolute right. We artists change our address so frequently. But, in the next week, perhaps more, you will find me at the Estuary Hotel, Edendale.'

Mr. Cork looked at the man sharply.

'Why, you look surprised? Is it possible that you are journeying to the same destination?'

'It is.'

'Then I shall undoubtedly have the great pleasure of meeting you again. Au revoir, Mr. Cork.'

Still smiling, he turned on his heel. Mr. Cork stood there watching as the man rejoined his companion and the car, a big American convertible, drove off up the single track road which ended at Edendale. Then he walked back thoughtfully to the place where Robert was waiting for him with the Bentley.

'What the hell do they think they're up to?' said Robert. 'They were driving like maniacs.'

'How far is it now to Edendale?' said Mr. Cork.

'About fifteen, I think, to the hotel. We passed the headwater loch a few miles back.'

'As I thought,' said Mr. Cork. 'Did you see the man who spoke to me?'

'Yes.'

'What did you think of him?'

'Looked like a bloody foreigner to me. And that suit!'

'An electric blue suit,' said Mr. Cork, reminiscently. 'A cast in his left eye and a permanent smile. That was Anna Pryde's description.'

He climbed back into the car.

'Drive on, Shipley,' he said. 'It's evident that we're expected.'

Five

THE Estuary Hotel clings like a limpet, and looks as squat and uninviting as a limpet, on a high promontory of rock which marks the point where the River Edendale joins the sea. Approaching it, you cross a stone bridge over the river, a bridge which is constantly patrolled by representatives of the local inhabitants keeping one sharp eye on the visitors and another on the salmon running up from the sea.

After crossing the bridge, you change gear. If you haven't got a car to change gear on, it's unlikely that you'll ever find yourself at Edendale because there's no way of getting there except across thirty miles of single-track moorland road. Thenceforward, you ascend a steep hill, past the village store and a single pump petrol station, which is normally closed, to Mr. Mackenzie's desolately-situated establishment at the top. The climb is worth it: not for the damp comforts of Mr. Mackenzie's hotel, but for the view.

From the wall which props up the drive in front of the hotel, you look southwards up the glen through the avenue of hills, coloured in blood reds and tartan greens, which encloses the winding watercourse of the Edendale. Northwards, you look out over the bay, with no land between you and the Pole. Below, you look down on the golden beach, where the river ends its exciting rush from the hills in a gentle progress over the sand-bar to the beckoning waves of the sea.

The gulls loop and squawk over the tidal debris. A few boats lie stranded off the edge of a grey stone pier. By the water's edge, a wooden hut, decked with nets and fish crates, marks the collecting point for the salmon, the smaller proportion of the fish caught, which are netted legally for the market.

Situated in a straggling curve round the sea shore is a row of small stone houses. On the near hills are a dozen grey-faced crofts and farmsteads. But, up the glen, the valley of the Edendale is as nature left it, untamed, uncultivated, unwelcoming and, by all but shepherds and sportsmen, unvisited.

In wintertime, the Estuary Hotel is closed, except for a bar at the back entrance which has to be kept open to preserve the continuity of the licence and to distract the marooned local inhabitants from thoughts of cutting each other's throats. In summer and autumn, the regular visitors from outside are the fishermen after salmon and the guns after grouse and red deer. The stalking in its season in the hills is magnificent but the fishing on the Edendale is among the finest on the northern seaboard of Scotland. Even in July, the riparian landlords are able to charge up to two hundred and fifty guineas a month for each of the six beats of two rods into which the river is divided. For the sake of the fishing, lowlanders are content to make the long journey through the Highlands; to shiver uncomfortably in Mr. Mackenzie's Estuary Hotel; to support themselves on a diet completely lacking in green vegetables which are unobtainable in Edendale because there's no soil to grow them in; and even to put up with the company of Lt.-Colonel Adrian de Crecy Johnson who, after twenty-nine fishing seasons, has become as much a part of the place as pulped swedes for dinner.

But Colonel Johnson has never been quite the same since July 4th, 1949, when he lost the fish of his life; and incidentally, brought a dead man to the surface. He had been found, about half-an-hour after losing the fish and fishing the dead man, lying exhausted by the side of his car. Jock, the hall porter at the hotel, who had been sent out to see what had befallen him, brought Colonel Johnson home prior to reporting the finding of the corpse to Edendale's local police sergeant. But it was too late. The combined effects of wet clothes, over-exhaustion and over-excitement had proved too much for his constitution. Gone were his hopes of killing two hundred salmon that season, never mind achieving a grand total of three thousand fish. He had taken to his bed with a bad chill and, even now, more than a fortnight later, he was still doubled-up in his joints. Dr. McCluskie, the local practitioner, would not allow him on the river. He was too obstinate to go home. And he had nothing whatsoever to do except post himself in the hotel entrance hall, facing the stone slab where the salmon which had been killed on the different beats each day were laid out for inspection, and snort at the inadequate bags brought in by the other anglers.

Colonel Johnson was sitting at his appointed station in the hall, under the moth-eaten trophy of a red deer, when Mr. Cork and Robert arrived at the hotel. He greeted them with a grunt of interest.

'If you want any fishing,' he said, 'you won't get any, because the beats are all taken.'

'Thanks,' said Mr. Cork, taking in the Colonel over the top of his half-glasses, 'but, as a matter of fact, we haven't come here entirely for the fishing.'

'Haven't you? Then what are all the rods for?'

'We thought we might spin for sea-trout in the Estuary.'

'Poor sport, I think. Still, every man to his taste. There's not much doing in this place if you don't fish for something. Dead as mutton up here.'

It certainly seemed so on first appearance. Apart from Colonel Johnson, the Estuary Hotel was temporarily deserted.

'Ring the bell if you want Mackenzie,' volunteered the Colonel. 'He's about somewhere. Jock's out in the yard feeding the fowls. But he ought to be back to unpack your bags in a few moments.'

Mr. Cork rapped at a round brass bell placed on a shelf outside the closed shutters of the reception box.

'If you'd come up here a few days earlier, I might have let you have my rod. My name's Johnson, by the way.'

'Colonel Johnson?' asked Mr. Cork blandly.

'You know me?'

'I've often heard people referring to your prowess as a salmon fisher.'

'Have you? That's very nice of them. I'm sure.'

Colonel Johnson purred with satisfaction.

'I suppose I have fished salmon rather more than most; rather more successfully than most, if I may say so. The pity of it is, you know, that I've been off-colour lately. Had an accident with the biggest fish I've hooked in m'life. I'll tell you about it sometime if you're interested.'

'I should be most interested,' said Mr. Cork. 'In fact, it would be a great pleasure to me if you would join me for a drink before dinner.'

'Delighted, my dear sir, delighted.'

'My name is Cork. Montague Cork. My young friend here is Robert Shipley.'

'Does he fish?'

'When I get the chance,' said Robert.

'Wish I'd met you both a few days earlier. I'd have let you have my rod with pleasure and, maybe, a few wrinkles as well. But there it is. It's too late now. A young woman came up here a few days ago, arrived unexpectedly just like you. Good-looking little filly for this benighted place; you wait till you see her. She said she wanted to fish and, as the vet won't let me out, I said she could have my rod. She doesn't know anything about it, of course. Hasn't brought in a fish since she got here. Much better if you had the rod. The river's stiff with grilse and they're catchable if you fish fine enough. Tell you what. You must get together with this girl—I'll introduce you at dinner to-night if you like—and make her share the rod with you. She won't mind. By the way, are you staying here long?'

'We don't know yet,' said Mr. Cork.

'Booked your rooms, I suppose?'

'We sent a wire.'

'Mackenzie will fit you in. There's a nice sitting-room if you want it on the ground floor overlooking the estuary. But take my advice and don't pay the old skinflint more than twenty-five shillings a day for it.'

There was a stir behind the closed panels of the reception box. Then, with a clatter, the sliding-doors thrust open. Mr. Mackenzie, sandy-haired, red-faced and blue-eyed, presented himself in the centre of the frame.

'You'll be Mr. Cork and party, I presume?'

'That's correct. You got my wire?'

86

'The Post Office forgot to deliver till this morning. But, fortunately, I have two rooms.'

He looked at the rods disapprovingly.

'You'll no' get any fishing. All the beats are let.'

'I've told them that already,' Colonel Johnson called out. 'They say they don't mind.'

'Very well then. Jock will collect your baggage and show you to your rooms when he's attended to the chickens. Dinner is at seven sharp and yesterday's papers usually arrive with the post after eight p.m. in the evening. Would you be wanting a sitting-room by any chance?'

'We should like one very much.'

'The charge is thirty-five shillings a day,' said Mr. Mackenzie.

'That's all right.'

Colonel Johnson rumbled to himself. Mr. Mackenzie produced the visitor's book.

'Sign the book, please.'

The hotel register was what Mr. Cork was waiting to see. As he and Robert signed themselves in, he ran his eye quickly down the list of guests. Anna Pryde had arrived all right. And, immediately above his own signature, he saw the name 'H. Kurt,' written in a spidery continental hand, and giving the vague address, London. Kurt's companion had also registered. The name, from the writing, was either F. Bowley or Bowyer, who also put in his address as London. For the rest, the guests seemed to be the typical salmon fishing crowd: Sir George Sanderson and his wife, who, Mr. Cork recollected, was a big industrialist in the Midlands; a Doctor McPeake and his family from Glasgow Infirmary; somebody called something hyphen Smith and, rather surprisingly, a woman, with a home address in France, who gave her name as

Breuvart. Mr. Cork wondered what a Frenchwoman was doing in Edendale.

True, it was unlikely that Madame Breuvart had any connection with Gabriel Daggers. But it was also an unlikely state of affairs to find a Frenchwoman at this remote place in North Britain. There might be an innocent explanation. Equally, Mr. Cork had an instinct that, in the matter of Gabriel Daggers' affairs, it was as well to assume that there was little which was either innocent or self-evident.

But, at that moment, Jock, the hall porter, arrived to unpack the baggage from the car.

In the interval before dinner, when all the guests would assemble in the dining-room, Mr. Cork made the most of his time. He was determined to learn at first hand more, if there was more to learn, about the drowning of Gabriel Daggers. Not that the information was difficult to come by. Jock, the sallow-faced hall porter, enquired if Mr. Cork had heard the news of the fatal accident, and started to tell him all about it while he was moving the baggage from the car to the bedroom. Mr. Mackenzie shook his head sadly and rolled out the story again as he introduced Mr. Cork to his private sitting-room. Colonel Johnson, accepting Mr. Cork's invitation to take a drink with him, was enchanted to discover that the new visitor had some whisky with him—a commodity which, as a direct consequence of all the comings and goings concerned with the procurator-fiscal's enquiry into the drowning, the hotel was temporarily out of stock—and, on the strength of it, insisted on giving Mr. Cork the details from his fishing diary of the height and colour of the water, the temperature, and the peculiar conformation of the bed of the pool called the Black Brae, over the second double.

But it wasn't very illuminating. In general, the people in the hotel only repeated the story which had been admirably reported in the *Northern Times*. It seemed that, over a number of years, Daggers had made a habit of disappearing from the hotel for several days at a time; but nobody seemed to know, or care, where he went to.

'He was a morose man,' said Mr. Mackenzie. 'Sometimes, he went for days without talking to anybody.'

Colonel Johnson seemed not at all surprised that Daggers should have drowned himself in the Black Brae. But Mr. Cork suspected that this was an expression of Colonel Johnson's pride in his own knowledge of the ways of the river, a knowledge which he was reluctant to give anybody else the credit for, rather than a conviction as to the peculiar dangers of the Black Brae. Even Colonel Johnson couldn't remember anyone being drowned there before.

The only new fact that Mr. Cork gleaned from half a bottle of whisky was a reference by Colonel Johnson to the mysterious man he saw, or thought he saw, watching him as he fished out the body, the man who disappeared when Colonel Johnson ran shouting from the river. Mr. Cork was curious; but he thought it wiser to refrain from asking the question that was uppermost in his mind. Instead, he asked if Daggers ever used a ghillie.

'You and I wouldn't call him a ghillie, Cork. We'd call him a damned poacher.'

'But he used a man?'

'Sometimes. Not always. Not the day he was drowned. But, quite often, he was out with a notorious ruffian known round here as "Snatcher." '

'Does "Snatcher" live in the village?'

'No, he lives in some broken down croft in the hills. Makes a living snatching salmon; hence his name. I complained to Daggers several times about his using a rogue like that as a ghillie and, when he ignored what I intended as a polite piece of advice, I reported it to the dempster on the river. But they were all afraid of Daggers, as afraid of him as they're afraid of the poachers who come out openly with their nets dragging the estuary there.

'The poaching up here is a public scandal, Cork. They ought to do something about it in Parliament. All the locals are mixed up in it, Wee Frees and all. Do you know the Wee Frees, Cork? These damned Sabbatarians. They're the curse of Scotland. The Wee Frees and the poachers. It's a wonder we catch any fish at all.'

'Why don't you report the poachers to the police?'

'I have. But it's useless, Cork, useless. They're all related to each other up here; police, water-bailiffs and poachers too. And they stick together. In fact, sometimes I think I'm the only man up here with any public spirit. The landlords won't do anything about it. Even old Mackenzie at the hotel here is in league with them at heart. I fight a lone battle. Why don't you write to the landlords, Cork? You're a big man in business, aren't you? Tell 'em what you think of 'em. I'll back you up.'

Mr. Cork assured the irascible Colonel Johnson that he'd think the matter over. But he didn't say which matter. He was a puzzled man and an anxious one.

Chain-smoking Passing Clouds, he was trying to piece together the possible relationship between Gabriel Daggers and the man with the permanent smile; H. Kurt, as he called himself, and his associate. F. Something-or-another. As they themselves had just arrived at the hotel, Colonel Johnson had nothing to say about them, beyond the fact that they were obviously non-fishers and therefore, in the Colonel's estimation, beneath consideration. Mr. Cork was anxious to arrange his thoughts before he met them, as he assuredly would, in the dining-room.

He had no doubt, from the man's extraordinary appearance, that Kurt was the same person who had watched for Anna outside the theatre and subsequently shadowed her to the offices of the Anchor. He was actually wearing the same astounding clothes which Anna described.

Assuming he was the same man, it seemed highly likely that he had followed Mr. Cork from London. Maybe, he had lost Anna's trail at some point, but, somehow, discovered Mr. Cork's association with her, either by seeing him when he visited her at the theatre or by intelligent detective work when she called at the offices of the Anchor. Anyhow, the coincidence of this man's appearance at Edendale was too remarkable for accident. Somehow, Kurt was involved in the business of Gabriel Daggers disappearance. But how?

There seemed to be only two acceptable suppositions to explain the presence of Kurt and his companion. Either they were Daggers' agents, connected with him in his mysterious and presumably criminal activities, or, alternatively—and Mr. Cork favoured the second possibility—they were not Daggers' friends but his enemies. Both ways, they had a very good reason for trailing them to Edendale. If they were Daggers' accomplices, they would obviously wish to discover what Mr. Cork, or Anna, were doing. If enemies, suspecting a conspiracy, they might well expect that Daggers' girl friend, or the girl friend's friends, would lead them to the man they sought.

The probability that they were Daggers' enemies, rather than his associates, was underlined by Anna's own description of Daggers. By all accounts, he was not companionable. And it seemed highly unlikely that a man who resented renewing an acquaintance with a wartime comrade, as Anna recounted of him, would share his darkest secrets with a crowd. It was easier to believe that these people who were trailing Anna, or him, might themselves be the cause of Daggers' disappearance. If Daggers was drowned, they might well have had a part in it. If Daggers lived, then they might be able to tell whose body it was that had been found in the Black Brae.

Meantime, Mr. Cork had no intention of underrating his opponents. Kurt's effontery, when they nearly crashed on the road to Edendale, was something Mr. Cork was unlikely to forget. Robert had a theory that, from the way the car came up behind them, it was a case, not of reckless driving, but a deliberate attempt to ditch the Bentley. Mr. Cork thought it was more likely a ruse to have a closer look at himself and Robert. One thing was certain. It wasn't an accident.

However he viewed the situation, Mr. Cork was discomforted by the prospect. His confidence—that confidence which Phoebe, bless her heart, always reposed in him so completely—was waning under the sinister threat that seemed to brood in the hills around Edendale. He waited nervously for seven o'clock and the call to action of the dinner gong.

As the gong clanged, Mr. Cork poured himself, and Robert Shipley, a steadying whisky and soda. Thank Heaven that Shipley, at least, was completely undisturbed in mind. It appeared that the unpredictable future had no terrors for him. Mr. Cork, although outwardly as calm as a well-trained gun-dog, was as agitated as a pointer who has marked his bird.

'This is it, Shipley,' he said, emptying his glass. 'Let's see what we've got coming to us for dinner.'

'I'll wager it's uneatable, sir.'

'You're probably right.'

As they walked through the hall, four salmon, brought in by the guests in the hotel after the day's fishing, glittered silver and mauve on the grey stone slab. They went through a dark passage, lined with trophies, to the dining-room which had been stuck on, as an afterthought, to the original building. It was a low-roofed annexe with a window along one side looking out over the bay. About a dozen tables, decorated with paper flowers and a formidable armament of musty sauce bottles, were attended by two pudding-faced lassies under the direction of Jock, who had exchanged the green baize apron which he wore in his capacity as hall porter for the white linen jacket of head-waiter, wine-steward and receptionist.

About half the tables were occupied. Colonel Johnson, sitting alone in the corner by the door, had already finished his soup. In the middle of the room, a party of five, perhaps Dr. McPeake and his family, were just starting their meal. At the table against the window which had the best view of the sea, an elderly couple, obviously Sir George and Lady Sanderson, watched Jock unwire for them a bottle of champagne.

Two other tables had people at them whom Mr. Cork was unable to identify. Anna Pryde was not there. But, on the window-side of the room, the man with a smile, and his associate, were already in their places.

As Mr. Cork and Robert stood by the door, waiting for Jock to show them to their table, the other guests peered at them curiously. Colonel Johnson flourished his napkin in friendly greeting.

'Hello, Cork. Soup's cold already.'

Mr. Cork nodded. His eyes were on the two men in the opposite corner. Kurt, who was facing him, half rose to his feet and, unabashed by Mr. Cork's cool gaze, gave a familiar wave of welcome. His companion, a thickset man with rounded shoulders and clothes which were obviously too tight for him, turned his head and, at a remark from Kurt, grinned broadly.

'I'd like to knock that smile off their faces,' muttered Robert.

'So would I,' said Mr. Cork grimly.

'What's that?' asked the Colonel.

'I was wondering if you'd seen the young lady yet?' said Mr. Cork.

'Oh, her. The girl who's got the fishing, you mean. No, she hasn't come down yet. Messing about powdering her nose, I expect. You know what women are, Cork. I can't think what her dinner will be like when she does get here. They've got no proper hot plates out there in the kitchen. I'm always complaining to Mackenzie about it, but it's no use. These Highlanders don't believe in anything unless it came in with Bonnie Prince Charlie.'

Jock was waiting to escort Mr. Cork and Robert to their table.

'Would you be minding sitting at the window, next to Sir George?'

Mr. Cork agreed. Sir George and his wife would set up a solid screen between himself and Robert and the two ruffians in the corner. It was also a strategical position from which to watch the room.

'Soup?' asked Jock, brushing the tablecloth.

'What soup?'

'It's usually broth.'

94

'Very well.'

'After that, you can have salmon, caught by Dr. McPeake, or broiled chicken.'

'Salmon for both of us,' said Mr. Cork.

He wanted to get the ordering over. A newcomer had appeared in the dining-room. She was a woman between thirty and thirty-five, younger rather than older than she appeared. In figure, she was big-breasted and heavy-hipped with the short thick thighs and calves of the peasant. She had brown hair pinned on the back of her head in a loose, old-fashioned bun. Her complexion was sallow, and she wore no make-up except a touch of lip-stick on her big and sensuous mouth. She was dressed in a practical-looking woollen jumper and tweed skirt. In a homespun way, she was a handsome woman.

'Colonel Johnson is signalling that she's not who you think it is,' said Robert.

'He means it's not Anna Pryde.'

'Now, he's hopping his hand over the table.'

'He's imitating a frog,' said Mr. Cork. 'He's clearly indicating that this is Madame Breuvart, the Frenchwoman.'

With lowered eyes, as if she meant to avoid an exchange of courtesies with the other guests, she went to a table on the opposite side of the door to Colonel Johnson. Not till she had given her order to one of the pudding-faced waitresses did she sneak a glance round the room. Her eyes passed over Mr. Cork and Robert without interest. But, as she spotted Kurt in the corner, her expression changed. Surprise, and other emotions too, showed in her face. From where he was sitting, Mr. Cork couldn't see how Kurt himself reacted. But, after a moment's hesitation, Madame Breuvart moved back her chair and walked quickly out of the dining-room.

95

The other guests stirred with mild curiosity at the spectacle of Madame's sudden departure, then quickly subsided over their own affairs again. Robert looked to Mr. Cork for enlightenment, but the G.M. was sipping steadily at his broth. He was waiting for Anna.

She came into the dining-room when most of the other guests were drifting out for coffee. Colonel Johnson, who had been laying in wait, button-holed her at the door; but not before she had sighted Mr. Cork and, apparently, Kurt as well. She gave no outward sign of recognition but, in her anxiety to be free of Colonel Johnson, she almost pushed him out of the dining-room. Then she went to a table in the middle of the room and deliberately placed herself with her back to the four of them.

It was Kurt who made the first move. He got up from his place and, with his companion swaggering behind him, walked across to Anna. She held down her head as if she half-hoped that he would pass by without accosting her.

'Surely I can't be mistaken?' said Kurt with one of his impudent bows. 'Miss Anna Pryde, isn't it?'

In spite of herself, Anna looked quickly over her shoulder at Mr. Cork. Kurt followed her glance.

'You know these gentlemen, too?' he said gaily.

'Yes,' said Mr. Cork, coming to Anna's table. 'Miss Pryde and I are old friends.'

'But wonderful. Miss Pryde is a very old friend of mine. This is indeed an unexpected pleasure.'

'Unexpected?' said Mr. Cork.

'But yes. Of course. Fancy meeting the great and beautiful ballerina, Anna Pryde, in this awful dump.' He threw up his hands in mock despair.

The man's perpetual smile was exasperating. The cast in his eye—Mr. Cork suspected that, maybe, he was blind in it—meant that you were never sure whether he was looking at you or not. He had a parchment-coloured skin which looked as if it never needed a shave. And his smoothness of manner was beyond belief. Mr. Cork considered it was high time to squash him, and squash him hard. He said to Anna:

'I met these gentlemen on the road up here in extremely unpleasant circumstances. Their reckless driving very nearly involved us in a serious accident.'

'It was a little mistake.'

'A very big mistake, Mr. Kurt.'

Momentarily, Kurt's smile seemed to fade. But he quickly recovered himself.

'As you choose,' he said.

'Is this gentleman really a friend of yours?' Mr. Cork asked Anna.

'I'm not aware that I have ever met him in my life.'

'Oh, come, come, Miss Pryde. You pretend you do not know Kurt. I have photographed you so many times; in Lac, in Carnival, in the Sleeping Princess . . .'

'I don't remember it.'

'But you must,' Kurt wheedled.

'Suppose you stop reminiscing,' said Mr. Cork, 'and tell us what a famous photographer, as you say you are, is doing in a remote place like Edendale.'

'It is a very great secret,' said Kurt, tapping his finger on the side of his nose and turning for confirmation to his companion. 'But, if Miss Pryde will confide in me what she is doing in Edendale, I will tell you, very confidential, what we are doing. That is British fair play, is it not?'

'What Miss Pryde is doing is no secret. It's been published in all the papers.'

'Ach,' said Kurt, with a deprecating gesture, 'but that

is a publicity stunt. What is the real reason, eh, Miss Pryde?'

'That is the true reason.'

'So,' said Kurt with a shrug, 'if you will not trust me, I will not trust you.'

'Is this the man who followed you in London, Miss Pryde?'

'Of course it is.'

Kurt's eyes narrowed and his companion drew closer to him.

'You say I followed you?' he said.

'That's what I said,' said Anna. 'Why did you do it?'

'I cannot understand what you mean. Ah yes. I have it. You saw me outside the theatre, perhaps, the other night?'

'You followed me.'

'But no, of course not. I am Kurt, the news photographer. I am always looking, looking for pictures.'

'Is that what you're doing here?' Mr. Cork asked.

'Do you think we can tell them?' said Kurt to his friend in his mocking tones.

'Aw, it's nothing,' said the other man. 'Spill it.'

Kurt's companion might have been a hanger-on in a boxing booth, or a type in a tough Soho dive. His head was deep-set in his shoulders, and he was running to fat. He talked out of the corner of his mouth, and held his cigarette, Cockney-wise, with the head under the cover of his palm. Mr. Cork thought he had probably seen the inside of a prison, more than once, and suspected that he might have a cosh, or even a pistol, inside his jacket. If Kurt hadn't been there for comparison, Mr. Cork would have regarded him as an extremely unpleasant person. But, compared with Kurt, he seemed almost likeable.

'What we are here for is a very, very big story,' said Kurt, lowering his voice. 'You have heard of the salmon-poaching up here? Of course you have. It is big, big news.'

'Well?'

'Can't you guess? I am going to get the big exclusive pictures of the salmon poachers at their work, and my friend here, Fred Bowley, he will write the story.'

'That's the ticket,' said Fred.

'It is, of course, very, very dangerous. They are fierce men, these poachers. But a little bit of this,'—Kurt rubbed his thumb on his fingers—'and a little bit of that,'—he pretended to stroke Anna's back—'and we have it in the bag. It will be big news. Absolute terrific.'

Kurt clenched his fists, and threw wide his hands to emphasize the importance of his mission. Then he looked to Fred for confirmation.

'That is right, Fred?'

'Sure, Smiler, it'll be a crackerjack feature.'

'There!' said Kurt.

He folded his arms and smiled at them with cool challenge. He was right. He had won the first round.

The waitress brought Anna a plate of cold chicken.

'If you'll excuse me . . .' she said.

'But certainly,' said Kurt. 'We are imposing on your privacy.' With a sweep of his hand, he placed the responsibility firmly on the shoulders of Mr. Cork.

'Charming woman,' he said, as the four of them left the dining-room. 'Exquisite dancer. But temperamental. Definite temperamental.'

Six

'HAVE you seen Miss Pryde this morning?' enquired Mr. Cork, as he finished his breakfast porridge.

'Aye,' said Jock.

'Do you know where she is now?'

'I do.'

'You seem very secretive about it.'

'I was only thinking that you're all asking the same question.'

'Oh! Who has been asking?'

'The Colonel, for one; and the foreign gentleman and his friend in the corner.'

'And what have you told them?'

'That I drove her myself to Beat 6 this morning.'

'In the hotel car?'

'There's no other.'

'You must have gone out very early.'

'The young lady insisted. I told her it was noo good. The glass is falling, I said, and it's noo day for a fush.'

'But she wouldn't listen?'

'Mistress Pryde is a very determined young lady. Will you be wanting any sandwiches?'

'Yes, Jock, we will.'

'I'll have them made up for you.'

'By the way, is Madame Breuvart about?'

'Noo, she isn't doon yet.'

'Is she a fisherwoman, too?'

'Noo. She's a foreigner, Muster Cork.'

'Have you any idea what she's doing here?'

'I wouldna know a thing like that, except she rides aroun' on a bicycle. Will that be all?'

'Yes, Jock.'

Mr. Cork didn't press the conversation further. On his way down to breakfast, he had discovered from the visitors' book that the Frenchwoman's arrival at the hotel had followed closely on the discovery of Gabriel Daggers' body. But the elucidation of Madame Breuvart's conduct when she saw Kurt in the dining-room last night would have to wait. Mr. Cork had an urgent appointment at Beat 6.

The way the fishing was arranged on the Edendale, each rod had a different stretch of the river each day. Colonel Johnson's rod, which he had sub-let to Anna Pryde, gave him Beat 6 on Thursdays. So Anna was presumably making her first acquaintance with the actual place on the river where Gabriel Daggers' body had been found. Mr. Cork wanted to keep an eye on her. He also needed to make some investigations on his own account. When Colonel Johnson watched him and Robert leaving the hotel, he would have been outraged could he have known that, disregarding all the proprieties of salmon-fishing, Mr. Cork had instructed Robert to wear swimming trunks beneath his trousers.

'Sorry, Cork, I couldn't fix anything with the girl last night,' he said in parting. 'She seemed somewhat distracted. But you'll find her up on Beat 6. Say I sent you if you like. You'll be lucky if anything's moving up there to-day. River's dead low and atmosphere's too close. Thunder about. But you'll see the Black Brae, that pool where I got stuck into a sixty pounder.'

It was a long journey because Mr. Cork himself insisted on driving. As they followed the twisting road up the river, they passed, one by one, the motor cars of the other fishers from the hotel. Sometimes, they saw the anglers themselves casting over the pools. Mr. Cork counted the cars that they saw parked on the roadside. They should leave five behind them before they reached their own beat. Then, according to Colonel Johnson's instructions, they would know Beat 6 by the landmark of Wully Sutherland's deserted croft on the slopes of the hill called Cnoc Craggie on the right of the road. By that time, they would be about two miles from the nearest fishers below them. Apart from the remote possibility of meeting a passing shepherd, they would be quite alone and undisturbed.

As Mr. Cork dragged the huge car round the hairpin bends and over the crumbling surface of the road in the last few miles of the journey, he noticed that the rabbits were out on the turf and the fitches were hunting along the verges. It was a fairly sure sign that nobody had passed by since Jock had brought Anna up the river in the early morning.

It was Robert who spotted Wully Sutherland's croft. As they came to it, he pointed out a parking-place in a half-circular cutting, obviously excavated when the rubble was being taken from the hillside to build the road. The road, such as it was, was sliced into the slopes. Above them, Cnoc Craggie, scarred with dark rocks and peaty burns, climbed steeply into the mists. Below, a sheep-track through the bracken led to the Black Brae, hidden from the road by the high rocks which enclosed the pool. The river, winding down the glen, looked as black as steel. The air was thundery and close. And the sky was overcast with dark threatening clouds.

When they got out of the car Robert led the way through the bracken to the pool. They walked cautiously, feeling their footing in the boggy ground and starting, in spite of themselves, at the snipe which, with sudden scaups, jumped up at their feet. Robert, wearing the old tweeds in which Mr. Cork had told him he looked like a commission agent, tried to convince himself that he was still on the payroll of the Anchor Accident Insurance Co. Mr. Cork, in the deerstalker hat, Norfolk jacket and knickerbockers which he clung to for fishing in the same determined way that he insisted on a wing collar, black suit and striped trousers for the city, tried to imagine himself sitting comfortably at home with Phoebe, or dozing after lunch in the solid safety of the Cornhill Club. Neither of them, on the brink of the Black Brae, could escape a feeling of complete unreality.

'There's Anna Pryde,' said Robert.

He stopped and pointed. In slacks and sweater, with her dark hair tumbled about her face, she was squatting on a shelf of rock, holding her rod over the water in the manner of a coarse fisherman angling for roach in the Thames.

'She hasn't got a clue,' whispered Robert.

With a smile, Mr. Cork walked up behind her, and watched. Anna, setting her jaw, pretended not to notice him.

'You might find a salmon who's fool enough to take you, Miss Pryde, but I think it very unlikely. Have you got a fly on your cast?'

'Of course I have,' said Anna, without moving. 'I know what I'm doing.'

'You haven't the first idea what you're doing, young woman, and don't pretend that you have.'

Anna wound in her line angrily.

'Why the devil can't you leave me alone? Why have you followed me to-day? It's no business of yours what I do.'

'Colonel Johnson suggested that you might care to share your rod with me.'

'He's an interfering old ass.'

'Like me?'

'If you say so. Oh, I know you mean well. But you're wasting your time up here.'

'Am I? What are you doing then? You're wasting your own time if you're meant to be salmon-fishing. Let me show you the proper way to use a rod.'

Mr. Cork picked up the double-handed rod and, drawing off line, made the cane hiss in the air. Then, with a flick, he shot the silk plait over the water.

'There,' he said.

'I can do that if I want to.'

'I expect I could do a pas-de-chat if I wanted to, Miss Pryde. But I've never tried.'

Anna did her best to hide a smile.

'Who's the boy friend?' she said, indicating Robert.

'Somebody I've brought up here to look after the two of us. Let me introduce you. This is Robert Shipley. Shipley, meet Anna Pryde.'

'I've seen you on the stage,' said Robert. 'It's a great pleasure to meet you.'

'I wish I could echo your sentiments,' said Anna coldly.

Mr. Cork looked at her seriously.

'I think the time has come, Miss Pryde, to finish with shadow-boxing. It must have been evident to you last night that all three of us have good reason to feel alarmed.

I am convinced that this man Kurt is dangerous. I suppose there's no doubt in your own mind that you haven't met him before?'

'Of course not.'

'Then the story that he's a famous photographer is an invention?'

'I've never heard of him.'

'Or his friend, Fred Bowley, who's supposed to be a journalist?'

'I'm glad to say I've never heard of him either.'

'Do you know the Frenchwoman, Madame Breuvart, who's staying in the hotel?'

'I've seen her in the dining-room.'

'She knows Kurt.'

'Are you sure?'

'Fairly sure.'

'Why do you tell me this?'

'I want to impress on you my own presentiments.'

'All right. What next?'

'Assuming that Kurt and his accomplice are telling the story of a photographic assignment as a cover for some other activity, what do you think is their real purpose in following you, or me, or both of us, to Edendale?'

'I can't imagine.'

'Now, it's you who are not telling the truth, Miss Pryde. Do you think it conceivable that Kurt and this man Bowley share our suspicions that Gabriel Daggers is still alive?'

'You mean your suspicions.'

'Mine and yours: unless, of course, in your case, Miss Pryde, suspicion has grown into certainty. Don't let's fence about it. You have come up here looking for Gabriel Daggers. So have I. These men are either Daggers' friends or his enemies. Whichever they are, I don't care. All I care about is that I'm sure that they're your enemies. And, whether you like it or not, henceforward I'm going to keep an eye on you.'

'And if I refuse?'

'I shall report my suspicions to the police and demand a guard for you. Well?'

'You know that I don't want you to go to the police,' said Anna in a low voice.

'Then that's settled.'

'Well, sir,' said Robert, in an attempt to relieve the tension, 'what do we do next?'

Mr. Cork looked over his glasses.

'What we do next,' he said, 'is a job I'm reluctant to pass on to anybody, Shipley. Have you got your swimming trunks on?'

'Yes, sir.'

'You know that this is the place where they found the body. I understand that, subsequently, it was thought unnecessary to drag it, although it seems that part of Gabriel Daggers' fishing tackle was never recovered. If we can find anything like that, it might help us to discover exactly what happened here when the accident occurred. It's an unpleasant job but I want you, if you will, to go in and have a look.'

Robert grinned, and started pulling off his coat. Tight-lipped, Anna looked on.

The stream, as Colonel Johnson had told them, was lower than it had been for a month. The salmon leap at the head of the pool was reduced to a narrow pipe of white water, too thin and too weak for the salmon to jump. The bed of the pool was as deep as ever but the flow of water in the roughs below, where Colonel Johnson had struggled into midstream to get on to terms with his fish, had fined down by a foot or more. The Black Brae was unusually settled and easy in current.

'Johnson tells me,' said Mr. Cork, 'that, under the fall there, it drops down about eight feet. Then the bed slopes gently upwards towards the tail. All you have to look out for, Shipley, are the four-pronged hooks which are bedded in concrete about the middle there.'

Robert nodded understanding. Strange how reminiscent all this was of war ops. The same quiet orders, the same feeling of misbelief, the same unforgettable schoolboyish exhilaration. And yet, hell, what did it all amount to? A plunge into a pool of cold water, slightly disconcerting because somebody had pulled a dead body out of it a few weeks before. What could possibly go wrong? Robert slid down the shelving rocks to the water's edge, enjoying the flex of his muscles on the lichen-covered sharp-edged granite. Then, with a gasp as the icy water enclosed him, he slipped in, working his limbs violently to warm himself for his task.

Mr. Cork, watching the young man earnestly, reached in his pocket for a Passing Cloud. Anna drew close to Mr. Cork's shoulder. Robert turned on his back, shook his tousled head, and trod water.

'I can't find bottom here,' he said. 'I'll work down the pool till I get my bearings.'

'What's the current like?' said Anna.

Surprised by her show of interest, Mr. Cork glanced over his shoulder at her.

'Of course,' he said. 'I'd forgotten you were a swimmer.'

'Current's all right,' Robert called out. 'There's a bit of a pull round the fall in the deep part. But down here, it's easy. O.K., I'm touching bottom now.'

He stood up, with his shoulders sticking out of the water about halfway down the pool.

'Are you cold?' asked Mr. Cork.

'I'm feeling fine, sir. Enjoying it. I'll start diving.'

Porpoising into the water, he kicked his legs and disappeared. He came up again under Mr. Cork's bank.

'It's damned dark down there,' he said, 'but the water's clear and I can see bottom. I think I've sighted the poacher's hooks. I'll try again.'

He did, and came up gasping.

'Too long,' he spluttered. 'I managed to catch hold of the hooks, but I can't see anything else. No, wait a minute. There's something here now.'

Treading water, he doubled forward and reached below him. Then, out of the water, he pulled a piece of line.

'Is this of any interest, sir? There seems to be miles of it.'

Robert pulled the line out yard by yard.

'It's Daggers' fishing line,' said Mr. Cork. 'They said that when they recovered the rod, the line had been stripped off the reel. That's it.'

Robert brought it to the side, scrambled half up the rocky side of the bank, and passed the loop of line to Mr. Cork. Yard by yard, Mr. Cork dragged it out of the water.

'It looks as if the cast is still attached to it,' said Robert, as Mr. Cork steadily pulled it out. 'And, look, the fly as well.'

Mr. Cork drew the line towards him till the fly was in his hand.

'The official theory,' said Mr. Cork, 'is that Daggers was drowned trying to hold a fish. This all fits in. Furthermore, this is Daggers' favourite fly.'

The fly was dressed in yellow deer's fur with a gold body. An unusual fly for most salmon fishers. But Shirt, the Anchor's enquiry agent, had discovered from the tackle shop that the 'Garry Dog' was the fly which Daggers nearly always used. Such evidence as it provided was confirmation, rather than otherwise, of the official story.

'It doesn't help us, I'm afraid, Shipley. I'm sorry. But we must have another look. Try down there in the deep hollow on the edge of the fall.'

'Aye, aye, sir,' said Robert. Leaning back on his arms he thrust his legs forward, and projected himself neatly from the wall of rock into the pool.

Mr. Cork watched anxiously as Robert dived again and again for the bottom. He was becoming tired. And, so far, they had found nothing in the search of value.

'I'm sorry, sir,' said Robert at last. 'I've searched the bottom fairly thoroughly. But, so far, I can't make it in that deep corner between your bank and the fall. It must be nearly ten feet. I'll have another go when I've got my breath.'

Eagerly watching Robert, Mr. Cork hadn't noticed that Anna had left his side. The first indication he had of it was the sight of her small white body flying through the air between the top of the bank and the water. She dived in with hardly a splash and, in a moment, her hair bedraggled over her face, she was treading water at Robert's side.

'Good God,' said Mr. Cork. 'Come out at once, Miss Pryde.'

Anna, exhilarated by the icy cold of the water and the excitement of action, laughed.

'But it's not safe there.' Mr. Cork was beside himself with anxiety.

'Don't be ridiculous. I'm a far better swimmer than he is. Look out, I'm diving.'

With a plunge, and a wriggle of her toes, she disappeared below the water. Robert fell back in the current to give her room. When she came up, Mr. Cork was flat on his stomach hanging over the edge of the pool.

'There's nothing there,' she gasped.

'Are you sure?'

'Of course I'm sure. I was down long enough, wasn't I?'

'Have another try, Shipley,' said Mr. Cork.

'He won't find anything.'

Robert took a deep breath, and dived again. To Mr. Cork, it seemed like minutes that he was under. He came to the surface, thrashing the water and dragging up a weight from the bottom.

'I've got it,' he said.

'Got what?'

'A canvas strap. I think there's a bag on the end of it. It weighs a ton.'

Slowly dragging the weight, he worked into the bank, and, with his other hand, gripped a rock on the edge for leverage. With another heave, the weight moved and Robert dragged it to the surface. It was a fishing bag, heavy with water and something else. Robert pushed it up the rocks to Mr. Cork. Then, followed by Anna, he scrambled after it.

'So, there was nothing there, Miss Pryde,' said Mr. Cork sardonically.

'She might easily have missed it,' said Robert gallantly. 'It was stuck right in a crack in the rocks at the bottom.'

'You forget, Shipley. Miss Pryde is an expert swimmer. Far better than you are.'

With an embarrassed grin, Robert winked at Anna. Recognizing a friend in need, she gave a quick smile in return. Mr. Cork was far too interested in the dripping bag to notice the exchange. He carefully unstrapped it.

'He seems to have carried a heavy load of tackle about with him,' said Robert.

Mr. Cork threw back the flaps. The pockets on the front, the compartments inside, were heavily loaded with stones.

'What on earth did he do that for?'

'Can't you guess? This fishing bag—it's Daggers' bag all right, it's got his initials on it, quite apart from the initials on the fly box here—this fishing bag has been deliberately weighted to sink. A man doesn't do that when he's drowning. But, if a man wants the world to believe he's been drowned, and if he also wants to make sure that no one discovers the fact until it's too late for a proper identification of the body, he takes good care that nothing comes floating to the surface. He jams his rod on to the bottom, he fastens the body which is meant to be his on the hooks in the bed of the river, and he weights his fishing bag with stones. Well, Miss Pryde, what have you to say about that?'

Anna, half-dressed and soaking wet, with Robert's jacket over her shoulders and teeth chattering with cold, looked at Mr. Cork with white-faced hatred. Stooping down, she picked up the soused fishing bag and, with sudden exertion, tipped the contents into the river. Then she threw the bag, empty, at Mr. Cork's feet.

'What's your evidence worth now?' she said. Then she broke down in tears.

Mr. Cork, signalling Robert aside, took her by the arms and shook her violently.

'Get hold of yourself, Anna. Get hold of yourself. I know you love this man Daggers, and I don't blame you for that. I don't blame you for trying your best to protect his interests. I admire you for it. But it's got to stop now.

This man is a cold-blooded murderer. I don't know who he has murdered, or why he has murdered. We've got to find that out. But he's a murderer, a man unfit for the love of any woman and especially of a woman like you. For your own peace of mind, try and forget him.'

He let her go.

'Give her your shirt, or something, Shipley, to dry herself on. And start getting dressed, both of you. What this means, I'm afraid . . .'

Mr. Cork stopped in the middle of the sentence. Out of the bracken, somebody had stepped up behind them.

'It looks as if, maybe, you'll be in some need of assistance,' said the stranger.

Seven

HE was a tall, bony man, with a raw beef complexion and to Mr. Cork's disgust, a disfiguring mouthful of broken and blackened teeth. He stood there, dressed in the characteristic homespun tweeds and stalking hat of the Highlander, staring at them sourly, and purposefully grasping a heavy blackthorn stick.

In the lonely bowl of moorland where, theoretically, you could see anything that moved for miles around, the three people on the bank of the salmon pool had been surprised completely. In the first start of discovery they looked as guilty, and as foolish, as naughty children caught in some mischief by the keeper in a public park. Robert, naked to the waist, his tweed trousers hanging ludicrously down his legs, rose to his feet to cover Anna, who was kneeling on the rocks in wet underclothes with his jacket over her shoulders and his shirt in her hands. Mr. Cork, with the slight moral advantage of having all his clothes on, was unable to conceal his astonishment. To all appearance, the stranger had sprouted like a dragon's tooth from the ground.

Playing for time and inspiration, Mr. Cork reached in his hip-pocket for his cigarette case. Slowly selecting a Passing Cloud, he fixed the interloper with a steady gaze over the top of his glasses, an intimidating stare which he had always found useful when he needed to make up his mind what to do next. He continued staring until he observed, with satisfaction, that the stranger was shifting uncomfortably from one foot to another. Mr. Cork was not the general manager of a great insurance company by accident. He knew that the initiative had passed to him.

'Who told you to come here spyinground the Black Brae?' he said, with sharp authority. The stranger dropped his eyes.

'Begging your pardon, Muster,' he said, touching his hat. 'I was just passing by and, seeing you here at the Black Brae, I thought, maybe, you might be needing the assistance of a ghillie.'

'I'm obliged to you,' said Mr. Cork, 'but if I required a ghillie I should have hired one in the usual way in the village.'

He turned away and lit his cigarette; the interview was closed. Robert, carefully watching the stranger, noticed the knuckles whiten as his hand tightened on his stick. He was hesitating.

'This is a verra dangerous stretch of the river,' he said slowly. 'And I was thinking that you'd be well-advised to have a ghillie, or to keep away from the Black Brae altogether.'

With studied disinterest, Mr. Cork sat down on a ledge of rock.

'I could hardly fail to notice,' the stranger went on pertinaciously, 'that the young lady and gentleman have been in trouble here already.'

'The young lady and gentleman have been good enough to help me recover a fishing bag which had fallen in the water. We have had no trouble yet,' said Mr. Cork with brisk emphasis, 'and I trust we shall have no trouble in the future.'

'With all respect to you, Muster, you'll need to be careful here in the Black Brae. Haven't you heard at Muster Mackenzie's hotel of the fatal accident a few weeks ago?'

'Yes, we've heard all about it. Why?'

'This is the verra pool where poor Muster Daggers was drowned. It's a treacherous place.'

'You knew Mr. Daggers, then?'

'I was the poor gentleman's ghillie every season he came up here.'

Mr. Cork looked up with renewed interest.

'It was a great pity you weren't accompanying him when he was drowned.'

'Yes, Muster. It was a terrible pity. But there were times when Muster Daggers would insist on fishing by himself.'

'Do you happen to know why it was so long before Mr. Daggers' body was discovered?'

'There are strange currents which pull in this pool.'

'Perhaps, as you ghillied for Mr. Daggers, you know who the friends were he intended to visit over the hill?'

The stranger looked at Mr. Cork slyly.

'I wouldna know a thing like that, Muster.'

'Did you like Mr. Daggers?'

'He was a grand fisher. He cast a lovely line.'

'I wasn't asking that. I was asking if you liked Mr. Daggers personally.'

'Why shouldn't I like him? I was his ghillie.'

'Not many people did like Mr. Daggers . . . Snatcher.'

Mr. Cork rose to his feet, and advanced close to the stranger.

'That's your name, isn't it? You're Snatcher.'

'It's my nickname. Somebody must have told you. Colonel Johnson, was it?'

115

'It might have been,' said Mr. Cork. 'But what I want to impress on you is that I know a good deal more than is healthy for you. You've got a hide-out up there on the hill, haven't you?'

'I've a wee bit croft on the far slopes of Cnoc Craggie.'

'And you keep a sharp eye on this pool, don't you, Snatcher?'

'I sometimes pass this way.'

'To come up on us unawares in this place, you must have crawled through the bracken,' said Mr. Cork. 'You'd be wise not to try it again. Do I make myself clear?'

Snatcher cringed.

'I was trying to help you, Muster. That's all. If you don't need my services, you've only to say so.'

'I may need your services before long, Snatcher. When I do, I'll come after you. Meanwhile, you can keep out of the way. And, if you know what's good for you, keep your mouth shut, too. Keep your mouth shut . . . even if the ghost of Gabriel Daggers rises out of the waters of the Black Brae.'

Snatcher looked at Mr. Cork searchingly. Then he turned on his heel and, without a backward glance, went striding through the bracken up the sheep track to the road.

'Good show, sir,' said Robert admiringly, as the three of them watched Snatcher climbing the hill. 'You fixed him properly.'

'What do you think he wanted?' said Anna quickly.

'You know what he wanted as well as I do,' said Mr. Cork. 'He was Daggers' ghillie. He's still Daggers' ghillie. He was sent here to find out what's going on.'

'You think he knows where he is?'

'So you admit, at last, that Daggers isn't dead?'

'I admit nothing.'

'Has Daggers given any sign, apart from this, that he knows you're here?'

'No.'

'Sure of that?'

'Of course I'm sure.'

'You're shivering. It's time you put your clothes on. You too, Robert. We might be overlooked again.'

'Funny you should say that,' said Robert, screening his eyes and studying the face of Cnoc Craggie rising above them. 'But just now I could swear I saw the flash of field glasses near the top of the hill. Yes, there it is again. Somebody else is spotting us.'

'Don't let him see you've sighted him,' said Mr. Cork. 'And come down here under the cover of the bank.'

He pointed the way down a cleft in the rocks to a clearing of rubble on the edge of the salmon leap, which was invisible from above.

'Are you quite certain, Shipley,' he said, as he recovered from the scramble down the rock, 'that it is someone watching us?'

'Absolutely certain. It was one of the little things we got used to looking for in the war. If you didn't spot it, you'd had it.'

'Where's Anna?' said Mr. Cork.

'I thought she'd followed us.'

Robert looked over the top of the bank. Anna was standing where they had left her, gazing towards Cnoc Craggie.

'Come down here, Anna,' said Robert. 'Get under cover.'

Reluctantly, she obeyed.

'Is Snatcher still in view?' asked Mr. Cork.

'Yes, and will be, unless he goes to ground again, until he gets round the curve of the hill.'

'I wonder how long we've been watched.'

'You can't tell. I'd never have spotted the man if the sun hadn't peeped through the clouds for a minute or two and been reflected in his glasses.'

'Do you think he noticed that we'd marked him?'

'I doubt it. I was careful not to point. And you and Anna were looking in the wrong direction.'

'Good.'

'It looks as if it's our man, doesn't it?'

'It seems like it,' said Mr. Cork.

'I suppose, after sending Snatcher to find out what we were up to,' Robert went on eagerly, 'he couldn't quieten his own anxiety, or felt he couldn't trust Snatcher sufficiently to keep out of the way himself. I wonder what he's looking for?'

'I can make a guess,' said Mr. Cork.

'Anna?'

Robert, excited by his discovery, felt a surge of male protectiveness.

'Don't worry, Anna,' he said, patting her arm. 'This is where I come in.'

'And what precisely do you purpose doing?' said Mr. Cork.

'Go after him, sir.'

'How?'

'I've had a good look at the lie of the land up there on the hill. Given time, I think I could stalk him.'

'Then what?'

'Well, sir . . .' Under Mr. Cork's cool stare Robert's spirits were steadily deflating. 'I shall try to cook his goose, sir.'

'I rather suspected that that was your idea,' said Mr. Cork. 'There will be no cooking of geese, Shipley.'

'But we might never get a chance like this again.'

'I sincerely hope that we won't,' said Mr. Cork.

'What are we going to do then?'

'Are you satisfied that you can make a close approach to this man without his seeing you?'

'It's a good sporting chance.'

'Very well, Shipley. You can try. But I want to emphasize that you're not to take the law into your own hands unless you have to do so to defend yourself. Your instructions are to get a good look at this man, identify him if you can, without letting him get a sight of you. Is that clear?'

'Quite clear, sir.'

'How long will it take your to get up to him?' Mr. Cork continued.

'Perhaps an hour, perhaps more. I shall work downstream under the river bank and then stalk him to the top of the hill through the bracken on the side of the burn. If I can get as far as that without causing too much of a commotion, I shall be above him. The rest of the approach ought to be easy.'

'What do you want us to do?' Mr. Cork enquired.

'Pretend to fish and give the fellow something to keep him occupied. Whatever you do, don't look about you to see how I'm getting on. What is it, Anna?'

Anna had grasped Robert by the arm.

'Don't talk about it any more,' she said.

'What's the matter, Anna?'

'I want you to leave this to me, Mr. Cork. It's all right. I'm not going to pretend any more that Gabriel isn't alive. I saw him in the theatre that same night you came to my dressing-room.'

'You spoke to him?'

'No, I saw him sitting in the stalls while I was dancing. When I looked for him afterwards he was gone.'

'You should have told me.'

'Need we discuss that now?'

'Unless you prefer not to.'

'You don't know Gabriel, Mr. Cork. He had a terrible time in the war. He's not normal.'

'Do you know why he had to disappear?'

'No.'

'Did you ever suspect that something like this might happen?'

'Yes.'

'Why?'

'Things he wouldn't talk about.'

'What things?'

'Where he got all the money he had. Why he mistrusted shadows in the street.'

'He was in fear of something?'

'Not in fear. Gabriel wasn't that sort of man.'

'He was wary but unafraid? You taxed him about it, of course? What did he say?'

'He said that it would all come right in the end.'

'And now that it's all gone wrong? What do you want to do?'

'I want to see him.'

'To warn him?'

'To prevent him murdering again. You mustn't let Robert go up there.'

'Don't worry about me,' said Robert grinning. 'Mr. Cork will tell you that, as an insurance clerk, I'm expendable.'

'Suppose, as you suggest, you go to him yourself, Anna. What good will come out of it?'

'I can talk to him.'

'And you think you'll be safe with him now that he knows that you know he's a murderer?'

'I'm ready to take that risk.'

'I'm not,' said Mr. Cork.

'You mean that Robert isn't to go either?'

'Robert is better able to look after himself.'

'But I've told you everything you want to know. There's nothing else to discover.'

'Isn't there?'

'So you intend to go on with this?'

'I do. And, if you as much as blow your nose, by way of warning, I shall treat you as Daggers' accomplice.'

'So you're threatening?'

'You've done your best, haven't you, to frighten me?'

Mr. Cork took her amiably, but firmly, by the arm.

'All right, Shipley,' he said. 'Get going; and good luck to you.'

'What about Anna?'

'Anna and I are going to give each other a fishing lesson,' said Mr. Cork.

The first part of the stalk was easier than Robert had anticipated. The action of the stream had rubbed a shelf under the bank and, thanks to the lowness of the river, there was never less than three feet of cover between the top of the bank and the surface of the water. He had no difficulty in feeling his way under the rocky walls of the Black Brae. As he crept on hands and knees along the edge of the rough water below the pool, pressing into the clay bank, pitted with rabbit holes, and guarding himself from slipping off the soft earth into the scummy holes on the edges of the river, he was only fearful that the watchful herring gulls and the oyster catchers perched on the exposed rocks of the river bed would sound the alarm. If the sea-birds rose in a squawking and protesting crowd over his head, he could scarcely hope that the watcher on the hill would fail to notice it.

He cursed a moorhen which burst out of the rushes within a few inches of his nose and skimmed noisily across the river to the other bank. He froze in his tracks when a pair of mallard broke out of the rushes in front of him and, with a startled quack of alarm, circled over his head. But the warning didn't arouse the other creatures of the river. He calculated that he had achieved the first dangerous part of his stalk without revealing his presence to the watcher on the hill above.

Robert was pleased with himself. Mr. Cork might have no use for his brains but, when it came to action, he could give the old boy his money's worth. If he made a success of this job, under the very eyes of the G.M., the Anchor could hardly fail to give him a decent rise and, with any luck promotion too. He might even stick in insurance after all. Who could have guessed, sitting at a desk under those beastly green table-lamps in the city, messing about with dusty ledgers and dreary policies, that the insurance business could be as exciting as this? If this was typical of the sort of thing that was going on behind the scenes, Robert felt that he had indeed discovered his vocation.

What a smashing girl, too. He felt that he could go for Anna in a real big way. Pity that she was besotted by this fellow Daggers. But perhaps she'd change her mind when he himself had got the measure of him. Daggers was obviously one of those Commando types who, because they'd done a battle school course and lived on raw potatoes, thought they were the toughest boys in army boots. When he shot a line, Anna, who only had the queens in the ballet for comparison, was probably impressed. But not Robert.

Even in the laborious excitement of crawling along under the river bank, he imagined himself at the wheel of Mr. Cork's Bentley, with Anna's head nestling on his shoulder, telling him what a mistake she had made in thinking that she had ever loved anyone else.

They say that cold water is the best antidote to sentimental yearning and, as he crawled round a curve under the bank, Robert realized that he faced the prospect of cold water. Between him and the point where the burn joined the main stream, the clay bank, under which he was crawling, crumbled away. A wide belt of shingle, exposed by the fall in the level of the river, separated him from the cover of the deep ravine in the rocks—the watercourse known as Baile an Or—by which he intended to make the climb up Cnoc Craggie. The open bank offered no protection from the glasses of the watcher on the hill. To conceal his approach Robert realized that he had no alternative but to take to the river, keep his head down, and float quietly with the current.

A deep and narrow run—the very run where Colonel Johnson fought the great fish after the race up the Devil's staircase—curled round the outer edge of the shingle towards the foot of the burn. Robert, with a wary eye for the white water beyond it rolled off the bank into the river.

Keeping his arms under the water and working his legs slowly, he moved downstream with the current. He thought to himself that the water was warmer than it had been in the Black Brae. But when he got to the bottom of the run and under the shelter of the high rocks of the burn, he realized that it was the protecting warmth of his clothes that had deceived him. Now he felt cold and uncomfortable, and even the memory of Anna left him strangely indifferent. He scrambled out of the river hurriedly. Shaking himself and squeezing the water out of his clothes, he tried to build up his circulation again by flogging his arms round his chest. And, in doing so, he almost ruined his chances.

Three or four gulls swung up from the river, screaming overhead. Blasting them, Robert lay still, and in a few moments they settled down to their preening and fishing. But it was a warning. Robert, blue with cold as he was, started the difficult journey up the ravine cautiously and slowly.

Beyond the bridge, the burn oozed down a cleft in the rock which, in times of rain, became a waterfall. Above that, the line of the stream was marked by a ragged black scar drawn across the northern slopes of Cnoc Craggie, veining out near the cap of the hill into smaller tributaries. The sides of the burn on the upper slopes were conveniently lined with a rank growth of bracken. Robert monkeyed up the cleft in the rock and, with a feeling of relief, sneaked into the cover of the foliage.

But the relief was short-lasting. In the hot thundery weather every frond of bracken was populated with clegs and flies. They closed on Robert's steaming body delightedly. Miserably wiping the flies off his face, hacking himself on the sharp stones lying along the edge of the burn, he climbed obstinately upwards till his breathing became heavy and tickling drops of sweat mingled with the damp of his clothes. He was three quarters of the way up the hill, and he was tired. He decided that it was time to rest. He turned on to his belly and, parting the bracken, peered down into the Black Brae.

Mr. Cork and Anna were doing their stuff. Outlined on the river bank below, and to the right, Robert could see them together fishing the pool just above the place where the fall tumbled into the drain hole of the Black Brae itself. With his sharp eyes Robert could even sight the splash of a salmon rising under the bank opposite them, probably the fish that Mr. Cork was casting to. But he wondered how much enthusiasm Mr. Cork was putting into the job. Or Anna. Especially Anna.

He thought to himself how slight and graceful she looked, standing there at Mr. Cork's side. He recalled, in shameless detail, the body she had revealed when she dived in beside him into the Black Brae. And he felt rather the better for it.

He turned over, and went on with the last leg of his climb. As he neared the top, a breeze stirred. Heather replaced the bracken. The flies faded away. Forgetful of the physical effort he had made, unconscious of his damp clothes, Robert was gripped with the thrilling knowledge that he was within striking distance of his man. He estimated that he himself was now about a hundred feet above him. And, if the watcher was still there, his attention would be directed towards the river; not behind him.

Robert decided to take a chance. Getting to his feet and bending double, he made a rush to the top. On the far slope, he found a sheep track. There, in a concealing fold, he recovered his breath and started to stride out, pace by pace, a thousand yards. At a thousand paces he turned up the hill again, falling to ground as he reached the top. He crawled round a little while in search of an observation place. Then he raised his head slowly and spied out the ground. There was nobody in sight.

Disappointed, he slithered forward, foot by foot, search-ing the hollows and the shadows behind the rocks. Senses taut to every sound and movement he stiffened at the warning call of an old cock grouse in the heather to the right. The birds were upwind of him and it was odd that they had got his scent so easily. Flattened to the ground, fingers digging into the peat, he rolled his head to get a look on his flank. As he did so, the grouse burst out of the heather like shrapnel and, with a whirr of wings, drove straight towards him. It couldn't have been Robert who had alarmed them. It was someone else.

The covey jinked as the old birds were surprised by the white dial of Robert's face. Raising himself on his arms, he peered along the curve of the hill. Lying in a hollow, his field glasses dangling on a strap round his neck, was the man Robert had been stalking.

The two of them sighted each other while the length of a cricket pitch still divided them. The man in the hollow pulled out an ugly-looking bludgeon from his pocket and, springing to his feet, came for Robert. Robert himself took a deep breath and, getting on his toes like a runner await-ing the start gun, measured the distance. If the fellow wanted a scrap, he could have it. He waited until there was ten yards between them; then he rushed his man.

Robert weighed thirteen stone and he made a flying tackle at his opponent's legs with all the extra force of his charge. The cosh flew out of the man's hand and the two of them came down with a grunt on the stony ground. For a moment, they lay there half-stunned. Then, together, they rolled and wrestled for an advantage. The man was powerful and Robert was tired after the exhausting climb up the hill. To win, he realized that he must make a more open fight of it. Raising his knees, he pushed out hard and threw himself out of the clinch. His opponent, far from making any attempt to stop him, rolled back too and, raising himself, plunged his right hand into his coat.

The pistol was half-drawn before Robert appreciated his mistake. He pitched in again just in time to feel the explosion as the bullet passed over his head. He grabbed the man's wrist and forced the barrel of the smoking gun into the ground. Desperately he closed his teeth on his opponent's hand. The pistol exploded again. A fist came down heavily on the back of his neck and he felt sick. But, somehow, he managed to bend the gun arm behind his opponent's back. The pistol dropped out of the man's hand and, as he tried to free his arm, he gave a sudden turn of his body. Robert rolled over but, as he went on to his back, he straddled his legs round his opponent's trunk and threw all his weight into twisting himself on top again.

With a lurch, the two struggling figures spilt over on the steep slope of Cnoc Craggie. For twenty or thirty bruising, bumping yards they stuck together. Scraping on the rough heather, cutting themselves on the outcrop rocks, they fought drunkenly on. Then, with another lurching roll, they parted.

Robert's head hit rock and for a few seconds he was knocked unconscious. He came to feeling heavy and with a warm trickle of blood trailing down the side of his face. Then he saw his man reeling desperately down the hill far below him. He had no hope of catching him. But he couldn't stop.

He climbed to his feet, shook his head wearily, and started tumbling and falling down the hill after his opponent. Half-a-dozen times he slipped and fell as, bleary-eyed and light-headed, he misjudged his footing on the slippery pot-holed slope of the hill.

He kept on until his head cleared sufficiently to let him see that the chase was hopeless. He saw Anna and Mr. Cork running towards him from the river bank. He saw his opponent sliding madly down the final slope of the hill on to the road.

First, he shouted to Anna and Mr. Cork to keep out of the way. Then, sitting there on the hill, he wondered where on earth his man was heading for. Surely he didn't expect to get far on his feet. And, as the thought struck him, he saw the answer. The man was on the road now and heading straight for old Cork's car. Please God they hadn't left the ignition key in the dashboard.

Robert roused himself and started down the hill again. He saw the man throw open the door of the Bentley and jump in. The ignition key was there all right. He heard the roar of the engine as the man put his foot down hard on the accelerator. The car swung out of the bay and turned towards Edendale.

Down below Robert glanced at Mr. Cork and Anna gazing after it. He himself felt a wave of utter misery. He had failed, hopelessly and completely.

He stood there watching as the Bentley gathered speed and weaved along the twisting road to the hairpin bend over the bridge that spanned the burn. He thought to himself idly that the driver seemed to be taking it unnecessarily fast. Then he saw that something was wrong. The silver car was reeling wildly across the road. It lurched over the verge towards the river, swung giddily for a moment on the edge of the burn below the bridge, and then, with a crash, nose-dived into the deep rock gutter where the burn joined the main stream.

Robert started to run again.

Eight

'ARE you all right?' gasped Mr. Cork.

He and Anna scrambled over the turf parapet between the brackened slope of the river bank and the road at the same moment that Robert, bringing with him a shower of rubble, slipped down into the cutting where the car had been parked at the base of the hill.

'I'm all right, sir,' panted Robert, running in the direction of the wreck. 'Just a bang on the head. Sorry I made a blot of it. He was too good for me. Out of training, I'm afraid. Too much sitting at an office desk.'

Robert shouted the last remark over his shoulder. Mr. Cork, with the handicap of his years, had come to a halt. Anna, in the hard training of a professional dancer, ran easily at his side.

'I suppose you heard the gun go off,' he said to Anna. 'He was armed.'

Anna made no comment. Robert, pressing his hand on his chest as he recovered his breathing, stopped. Anna stopped too, and looked at him coldly. With a worried gesture, he pushed back his dishevelled hair, making a smear of the blood coursing down the side of his face.

'I couldn't help it,' he said. 'We walked into each other, and he came straight at me with a cosh.'

'You shouldn't have gone up there. Come on, we must keep going.'

They started running again, jolting through the bracken as they made a short cut to the gully below the road bridge where the burn joined the river.

'What do you think happened to the car?' said Anna.

'It looked to me as if the steering went wonky. Apart from that, he was driving damned fast.'

Anna, running behind Robert, grabbed his coat and pulled him to a halt again. Robert turned and faced her.

'Tell me the truth,' she said. 'Do you think he's dead?'

'What do you want me to say?'

'I don't know.'

'You wait here for old Cork and I'll go on and look.'

'I'm afraid.'

'I can't imagine there's much to be afraid of now.'

'I'll wait. Don't be long.'

She watched him turn towards the wreck of the car, pushing his way through the bracken to the burn; the same burn which, a little while ago, he had negotiated during his stalk up the hill.

Standing on the side, Robert looked down the rocky cleft to the peaty trickle of water at the bottom of the gully, fifteen feet below. The Bentley, with its nose crushed into the bed of the stream, was lying there like a silver beetle, impotent on its back.

Robert climbed down the granite wall of rock. A glance was sufficient to confirm that his opponent was dead. The steering column had plunged into his stomach. The man who, only minutes before, had been so quick and muscular and wilful to live was twisted up in a grim heap. His eyes were still open in a horrified stare. Wax-faced, he was looking at Robert upside down.

Robert, accustomed in years of war to the sight of violent death, looked at the man carefully. He tried the doors of the car, but the framework was so twisted he could not move them. With an experienced eye, he looked at the base of the upturned chassis. Then he climbed up to the top of the bank again.

Mr. Cork was standing there with Anna.

'Well?' he said.

'He's dead all right,' murmured Robert casually. 'He hadn't a hope. Somebody has interfered with the car.'

'What?'

'The drop-arm of the steering has been sawn through with a hacksaw.'

'Are you sure of that, Shipley?'

'Positive. The car is on its back and you can see the saw-marks where the drop-arm has been tampered with. By a jewel saw, I should think.'

'What's a jewel saw?'

'A very fine toothed saw used by precision engineers, metal-workers and such like.'

'By jewellers, too?'

'I suppose so. Anyhow, the chap who did this job was a good mechanic. He knew what he was up to all right. He must have cut through about three quarters of the tube on the leading-edge so that when the car made a sharp right-hand turn the control snapped. As soon as our chap picked up speed and spun the wheel at that hairpin bend over the bridge, he'd had it.'

Mr. Cork pursed his lips between his fingers. Anna looked at Robert as if she was trying to make up her mind about something.

'I must see him,' she said suddenly. 'I must see the man in that car.'

'I shouldn't,' said Robert. 'He's not very pleasant to look at.'

'Describe him, then.'

'That's easy enough. He's fair-haired and tall, about my height, with blue eyes and several days' growth of beard.'

'Are you sure?'

'Of course I'm sure. When you've looked at a man down the wrong end of a gun, it's remarkable how observant it makes you. But why do you ask? You're supposed to know the fellow.'

'Not this man,' said Anna quietly. 'If your description is correct, it can't be Gabriel.'

'How would you describe Daggers.'

'Gabriel was short, about five foot seven. He had black hair, and his eyes were . . .'

'Never mind about his eyes,' Robert interrupted. 'I can tell you now that that poor devil down there in the burn isn't Daggers. Daggers might have changed the colour of his hair, and I might be wrong about the colour of his eyes. But he couldn't have put inches on his height. This fellow is a big chap. Didn't you see him tumbling down the slope?'

'We were too far away. We weren't even sure which of you was which.'

'Then, if it's not Daggers, who is it?'

'Did you say he was fair-haired and tall?' said Anna.

'He did. What of it?' said Mr. Cork.

'When I came up in the train here, a tall fair-haired man was in the next sleeper. He watched me get into the train. And, when I changed at Inverness, he changed too. I didn't see him again after that.'

'Did he look like a foreigner?' asked Robert.

'He might have been.'

'Like Kurt?' said Mr. Cork.

'I think he was following me . . . like Kurt.'

Instinctively, Mr. Cork felt in his pocket for his cigarette case. Instinctively, Robert took Anna's arm, and she didn't withdraw it. Instinctively, the three of them walked away from the tragic remains in the burn. They sat down together behind the grass bank on the edge of the road.

'I'm sorry about the car, sir,' said Robert, tenderly dabbing his head with a wet handkerchief. 'I'm afraid she's a write-off.'

'Never mind the car,' said Mr. Cork. 'Just thank God we weren't in it.'

'You think the steering was fixed for our benefit?'

'Who else could it have been for?'

'Snatcher must have done the job after we got rid of him. After all, we let him out of our sight as soon as I spotted the man on the hill.'

'That's a possible explanation,' said Mr. Cork doubtfully. 'But who was this man on the hill? Why was he so interested in studying our movements? For what reason was he around? Why was he so anxious to get away that he stole the car? Obviously, he couldn't have known that the steering had been interfered with.'

'Suppose Daggers fixed the car to get rid of you and me,' suggested Robert, 'in a convenient accident. And suppose the man on the hill was an accomplice of Kurt's. The description tallies with the fellow Anna says she saw on the train.'

'But what can they possibly want with me?'

'Perhaps they hope you'll lead them to Daggers,' Robert suggested. 'Perhaps they're friends of the man he murdered.'

'That's what I thought,' said Mr. Cork, 'before I made

133

Kurt's better acquaintance. But he doesn't strike me now as the sort of man to nurse a vendetta. There must be a more valid reason for his interest than that. Suppose that Kurt and his friends—we'll assume that the man on the hill was associated with Kurt—think that Daggers is dead; can you imagine any secret that Daggers might have had, Anna, which they could believe had been passed to you?'

'No.'

'What about Daggers' money?'

'I've told you I didn't know where it came from.'

'But these men might believe you do know.'

'How did they know where Anna was to-day?' Robert asked.

'That's easy. Kurt asked Jock. It increases the likelihood that this fellow who has been killed was in league with him.'

'But what did they expect to discover, watching Anna fishing?'

'Not how to catch salmon,' said Mr. Cork. 'Maybe they wanted to know, like Snatcher, what your real intentions were, Anna, at the Black Brae. But why the Black Brae?'

Defeated, Mr. Cork lit a cigarette.

'Well,' said Robert, 'what do we do next? I could do with a hot bath.'

'We must walk to beat five down the river, where they'll be fishing, and get some help. Next, we must report this to the police. Are you feeling fit to move, Shipley?'

Robert got to his feet and shook his damp clothes. As Mr. Cork bestirred himself to follow, Robert checked him.

'Wait a minute,' he said, 'there's somebody coming up the glen.'

He dropped down again quickly under the shelter of the grass bank.

'What sort of somebody?' said Mr. Cork.

134

'Somebody on a bicycle.'

'A bicycle?'

'Why not?' said Anna.

'Yes, why not?' said Robert. 'What on earth are we hiding for? It's probably a keeper or a shepherd. We can send him to get help.'

Robert started into the road again.

'No, come back,' said Mr. Cork quickly. 'You may be quite right, Shipley. And it may be that I'm becoming excessively cautious. But I'm a nervous man by nature and, to-day of all days, in this place of all places, I'd like to make sure. We'll wait and see who this cyclist is before we show ourselves. How far away is he?'

'I saw him coming round a bend in the road about half-a-mile down river.'

'Then he won't get here for a few minutes. Come along,' said Mr. Cork. 'We'll watch for him behind the bridge wall.'

Mr. Cork, with his nose on the ground like an old dog on a hare, crawled heavily towards the bridge about fifty feet from where they had been sitting. Anna and Robert followed. On the sloping bank behind the bridge wall, Mr. Cork hauled himself from the ground and, with the other two crouching behind him, peered cautiously down the road.

They got into position just in time. The cyclist was pedalling rapidly along the curve of the road. And one glance was enough. As the three of them ducked into hiding again, Robert gave a low whistle.

'It's the Frenchwoman,' he whispered, 'wearing slacks.'

'Twelve miles from base,' said Mr. Cork, 'riding a bicycle up the glen. I wondered how Madame Breuvart fitted in. Now, maybe, we shall find out.'

'You really think she has something to do with this Daggers business?' Robert asked.

'She knows Kurt and I've been asking myself ever since I got here: what brings a lone Frenchwoman to North Britain?'

'She must have a good reason.'

'That's self-evident, Shipley. Quietly, here she comes.'

They waited silently until they could hear the clicking of the chain as the cyclist free-wheeled up to the bridge before braking round the hairpin bend on the side where Mr. Cork, with Robert and Anna, was hiding. When she was safely past them, Mr. Cork peered up the road after her. She still pedalled on, but he noticed that she was looking about her as if she were searching for a landmark or a signal. As she arrived opposite the deserted croft on the hillside, she slowed down and dismounted. With a quick look about her, as if she was making sure that she was unobserved, she ran her bike off the road and concealed it in the bracken. Then she hurried towards the river.

'She seemed to be quite sure where she wants to get to,' said Robert.

'Somebody else with an interest in the Black Brae,' said Mr. Cork.

'Do we follow her?'

'As soon as she's out of sight of us, we'll walk down to the river and collect the rod we've left on the bank,' said Mr. Cork. 'Then we'll discover whether she's got as good an explanation for being at the Black Brae as we have.'

The woman disappeared, as Mr. Cork had guessed she would, below the rock bank of the pool. Once again Mr. Cork, with Robert and Anna, zig-zagged along the sheep-tracks to the river. He walked slowly and thought hard. He calculated that whether or not he got any information out of Madame Breuvart depended to a large degree on surprise; on how shrewdly he could guess the square she occupied in the complicated chess problem of Gabriel Daggers' disappearance. That Madame Breuvart, like Kurt, was in some way involved with Gabriel Daggers, seemed to be beyond question.

But what was she interested in? The reasonable explanation seemed to be that she also was puzzled by the circumstances of Gabriel Daggers' drowning. If that was so, she and Mr. Cork had a common interest. But Mr. Cork had been brought to Edendale for the very solid reason that he needed to check an insurance claim. What was the reason that had brought Madame Breuvart to the Black Brae? Was it the same reason as Kurt's? On what he knew so far Mr. Cork considered two possibilities, and made one inspired guess. It was enough to be getting along with.

He looked over his shoulder at Anna and Robert, and signalled to them to move quietly. Then, choosing his way carefully through the undergrowth, he showed himself on the bank of the river at the tail of the Black Brae. It gave him a complete view through the high rocks on either side of the pool to the salmon leap at the mouth.

At first, peering over the top of his glasses, Mr. Cork could not see the Frenchwoman at all. She was lying full length on her stomach, facing upstream, on one of the flat stones which guided the fall of white water at the head of the pool. Her left arm was plunged into the river, almost up to her shoulder. She appeared to be fumbling about in the pot holes and clefts in the rocks under the surface. When she raised her arm out of the stream to change her position Mr. Cork saw that she had in her hand a gaff, one of those metal hooks on the end of a telescopic rod which anglers use for lifting salmon out of the water. But Madam Breuvart was not snatching for salmon. When a fish jumped in the pool opposite her, she didn't look up. She was searching the Black Brae for another sort of quarry. And she was so closely engaged that she even failed to notice the figure of Mr. Cork standing on the bank about thirty yards below her. He watched her for several minutes and then, beckoning Anna and Robert to follow, he circled round the outskirts of the pool to a point exactly opposite where the Frenchwoman was lying. He walked forward to the crown of the rock overlooking the river and, with his foot, deliberately toppled a pebble into the water by the side of the prostrate Madame Breuvart.

With a cry of alarm, the woman rolled on to her back and sighted the figure outlined on the rock above her. Before she had drawn her left hand completely out of the water, her right went to her breast and she levelled a pistol at Mr. Cork.

'Don't move.'

Mr. Cork eyed her imperturbably as she drew herself into a sitting position and got warily to her feet. As she watched him, she balanced the pistol with practised care against her stomach, the muzzle never wavering from its target. Mr. Cork reflected that she was probably highly efficient in everything she undertook: making love, cooking a dinner, or using an automatic pistol.

'What do you want?' she said.

'That's a question I might more properly ask you,' said Mr. Cork. 'For my part, I am fishing this beat on the river. What is your business, Madame Breuvart?'

'You know my name?'

'We are both of us resident in the Estuary Hotel. I happened to notice your name in the hotel register.'

'Of course.'

She gave a wan smile of relief.

'Further, I had the pleasure of seeing you in the hotel dining-room last night.'

'I was taken ill,' she said defensively.

'I guessed that something like that must have happened. Please accept my sympathies.'

'Thank you.'

'Now that I've explained myself, Madame Breuvart, will you please point that dangerous weapon in another direction. I assure you that, personally, I am quite harmless.'

For a moment, she hesitated. Then she tucked back the pistol into what looked like a holster under her blouse.

'I am sorry, monsieur. Unfortunately, I have many enemies.'

'So it seems.'

As Mr. Cork spoke, Robert, who had crept round behind the Frenchwoman, relaxed his watchfulness and sneezed, the consequence of several hours in wet clothes. At once, she jerked the pistol out again and swung round.

'You are not alone,' she said fiercely.

'We are friends of Mr. Cork's,' said Robert. 'You have nothing to fear from us either.'

'Then why did you creep up behind me?'

'You have a pistol. And you seem to be the sort of person who wouldn't be afraid to use it.'

Madame Breuvart looked suspiciously from one to the other.

'May we introduce ourselves?' said Mr. Cork. 'This lady is Miss Anna Pryde. You must have seen her in the hotel. The gentleman is Mr. Robert Shipley, and my name is Cork, Montague Cork.'

'My name, as you know, is Rita Breuvart. I beg you to forgive my misunderstanding.'

Once again, with more confidence this time, she put away the pistol.

'We've told you that what we're doing here is fishing,' said Mr. Cork. 'Will you think it impertinent of me if I ask you again what you yourself are doing here, Madame Breuvart?'

'I am interested in rocks. I am what you call a geologist.'

'I don't believe you. No, please don't bring out that pistol again. If I may make a guess, I think that what you're interested in is something more exciting than rocks.'

Watching the woman closely over the top of his glasses, Mr. Cork saw a change in her eyes. His inspired guess was not so far out.

'Was Gabriel Daggers a friend of yours?' Mr. Cork asked casually.

'Daggers a friend of mine?' Madame Breuvart spat the words out of her mouth.

'So you knew him?'

'No, no. I do not know him. I do not know who you mean.'

'And yet you've come all the way from France . . . you don't deny that I suppose?'

Madame Breuvart shook her head.

'You've come from France to the very pool on the River Edendale, the Black Brae, where Gabriel Daggers was drowned a few weeks ago. But perhaps you knew him better as the Black Bastard?'

'I tell you I do not know him. I do not know where he is or anything about it.'

But Mr. Cork was certain that she was lying again. One of the two possibilities he had considered to explain

Madame Breuvart's presence, in addition to the inspired guess, had had startling confirmation. Mr. Cork tried the other possibility.

'I can't help noticing, Madame Breuvart, that although you say you know nothing of Gabriel Daggers, although I've told you that he was drowned here a few weeks ago, you persist in speaking of him as if he were still alive.'

'Why are you so interested in this man?' countered Madame Breuvart.

'Like yourself, I have my reasons. But, since you are disinclined to be frank with me, you mustn't be surprised if I am not frank with you.'

She hung her head in a sulky sort of silence. It was evident that she was taking time to make up her mind whether to talk or not. She decided against.

'I repeat, Monsieur, I know nothing.'

'Very well, Madame, we'll leave it at that. But now I have to ask you a favour? My friends and I are in trouble'.

'What sort of trouble?'

Madame Breuvart showed a mild, but still sulky, interest.

'I'm afraid we have had a serious accident with our car. You have a bicycle. On your way back to the hotel, will you please speak to the first fishing party you meet, probably a few miles down river, and ask them to bring help as quickly as possible?'

'It is a pleasure,' said Madame Breuvart. 'But what sort of accident is it?' she persisted.

'A very bad accident, I'm afraid. A man has been killed.'

'One of your party?'

'A man that none of us has seen before in our lives. A man, like yourself, who was also interested in the rocks of the Black Brae.'

Mr. Cork spoke slowly and emphatically. But there was

no necessity to impress the significance of his words on Madame Breuvart.

'Where is this man?'

'He's lying in the wreck of my car at the bottom of the burn a little way down the river.'

'Then I must see him,' said Madame Breuvart. 'No, you must not ask me questions. But I must see him.'

She started to climb the bank. Robert offered a hand to help her. As he did so, he looked at Mr. Cork, who gave him a slight nod of agreement.

'I think I ought to tell you,' said Robert, 'that this man has died a particularly violent death. It's not really the sort of thing . . .'

'I appreciate your thought for me,' interrupted Madame Breuvart. 'But, in the years of the war, we people in France have unhappily had experience of these things. Where is he?'

Robert pointed.

'There?' said Madame Breuvart. 'Good.'

She walked purposefully in the direction of the burn, seemingly careless whether the others accompanied her or not. Mr. Cork and Robert kept on her heels, with Anna a few yards behind.

Slipping down the wall of rock on her stocky strong limbs, she splashed into the puddles of the burn and put her head on one side to examine the upside-down corpse of the man in the car. Robert was still helping Mr. Cork down the slope as she tried to open the car doors. But they both heard the Frenchwoman's first startled exclamation when she saw the body.

'Mon Dieu,' she said, and then in a whisper, 'it's him.'

By the time they were standing beside her, she had turned away.

'I have seen enough,' she said.

'You know this man?'

'It is useless for me to deny it.'

'Who is he?'

'What interest is it of yours?'

'I want to know, as I think you do, what's happened to Gabriel Daggers. I believe this man is mixed up in the business.'

'I see.'

'I believe too that he may have been an associate of a man named Kurt, who is a guest at the Estuary Hotel.'

The Frenchwoman shrugged.

'You may not recognize him by the name of Kurt. But he was sitting in the corner of the dining-room last night and it was the sight of him, I think, that put you off your dinner.'

She still stared expressionlessly at Mr. Cork.

'Are you still going to pretend that you don't know who I'm talking about?'

'I know the man you mean,' she said quietly.

'Was this fellow here an accomplice of his?'

Madame Breuvart nodded.

'What sort of man was he?'

For answer, Madame Breuvart turned to the wreckage of the car and spat.

Nine

THE storm-clouds, which had been gathering all day, settled darkly over Edendale. Rain was falling up the glen, loading the burns with foamy brown water and clothing the hills in folds of white mist. At the mouth of the river the air was so breathless that the sound of a piper, wailing a lament down in the village, penetrated to the Estuary Hotel on the promontory of rock overlooking the bay. Montague Cork, at the open window of his sitting-room, stood there listening.

Although it was past eleven o'clock, well past his regular bedtime, he was reluctant to retire to his room. He had already broken two golden rules of personal conduct by drinking a stiff whisky and soda after dinner, and filling his cigarette case for a second time in a single day. Whether it was the oppressive effect of the impending storm, the nervous strain of the events of the past day, or the nagging wakefulness of his thoughts, Mr. Cork was filled with foreboding. He stood there, alone at the window, like a tired sentry, fighting sleep and searching the shadows for intangible enemies.

In the gloom of the room behind him, Robert's rhythmic breathing from the armchair told Mr. Cork that sleep had already overtaken his young accomplice. He should have gone to bed earlier, like Anna. But Robert, exhausted as he was by the physical effort of the fight at the Black Brae and all that had come after, had nevertheless insisted on sitting up with Mr. Cork. It was better that he slept. Anna, too.

Anna had been pale and silent after dinner, as if she too shared Mr. Cork's fears for the night. Mr. Cork was relieved when she said, early in the evening, that she was going to bed. She was safe there, behind a locked door and in a room guarded from approach through the window by the precipitous rock of the bay. Mr. Cork took comfort from that.

And yet, what was it he dreaded? There was nothing, or almost nothing, which had happened during that eventful day on the Black Brae which would not be explained, as Colonel Johnson and Mr. Mackenzie and the Police Sergeant explained it, by that one word 'Poachers.'

'Mark my words, Muster Cork,' said the Police Sergeant firmly. 'The poachers up here are verra desperate men.'

'What do you expect,' said Mr. Mackenzie phlegmatically, 'with fush fetching nine shillings the pound?'

Nothing that Mr. Cork said could shake local opinion. The Black Brae had always been a favourite pool of the netters; hence the hooks which had been sunk in the bottom. It was typical of the poachers to send a man to spy out the land. And, if they were interfered with, the poachers would stop at nothing; even stealing a car.

Mr. Cork protested that this fellow was armed. But the police sergeant, rejoicing in the news that the man who had been killed was a stranger, and that he himself would not get into bad odour in the village by pursuing the case, expressed no surprise. That the Frenchwoman had identified him was simply regarded as valuable confirmation

145

that this was a gang of poachers from far afield. The police sergeant mollified Mr. Cork by promising that immediate measures would be taken, first thing in the morning, to trace Kurt and his companion, who had temporarily disappeared. He also undertook to take a statement at the earliest opportunity from Madame Breuvart who, after leaving Mr. Cork and getting help from Sir George Sanderson, fishing the next beat down the river had also not been seen since. But nobody worried about that except Mr. Cork. The police sergeant was anxious to make his report and summon help from the headquarters at Dornoch.

After an hour's talk with the local authorities, Mr. Cork became almost ashamed of his own fears. After all, if he were right, the County Police would ferret it out when they came over in the morning. Meanwhile, it was worse than useless to take anybody into his confidence about Daggers.

Gabriel Daggers was officially dead. Even the fishing bag loaded with stones could be fitted in with the poacher theory. Suppose Snatcher, for example, himself poaching salmon in the Black Brae, had inadvertently discovered the body and the fishing bag? Wouldn't it have been his first thought to keep out of trouble by weighting the bag and leaving it to somebody else to make the discovery?

There might even be a reasonable and fairly innocent explanation for the Frenchwoman's interest in the Black Brae. Was it possible that Madame Breuvart, like Anna, had at some time been the victim of Gabriel Daggers' unwelcome attentions?

But, while Mr. Cork was reasoning his way from one improbability to another, while the local Police Sergeant was still pencilling in his notebook, the conviction that he

146

was right and that all the others were wrong, became a sickly certainty again.

Jock, the porter, brought the news that the telephone lines were out of order. The fact that the phone was dead was discovered when, in anticipation of the social needs of another Fatal Accident Enquiry, Mr. Mackenzie had given instructions to call Dornoch for urgent supplies of whisky. Finding the hotel instrument out of order, Jock had gone down to the doctor's house to phone from there. But Edendale was cut off. Somewhere along the twenty miles of moorland road between the coast and the south, the lines were down.

'The storm is responsible,' said Mr. Mackenzie, looking up the glen. And the police sergeant agreed.

So they were cut off from the outside world altogether until Jock, the hall porter, accompanied by the police sergeant, took the car into Dornoch in the morning: the sergeant to report the accident to his superiors, and Jock to carry out the more solemn duty of trying to raise a few cases of whisky for Mr. Mackenzie's hotel. Nobody, except Mr. Cork, thought anything more about it. Edendale was accustomed to being cut off.

Robert, fortunately, had got through to Mr. Cork's branch office in Inverness before the lines came down. Another car for Mr. Cork would arrive to-morrow. But Mr. Cork's own nightly call to Phoebe had not come through in time. Phoebe would, of course, wonder what had happened. If she telephoned herself, the Exchange would discover that the lines were out of order. If it wasn't a serious hitch, they might make a quick repair. But if somebody had deliberately cut the lines . . .

If somebody had deliberately cut the lines . . .

Mr. Cork, looking at the glowering sky, lit another

cigarette. What had happened to Madame Breuvart? What was the woman up to, out on the hills on a night like this? They had exchanged no word since the Frenchwoman had identified the corpse; or pretended to, because that was a possibility, too. But assuming Madame Breuvart was telling the truth; what was the link, if there was a link, between this Frenchwoman, Kurt, who was presumably of middle-European extraction, and Gabriel Daggers? Daggers, remember, was in the Commandos. Might it not turn out that what had brought these three people together on the Black Brae was something in which they had all been involved during the war? It was possible. Some strange and violent story of those strange and violent years which had begun, perhaps in France, and was culminating now, of all places, in the remote Highlands of Scotland.

Mr. Cork was disturbed in his theorizing by the sound of a car starting up in the yard behind the hotel. He wondered if it was Jock parking one of the guest's cars for the night. But, within a few seconds, he saw the headlights as the car nosed round the yard to the front of the hotel and then through the gates down the hill to the village. He watched the car cross the bridge and head up the moorland road. Perhaps Mackenzie had decided after all to send Jock to Dornoch. Knowing Jock, Mr. Cork could imagine his sullen Scottish disapproval of taking to the road at a time of night like this. Mr. Cork looked at his watch, and yawned. It was after half-past eleven. He would have to shake up Robert and get to bed.

Turning back into the room, he switched on a table-lamp and smiled at Robert sprawled on the couch among the newspapers of the day before yesterday. Then he opened the door and looked out into the hall lined with stags' antlers, coloured fishing prints and a collection of unspeakable brass pots arranged on carved teak furniture which Mr. Mackenzie, or Mr. Mackenzie's father, had brought back with him from India years before.

The hall, as Mr. Cork expected, was unoccupied. Even the stone slab adjoining the office, where the salmon were laid out for admiration at the end of each fishing day, was empty. Jock had presumably packed up the fish and labelled them in readiness for the carrier in the morning. The sight of the empty slab suddenly reminded Mr. Cork that, while Robert was climbing Cnoc Craggie on the ill-fated stalk of the watcher on the hill, he had actually killed a fish himself. Normally, Mr. Cork would have been as pleased at killing a fish as a dog with two tails. Normally, he would have celebrated with a bottle of champagne for dinner and relived the experience after dinner by describing every detail of how he caught it in a long distance conversation with Phoebe over the telephone. It was measure of his agitation to-day that he had completely forgotten all about it. He had left the fish on the grass where he had gaffed it because, at that precise moment, they had heard the pistol shots as Robert closed with his opponent on the hill.

Looking around him, Mr. Cork was surprised to notice that the front door of the hotel was wide open. Normally, Jock locked it as soon as he went to bed about 10.30 p.m. None of the guests ever used it after that. Most of them, lazy after fishing, retired early. The only explanation was that the door had been left open by the person who took out the car. Mr. Cork, with his tidy ways, went over to the door to lock it again, but he was stopped before he could get there by a voice on the stairs.

'Is that you, Cork?'

He looked up. Outlined on the banisters was the

dishevelled figure of Colonel Johnson, his skinny frame wrapped closely in a dressing-gown and his feet tucked in a pair of red slippers.

'Did you hear that car driving off just now, Cork?' Colonel Johnson spoke in a hoarse whisper.

'Yes, I did,' said Mr. Cork. 'I wondered who it was.'

'So did I.'

'I thought maybe it was Jock going to Dornoch.'

'At this time of night? Never heard of such a thing.'

Colonel Johnson shuffled down the stairs.

'I don't like it, Cork. You know, I'm not sleeping very well these days, not since I lost that big fish. My joints are giving me trouble. I was wide-awake when that car started up. And do you know what I think?'

Colonel Johnson joined Mr. Cork in the hall.

'What I think, Cork, from the sound of that car, is that it was mine. I intend to go out and have a look.'

'You ought to be careful, Colonel, you'll catch your death of cold. Are you sure it's your car?'

'Of course I'm not sure, Cork. But it's an old car. I've had it a long time and it coughs a bit, if you know what I mean, over the self-starter. I thought I recognized the cough.'

'What about the ignition key? Wasn't the car locked?'

'It hasn't got a key. You switch it on with a bit of wire.'

'Let me look for you,' said Mr. Cork.

'That's very decent of you, Cork. It would relieve my mind.'

'What does the car look like?'

'It's an old Morris, not the bull-nosed sort, later than that, and the wing is crumpled on the near side where some damn fool ran into me. I park it under the lean-to shed which you come to just as you enter the yard. You can't miss it.'

'All right. You go to my sitting-room and pour yourself a drink. You'll find my young friend, Shipley, there, sleeping on the couch. You'd better wake him and tell him it's time for bed.'

Colonel Johnson watched Mr. Cork go through the door and then, with a shudder of cold, he went through to the sitting-room. Outside the door, Mr. Cork took a quick look about him and went round to the yard at the back of the hotel.

Colonel Johnson's car had gone.

Mr. Cork had often noticed it there when he was parking his own. Somebody in the middle of the night had driven off with the Morris. Mr. Cork returned to the hotel.

'This is a scandal,' said Colonel Johnson, taking a long pull at his glass. 'We must rouse Mackenzie at once.'

Robert, still half-asleep, rubbed his eyes and stretched his arms.

'Sorry, sir,' he said. 'I just couldn't keep awake. What's the time?'

'Midnight very nearly,' said Colonel Johnson crossly. 'And somebody's stolen my car.'

'Your car?'

Mr. Cork briefly described what had happened. Robert looked at them both for a moment, then jumped quickly to his feet.

'Excuse me,' he said, starting for the door.

'What is it?'

'I must see if Anna's all right.'

'Anna?'

'Best to make sure, sir.'

Robert sprang up the stairs, three at a time, with Mr.

Cork hastening after him. Colonel Johnson, still clutching his glass, watched them from the hall.

Outside Anna's door, Robert tried the handle.

'It's still locked,' he said in a whisper.

'Knock at the door and see if she answers.'

Robert knocked, gently at first, and then with increasing determination. There was no answer. Bending to the keyhole, he called her name sharply.

'Anna.'

He looked at Mr. Cork.

'Shall I shoulder the door down?'

'No, it'll wake the entire hotel. She was very tired and she's probably sleeping heavily. Anyhow, nobody could get into her.'

'Suppose she came out?'

'Surely she wouldn't do that.'

'She behaved very strangely this evening. I'm sure she had something on her mind. And when we were on the river together, remember, she talked wildly of going to see Daggers. Suppose she's gone out looking for him in old Johnson's car?'

'Surely she wouldn't do a fool thing like that?'

'You know what women are,' said Robert.

'I don't,' said Mr. Cork. 'But you may be better informed, Shipley.'

He looked at Robert, as if he were searching his eyes for inspiration.

'Even if Anna had a silly idea like that, she couldn't do anything about it. She doesn't know where Daggers is any more than we do.'

'But suppose Daggers sent her a message. If he's the villain we think he is, he's probably feeling pretty desperate at the moment, and it's the sort of thing he might do.'

'But how could he pass a message?'

'That's easily answered. Jock told me earlier that Snatcher had been hanging round here this evening.'

'My God, why didn't you tell me that?'

'I didn't get a chance while everybody else was milling round. Apparently Snatcher's often in the bar at the back of the hotel. Well, there it is. Do we smash the door down, or take a chance?'

'We use the key,' said Mr. Cork, pointing.

The key was lying on the side of the passage, half-covered by the strip of carpet.

With a hot hand, Robert turned the lock and swung open the door. Although the electric light was off, there was light enough from the window to see that Anna's bed was empty. The clothes were thrown back as if someone had jumped out of bed in a hurry.

'What do we do?' asked Robert.

'We go after her,' said Mr. Cork grimly.

'Where can we get a car?'

'If we can't borrow one, we shall commandeer a car. Have you got that stalking rifle?'

'In my room.'

'Get it, and join me downstairs in the sitting-room. I must talk to Johnson. He can explain things to the people at the hotel.'

Mr. Cork and Robert divided; Robert to his room, Mr. Cork down the stairs.

'We're going out, Johnson,' said Mr. Cork.

'You're what?'

In his agitation, the Colonel poured out another drink.

'Miss Pryde has borrowed your car. Don't ask me why. I don't know exactly myself. We're going out to find her.'

'What in?'

'I'm afraid we shall have to take the hotel car.'

'Does Mackenzie know?'

'No, he doesn't.'

'Look here, Cork, if there's any monkey business going on, we ought to wake him.'

'I think it's better if we don't. Where does he keep the keys?'

'Do you realize that you're asking me to condone a felony?'

'You want your car back, don't you?'

'Yes, of course.'

'Well, where are the keys?'

'You can keep it to yourself that I told you. But they're hanging on the hook in the office beside the letter rack.'

Robert came into the room with the rifle under his arm.

'Great Heavens, what's that for?'

'Shooting salmon,' said Robert with a grin.

'Well, I'll be jiggered. I tell you honestly, Cork, I don't know what this place is coming to.'

'Neither do I,' said Mr. Cork. 'Good night.'

As Robert stowed the rifle into the boot of the hotel car, a flash of lightning signalled that the storm which had threatened all day, had broken over Edendale. Thunder reverberated round the bay and the rain broke through as if a sluice-gate had opened in the clouds.

'You drive,' said Mr. Cork.

'What's the objective?'

'We'll try the Black Brae first. That seems to be the fashionable rendezvous. And get there as fast as you can.'

'As fast as I can?' said Robert wonderingly.

'All right, as fast as this miserable car will go. I shall control my own nerves by keeping my eyes shut.'

Mr. Cork reeled in his seat as Robert, settling squarely over the wheel, swung out of the hotel yard, down the hill, over the bridge and on to the winding road up the river. Driving conditions could scarcely have been more awful. Even in fine weather, and in daylight, as Mr. Cork never ceased reminding Robert, these moorland roads were death-traps. At night, in a storm like this, conditions were nearly impossible.

The windscreen, sheeted with rain on the outside, fogged with mist on the inner. Robert dabbed at the cloudy glass with the palm of his hand and, ignoring the water splashes in the road, glued his eyes on the switch-back of the verge. The hills belly-rumbled with thunder. Lightning carved forked patterns in the sky. The car wobbled and wallowed in the mud holes. The radiator steamed under the frozen patter of the rain. The faltering beam of the headlights picked up the white lumps of Cheviot sheep hugging cover under stone walls and in earthy hollows.

Robert half hung his head out of the side window for better visibility of the road. The hotel car wheezed in its springs and the engine roared discontentedly. But, somehow, he rushed it round corners, raced it up hills and sent it snorting safely through water splashes. They were topping forty on half-a-road which nobody had ever manœuvred faster than twenty miles an hour before.

'Why on earth did Anna do what she did?' said Robert, as he skidded safely through a flock of frightened sheep.

'You know what women are,' said Mr. Cork. 'Or you said you did.'

'How shall we find her when we get there? . . . If we get there,' he added quickly as the car bumped ominously on the verge.

Mr. Cork opened his eyes to light a Passing Cloud.

'How shall we know where to look?'

'There's one person who can tell us.'

'Snatcher?'

'Yes. Take it easy now. We're coming to that hairpin bend over the burn. If she's here, we ought to see the car in one of the passing places.'

Robert reduced speed. As he did so, he felt a cold ring press sharply into the nape of his neck.

'You'll keep going,' said a soft Highland voice from the darkness behind them. 'And you, Muster Cork, you'll not be looking round.'

Ten

'SO it's you, Snatcher,' said Mr. Cork, looking straight in front of him. 'What do you want?'

'You're to drive awa' from Edendale.'

'Is it murder?'

'Nae harm will come to you if you do as you're told.'

'Like hell,' muttered Robert.

'Hold your blathering tongue.'

Snatcher jerked the muzzle of the pistol into Robert's neck.

'Where are you taking us?' Mr. Cork went on coolly.

'Where you'll no' interfere again in matters which don't concern you.'

'And where may that be?'

'You'll find out soon enough.'

'You won't get away with it, Snatcher. I'll have the police on you before the night's out.'

'Not where you're going, Muster. You'll have the moors to walk first.'

'So we're to be marooned in the hills while you and Daggers make your getaway. Is that it?'

'Muster Daggers is drowned.'

'Where's Anna Pryde?'

'For your own sakes, you'd do well to let her bide.'

'Why don't you let Daggers manage his own dirty business?'

For answer, Snatcher seized Mr. Cork by the coat collar and brought their two heads close together in the darkness.

'From now on, you'll mind your own affairs,' he said menacingly, 'or, by God, I'll . . .'

'I understand the position perfectly,' said Mr. Cork.

'You'd better.'

Dragging Mr. Cork half out of his seat, he thrust him violently into the windscreen.

'Are you hurt, sir?' murmured Robert.

'I'm all right.'

'Stop blathering.'

They drove on through the storm. In the glare of a lightning flash, Mr. Cork peered at the driving mirror and made out Snatcher's shape crouching behind them. The man must have laid in wait for them all evening outside the hotel; probably overheard the conversation with John-son through the open window when he and Robert decided to follow Anna in the hotel car. It might be true that the plan was to set them down in some isolated spot on the moors; but, equally, Robert could be right. Daggers had already made one attempt to eliminate them: why should he hesitate now when, clearly, there was some desperate business he planned to accomplish?

Robert, in his turn, was wondering if there was a way, any way, of getting out of the mess they were in. And, as the thunder rolled round the hills, he leaned down and fumbled at his feet.

'What are you playing at?'

'I'm moving my seat back. I want some more room for my legs.'

'You'll mind what you're doing, young gentleman, or you won't be needing your legs.'

'Very well. Then I shall have to drive more slowly.'

'You'll be safer if you go a wee bit faster.'

'Do as he says, Shipley. It's our only hope.'

Robert made no reply. He was driving with slit-eyed concentration, searching the shadows outside the beam of the headlights, probing the curtain of rain which thrashed on the windscreen, trying to recall in his mind the lay of the ground they had gone over in the morning. The intention forming in his mind was a desperate one; but the alternative was desperate, too. Pity he couldn't warn Mr. Cork; but he had to act faster than Snatcher could close his finger on the trigger. They both had to take their chance.

As they came round a bend, he saw what he was seeking; a slope on the near side of the road running down into a hollow; well-cushioned with young wood and vegetation. He guessed it was probably a bog but it was as likely a place as any for his purpose.

With a sudden swing of the wheel, he lurched the car into the thick of it. As they nose-dived off the road, Mr. Cork was toppled out of his seat on to his shoulder. Snatcher's gun slipped from his neck and went off somewhere behind him. Throwing all his weight on the wheel again, he gave it another strong turn to keep the car on its wheels. He watched the bonnet crumple up. The windscreen shattered into powder. And they swung to a stop, up to the running board in mud, in a wreckage of splintered saplings and a mesh of uprooted bramble.

For a moment, Robert sat there taking it all in, with Mr. Cork lying on his lap. Then, squirming out of his seat, he dived on to the prostrate Snatcher.

Mr. Cork just had time to realize that Robert was crashing the car. Then, half-stunned, he heard him shouting.

'Are you all right, sir? Are you all right?'

'I'm all right,' said Mr. Cork wearily.

'I've got the blighter cold,' Robert called out from the floor of the car.

Mr. Cork looked over the seat. Robert was straddled on the top of Snatcher, with his hands on his throat and hitting his head on the floor.

'See if you can find the gun.'

Mr. Cork felt around the floor but there was no sign of the pistol. Possibly it had gone through the window as the car crashed. He tried the doors but they were jammed. There was no way out except through the windscreen frame. He crawled through on to the bonnet and, slipping down, settled up to his calves in mud. He went to help Robert: but Robert was in no need of help. He had burst open one of the rear doors and was dragging out the unconscious Snatcher by his legs.

'Sorry, sir,' he grinned triumphantly, 'but it had to be done. I hope I didn't shake you up too much.'

'I shall be all right in a minute. What about him?'

'Knocked silly, that's all. Where's the pistol?'

'Not much hope of finding it in this muck. But we've got the rifle in the boot.'

'We can get along without it. Help me lean him against the car.'

They sprawled the unconscious man along the running board with his head resting on the shattered mudguard.

'The rain will bring him round in a moment or two. Then we'll see what we can get out of him.'

'Do you know where we are?'

'About half-a-mile above the Black Brae, I think. Right in the middle of the fun.'

Mr. Cork leant on the bonnet and felt in his pocket for

his cigarette case. Robert asked for the matches. Striking a light, he held it close to Snatcher's face. There was a flicker in the man's eyes.

'Remember me,' said Robert, bending over him. 'You had a pistol in the back of my neck a few minutes ago.'

Snatcher looked at him with a puzzled expression.

'The angel's are still singing for you, eh Snatcher? Ah, that's better. You remember me.'

Taking him by the shoulders, Robert pinned him like a naturalist's specimen to the wreck of the car. Mr. Cork stood over them, striking matches to light up Snatcher's face. He was trying to speak but his tongue was sticking to the roof of his mouth. Robert, eyes sparkling and his blood prickling deliciously in his veins, looked as dangerous as he was feeling.

'Can't talk, Snatcher? You were voluble enough a few moments ago. Who were you carrying that gun for? Daggers?'

Snatcher nodded.

'Who did he murder?'

Snatcher gulped and shook his head hopelessly.

'You'd better find your tongue soon. Where's Daggers now? Where's Anna Pryde? When did he give you that message to Miss Pryde that you delivered for him? Why did he want to get rid of us? What do you know about the Black Brae?'

With every question, Robert shook him fiercely by the shoulders. With his tousled hair, blackened teeth, and raw-boned face almost blue with terror, Snatcher was licked.

'Muster, if you'll only bide a wee, I'll tell you all I know. I swear I will. But don't kill me. For mercy's sake, don't kill me.'

F   161

'You didn't have any scruples about trying to kill us.'

'I told you nae harm would come to you. I was taking you awa' frae trouble.'

'What trouble?'

'I canna tell you.'

'You mean you don't know?'

He shook his head.

'Ask him if he interfered with the car this morning.'

'It was him himself, Muster.'

'Daggers was there, was he?'

'In the hut.'

'Which hut?'

'Wully Sutherland's.'

'What hold is it that Daggers has got over you?' interposed Mr. Cork.

'I was his ghillie.'

'That's not good enough. You'll have to do better than that.'

'Strike another match,' said Robert suddenly. 'I've got an idea. Ah, I thought so. Where did you get that khaki shirt? It looks like army issue. You're a youngish man. Were you in the army?'

Snatcher nodded sulkily.

'You weren't in the Commandos, by any chance? Come on, man, spit it out.'

'Aye, Muster, I was.'

'That's how you met Daggers?'

'Aye.'

'I've got it. I was in the army, too, and I know your type, Snatcher. I know why Daggers has got you where he wants you. I know why you're living up here miles from anywhere scraping a living as a salmon sniggler. You're a deserter, aren't you? You're wanted by the military police?'

162

'Don't give me up, Muster. I couldna' live awa' from the hills. I couldna' live.'

'We might feel more sympathy for you,' said Mr. Cork, 'if we didn't also know you are an accessory to murder.'

'I didna' kill anybody, Muster.'

'Somebody was murdered. Who was it?'

'I swear to you I never knew. I thought it was Muster Daggers himself who was drowned, till he came here days after he was dead and gone, like an evil spurrit out of the river, to haunt me.'

'How did Mr. Daggers explain his resurrection.'

'He didna' explain much. He's a terrible man. It was an accident, he said, and his eyes bored through me like a hook in the side of a fush.'

'I'm sure you're frightened of Daggers,' said Robert. 'But, at the moment, you've more reason to be frightened of me.'

Snatcher nodded appreciatively.

'Did you see anything at all the night that Daggers was supposed to drown? Come on, out with it.'

'I heard a car on the road by the Black Brae.'

He spoke hesitantly.

'I saw a stranger about here, talking to Muster Daggers, by the Black Brae pool. But you must never tell. He'd kill me if he knew I knew about it. You must never tell.'

'Daggers has put the fear of God in you all right. Do you know, by any chance, why he's so interested in the Black Brae? You don't, eh? Where is he now?'

Snatcher lowered his head.

'I shall count five,' said Robert, 'and then I shall get rough. One, two, three, four . . .'

'I'll tell you,' said Snatcher desperately. 'But he'll kill me, I know he will.'

163

'So will I if you don't hurry.'

Snatcher lowered his voice with terror.

'He's in Wully Sutherland's hut on the slopes of the hill.'

'Is the young lady with him?'

He nodded.

'Is that where he's been hiding up here in the hills?'

Snatcher didn't answer.

'Or have you been sheltering him in your croft?'

'We can soon find out,' said Robert. 'Your croft's on the far side of Cnoc Craggie, isn't it?'

'Are you going to try and take him yourself?'

'That's the idea.'

'You'll need to be careful, Muster.'

'I don't know why you should have any sympathy with me.'

'I'm afraid for any man who gets in the road of Muster Daggers.'

'So it appears,' said Robert drily. 'What I'm anxious to find out is why.'

'You'll find out now,' said a cold voice from the darkness.

Mr. Cork gripped Robert by the arm. Standing together in the bog, they stared into the night. Nothing stirred. There was no sound except the patter of the rain, the swish of the wind playing in the hills and the steady rush of water nosing through the burns and hissing angrily in the boiling pot-holes and creamy roughs of the swollen river.

'Did you hear that?' whispered Mr. Cork.

'Yes.'

'Can you see him?'

164

'Not yet. But he's not far off.'

As they listened, somebody laughed.

'It's the Muster,' Snatcher whimpered.

They saw him, a black shadow against the sky, standing at the top of the slope above them. He switched on a torch and cast the beam slowly from one to the other. When he came to Snatcher, he stopped.

'So you made a mess of it,' he said.

'You're not going to kill me?'

'Why, you haven't been talking, have you?'

The quiet voice had a razor edge to it.

'They crashed the car, Muster.'

'And, luckily, I heard the pistol shot. Now we can make a better accident of it. Don't move, you two,' he added sharply. 'I've got you covered with a rifle and I know how to use it. Turn out the tool box, Snatcher, and pick out a large spanner. Get on with it, you miserable devil. A spanner under the back seat.'

As Snatcher rummaged in the car, Gabriel Daggers came towards them. He came so near that they could hear the rustle of his waterproofs and the squelch of his boots in the mud.

'What do you mean to do?' said Mr. Cork.

'You give me no choice. You had your chance to get out of Edendale but you wouldn't take it.'

'Would we have fared any better?'

'Probably not.'

'So you're going to murder us here?'

'Murder?' said Daggers. 'There's been an accident, another motor accident. When the police come in the morning, the victims' bodies will be found in the wreckage of the car. Your bodies.'

'You'll hang for it all the same.'

165

'A dead man hang?'

'Who are you then?'

'A ghost.'

'And the man you murdered in the Black Brae?'

'Another ghost.'

Daggers laughed again.

'Killing us won't get you out of trouble,' said Mr. Cork. 'There are others who are curious about you. You can't go on murdering indefinitely. You're bound to be found out; bound to be found out in the end, Daggers.'

'Give me the spanner.'

Snatcher passed it to him in exchange for the rifle.

'Where's Anna Pryde?' demanded Robert.

'What's that to you?'

'I pity her in your tender care, that's all, you dirty bastard.'

Daggers closed on Robert and, swinging the spanner, caught him a glancing blow on the side of the head. Robert dropped into the bog. Mr. Cork, with the energy of desperation, stumbled into Daggers and, for a few moments, the two of them wrestled with open arms. As Mr. Cork's effort faded, an anxious shout from Snatcher checked Daggers' hand.

'Mind out, Muster.'

He threw Mr. Cork to the ground. The enquiring beam of car headlights was moving swiftly up the road.

'We'll get out,' Daggers said.

Plunging through the bog, the two men ran into the outer darkness as the car pulled up with its lights set on the wreckage of the hotel cab. Mr. Cork struggled to his feet.

'Help!' he called. 'Help!'

Two people got out of the car and came down the greasy slope towards them.

'So,' said a familiar voice. 'Another trifling accident, Mr. Cork. Very unlucky for you. But, for me, interesting. Definite interesting.'

Mr. Cork thought of the rifle they had put in the boot of the car; but what was the good? He had no notion how to use it and, if he had, Daggers would never yield a chance. Somewhere in the undergrowth, he was watching with his finger on a trigger. Kurt and the other fellow were stepping straight into the same trap. All that was possible was to give what help he could, while he could, to Robert. Grasping him under the arms, he hauled him through the boggy ground towards the car.

'Is he dead?' asked Kurt disinterestedly.

Mr. Cork looked over his shoulder.

'I don't know.'

'So.'

Kurt ran his hands over Mr. Cork's clothes.

'What's the meaning of that?'

'A little precaution. Just a little insurance, as you might say, against the possibility of any more accidents.'

'Are you satisfied?' said Mr. Cork, as Kurt withdrew his hands.

'I feel, shall we say, a little safer,' he smiled.

'Then perhaps you'll help me get this young man into the car?'

Kurt shrugged. Moving Mr. Cork aside, he lifted Robert easily into the back seat. Casually leaning over him, he raised his eyelids and felt his heart and pulse.

'Well?'

'He is luckier than the last person who had a car accident at Edendale. He was killed instantaneous. Definite instantaneous, eh, Mr. Cork?'

Still the man smiled. But his voice was threatening.

'Is this the start of a business talk?' said Mr. Cork.

'But of course.'

Kurt, his face a grinning white mask under the watery beam of the car lights, looked like a character in some evil harlequinade. His stooge stood patiently behind him in the mud, round-shouldered, pig-eyed and immeasurably wary.

'Is our business to be as unpleasant as I suspect?'

'Unpleasant?' smiled Kurt. 'Nothing in business is unpleasant unless one side or the other makes it so. You and I, Mr. Cork, have a great understanding of each other.'

'Have we?'

'But of course. Excuse please. What is it, Fred?'

'The guy in the car is coming to his senses.'

'So soon? Good, we may need him. But watch careful. He's the one who fixed Harry this morning.'

'So it was him.'

'It was no fault of his,' said Mr. Cork. 'I accept the full responsibility.'

'So.'

'Suppose you say what you've got to say and get it over.'

'Forgive me. You are a great business man, Mr. Cork. Me? I am the temperamental artist.'

'Do you still pretend that you two are newspaper photographers?'

'Commendable quickly, you come to the point. No more pretending . . . from me or from you, Mr. Cork. Let us admit quite frank we have both acted a part; you the big man of insurance, very good, and me the photographer. But now we talk business.'

'I'm listening.'

'Where is the girl?'

'I don't know.'

Fred made a threatening move but Kurt checked him with a gesture.

'Has she got the stuff, or have you?'

'I don't understand what you're talking about.'

'So you wish to make it unpleasant for yourself after all.'

'On the contrary. I will do anything in my power to avoid any more unpleasantness. But I can't tell you what I don't know.'

'Do you deny that you're in league with Anna Pryde?'

'I've been trying to help her.'

'You came up here with her.'

'I followed her, like you.'

'For the same reason?'

'I doubt it.'

'Aw, hell,' said Fred, jogging Kurt with his thumb. 'He's wasting time.'

'Not yet, my friend,' said Kurt.

'So,' he went on. 'You want us to believe that you followed this woman to Edendale because she was so charming you wished to help her. You go with her this morning to the Black Brae to catch salmon. But, while you're there, you search the bottom of the pool.'

'That's correct.'

'Ah, now you are being more reasonable. When you discover you are overlooked you are so alarmed that you arrange a convenient accident for the man I put there to watch you. You even sacrifice your expensive motor car. To-night, the woman goes out after dark. And, in a storm like this, you follow her here to the Black Brae. You drive so fast you crash the car. It is all circumstantial, definite circumstantial. But it is proof.'

'Proof of what?'

'You came here with the girl to find the hiding-place of the Pongratz jewels,' snapped Kurt. 'And you've got them.'

He paused while the smile slowly smeared over his face again.

'I want them. Please to hand over.'

Mr. Cork pressed his hand wearily to his head. His expression, as Kurt waited eagerly for an answer, gave no indication that he was other than bored. But his thoughts were racing. Suddenly, the dizzy pattern of events was beginning to fit together. So it was treasure that they were after; it was these Pongratz jewels, whatever they were, that had drawn these people to Edendale. That was what the Frenchwoman was raking about for in the Black Brae. That was why Daggers had committed murder. That was why Kurt was ready to risk murder now.

'You submit?'

'Entirely.'

Kurt's smile spread into a grin.

'No double-crossing,' said Fred suspiciously.

'What's the use? But I'm interested to learn, as a matter of professional interest, how you found out.'

'Surely everyone knows the Pongratz jewels?'

'I suppose so; but it was clever of you to trace them.'

'You flatter me, Mr. Cork. But I have a great experience of this collection.'

He kissed his fingers and threw up his hands in admiration.

'When did you first see them?'

Kurt gave a modest shrug.

'I was present, never mind how, when they were stolen.'

'Let's quit the talking, Smiler,' said Fred impatiently, 'and get on with the job.'

'There is no hurry now.'

'Maybe not. But let's get the stuff and get out.'

'How do you know the theft won't be discovered?' persisted Mr. Cork.

'But simple. Your own Allied Military Commission decided after the war that the Pongratz collection was irretrievably lost.'

'Yet you found out who had it?'

Kurt preened himself.

'Poor penniless alien that I was, I traced the man who had them. But he was a clever one, that Daggers.'

'He was.'

'For years, I hunted him. And then, when I found him, it was too late.'

'You mean he disappeared.'

'Shall we say he had an unfortunate accident, like my poor friend this morning? Who knows? But it was frustrating, definite frustrating, at the time.'

'It must have been.'

'But wait. I say to myself: Kurt, every man has his little weakness. In my case, I like to talk. In his, it was Anna, the beautiful ballerina. Voila!'

'Aw, chuck it,' said Fred. 'Let's get cracking.'

So much that had puzzled Mr. Cork in this extraordinary adventure he had embarked on was now clear that, listening to Kurt's triumphant revelations, he had almost forgotten his own desperate danger. It was evident that Kurt was convinced that he, Montague Cork, was not only a fellow crook and the possessor of these Pongratz jewels but Daggers' murderer as well. No wonder he had treated him so respectfully. As a double murderer and an international cracksman, he must obviously be regarded as a formidable opponent. He wondered what Phoebe would say when he told her.

When he told Phoebe . . .

Hot with apprehension, he realized the chances were that he would never see Phoebe again. Thank heaven he had said no when she suggested coming with him to Edendale. And Anna. What of Anna? And Robert. Poor Robert. He racked his brains to recapture some hazy recollection of having heard of these Pongratz jewels before. But he was too dizzy and weak to concentrate. A feeling of lethargy was creeping over him. Difficult to think . . . difficult to understand . . .

His legs gave under him and he fell forward into the mud. He had fainted.

He was at the bottom of the pool of the Black Brae, held down helplessly on the poachers' hooks in the bed of the river, struggling for breath, with the waterfall beating him in the face. He couldn't move, his lungs were bursting and a piston was beating inside his head. Then, slowly, the pain eased.

'He's coming round now,' said Kurt, standing over him.

'You shouldn't have wasted all that time gabbing, Smiler.'

'Shut your mouth and pull yourself together. He won't give us any trouble.'

The two men watched as the pupils rolled back to position in Mr. Cork's eyes. Coughing a little and blinking, he stared in a puzzled way at the black sky.

'You've fainted,' said Kurt. 'Do you understand?'

Mr. Cork licked his lips.

'I understand.'

He stirred himself and sat up.

'Well, where are the jewels? The Pongratz jewels?'

'Aw, let me take a hand, Smiler.'

Fred leant over him menacingly.

'Come on, spill it.'

'May I have a cigarette?'

'You'd better hurry.'

Mr. Cork took out his case and, with trembling hands, lit a cigarette. He puffed greedily. He felt clearer in the head now.

'Was it you who cut the telephone wires?'

'Of course. But don't try playing for time. I want information. Where are the jewels?'

'Why do you suppose there are any jewels left? How do you know Daggers hadn't got rid of them?'

'Stop that nonsense. Talk.'

Mr. Cork, comforted by the cigarette, began to realize that Kurt was reluctant to use force, whatever his thug of an accomplice intended. Presumably, Kurt realized that, if he bludgeoned him, he had sacrificed his chief hope, as he believed, of discovering the whereabouts of these jewels.

'The only person who knows where those jewels are,' went on Mr. Cork calmly, 'is the man who disposed of them. Contrary to what you imagine, Gabriel Daggers is not dead.'

'He's drowned. And you know it.'

'Officially, he's drowned. Unofficially, no. The man whose body was recovered from the Black Brae was not Gabriel Daggers.'

'Who was it then?' said Kurt unbelievingly.

'At one time, I thought you might be able to help me.'

'You're lying.'

'I'm not lying. The position I'm in—the position we're all of us in—is too serious for levity. I am simply telling you that Daggers is alive.

'You look worried,' he went on. 'And with good reason. It was Gabriel Daggers, not me, who was responsible for that man's death in my car. It is Gabriel Daggers who is probably trying to make up his mind how to deal with you now.'

'You lie. You lie.'

Kurt made no attempt to conceal his alarm. He screamed at Mr. Cork hysterically.

'You're wasting your breath shouting "you lie" at every statement I make. And it's no use your friend trying to bully me. If you hit me, I shall faint again and I shall be of no further use to you. I am an elderly man and I am already in a very shaken condition. I am also past frightening any more. I'm much too frightened already. I'm willing to tell you what I know, which I regret does not include the whereabouts of the Pongratz jewels, because I have no wish to prevent you or Daggers from cutting each other's throats. In fact, it would make a very satisfactory end to an unpleasant business.'

Mr. Cork, squatting in a bog, was establishing his authority again. Fred was clenching and unclenching his fists uncertainly. Kurt, as the man at his feet reiterated again and again that Daggers lived, had lost his poise. He was wavering; 'definite wavering,' Mr. Cork reflected grimly.

'Where is Daggers now?' Kurt demanded.

'I was afraid you were going to ask that. As you came up the road in your car, Daggers was here.'

'Here,' whispered Kurt.

'He went away when he saw your lights. As a matter of fact, your coming saved our lives.'

'Never mind that. Where is he now?'

'I haven't the slightest doubt that he's looking at you at this moment, along the sights of a rifle.'

Kurt put his hand purposefully inside his coat. The mask of his face hardened into grey stone and his cross-eyes glittered as he looked cautiously around him.

'Put out the car lights,' he said to Fred. 'No, stay where you are. If he sees you doing that, it might draw his fire.'

He looked at Mr. Cork again.

'Are you sure you're telling the truth?'

'I wish to God I wasn't.'

'What are we going to do?' Fred whined.

'You want the jewels, don't you?'

' 'Course I do. But I don't want a bullet in me. He's got Harry already, hasn't he?'

'You can stay here then, and keep an eye on the old man?'

'What are you doing, Smiler?'

'What do you think? I've waited for these jewels for five years. I've looked for Daggers for five years too.'

'You're going after him?'

'Yes.'

It was lighter now, the steel-grey and lemon light of first dawn. The rain had reduced to a steady drizzle and the short Highland night was nearly over. Mr. Cork was crouched against the back of the wrecked car with the humpy figure of Fred hugging cover behind him. Kurt, a vaguely-outlined shadow in the steaming mist, was moving guardedly round the perimeter of the hollow, passing his body lovingly from one starved tree trunk to the next one, drawing the ground like a fox wary for the spring of the trap.

Inside the remains of the car, Mr. Cork could hear Robert stirring to consciousness. At the back of him, Fred was breathing heavily and hotly. The sound of rushing water, water everywhere, was punctuated by a noisy drumming which he vaguely identified as the beat of his own heart.

The agony of waiting could scarcely be prolonged much longer. If Daggers was there, watching them, the moment for decision must come quickly. Mr. Cork wondered if it was true that the victim didn't hear the report of the bullet that killed him. If Daggers wasn't there, the alternative was almost worse. Kurt would believe that he had been tricked. But, at that moment, Mr. Cork's speculations were abruptly ended.

A splash of flame jetted among the trees. With a queer sense of relief, Mr. Cork heard the sound of the shot. Kurt was standing there, still and upright, with a smoking pistol in his hand.

A man's shape separated from a dark clump of foliage. Falteringly, with his hands pressed to his stomach, he came down the slope of the hollow towards the pool of bright light made by the headlamps of the car on the road. As his legs stuck in the mud, he stopped, blinking stupidly. Then slowly, unbelievably slowly, his mouth swung open, his knees hinged, and he folded up in the bright green stuff of the bog.

It was Snatcher.

The man Fred drew in his breath between his teeth in an involuntary whistle. Then he gave a low whine of alarm.

'He's got him,' he murmured.

Stumbling over Mr. Cork, he ploughed his way to the spot where Snatcher's body, spotlighted by the car, lay doubled-up in a sort of macabre curtsey. As he studied the human heap, and saw the blood seeping out of it, he drew the back of his hand across his mouth in horror. Then he looked up at Kurt, standing impassively at the same point where he had fired.

'Christ,' he said. 'You've done it now, Smiler. How we going to get away with this?'

The last words choked in his throat. Another shot whip-cracked in the air. But, this time, it wasn't Kurt who fired. Mr. Cork, as he snuggled against the cover of the car, saw Kurt spin round to face a challenge from somewhere behind him.

'Something's hit me,' said Fred.

He put his hand enquiringly to his side. Then, drawing it away, he looked down at his palm. It was stained a sticky red.

'I'm hit, Smiler. D'ye hear me? I'm hit.'

This time, the thug shouted hysterically. With a lumbering effort, he plunged panic-stricked out of the hollow towards the car on the road.

'Where the hell are you going?' shouted Kurt. 'Where are you going?'

Fred made no answer. He was wrenching open the car door. Kurt, avoiding the revealing beam of the lights, circled round after him. As he did so, there was another shot from high up the hill. Kurt turned, fired twice and then ran on to intercept his accomplice. Fred had opened the door, and, whimpering noisily with pain, was dragging himself into the driver's seat.

'Stay where you are, you swine,' Kurt screamed. 'You want the stuff, don't you?'

The lights of the car were switched off. Mr. Cork heard the whirr of a self-starter. Raising his head, he saw the car drawing away as Kurt reached it. As it gathered speed, Kurt jumped on to the running-board. The last Mr. Cork saw of him he was hanging on to the side fighting to burst open the door.

Eleven

'SHIPLEY,' said Mr. Cork, in his most managerial tones.

'Yes, sir?' said Robert.

'I'm sorry, Robert,' said Mr. Cork gravely.

'Sorry for what, sir?'

Robert was lying face down on the banks of a flooded burn making a cold compress for his head with a handkerchief. Mr. Cork himself was trying vainly to force a clip of cartridges into the rifle which he had retrieved from the back of the hotel car.

'I'm sorry for the mess I've got you, and all of us, into. I realize, only too well, that I have failed in my responsibility to you as a friend of your father's, as an employee of the company and—don't interrupt—as your senior in years and experience. Indeed, I confess it freely. I am extremely ashamed of myself. I have meddled in matters which are beyond my own strength and authority. And, as a consequence of my fecklessness, I have endangered your life, and probably Anna Pryde's. To put it bluntly, Robert, I have behaved like a damn fool.'

Such a confession from Mr. Cork, in addition to his addressing him by his christian name, took Robert's attention from the care of his head. Sitting up too quickly, he gave a wince of pain. Mr. Cork, grey-faced and plastered with mud, looked at him anxiously.

'Head no better?' he asked.

'It's nothing,' said Robert, touching himself tenderly. 'I've had a worse hang-over from beer.'

'Nevertheless, from now forward, I shall handle this terrible business myself. I'm going back to the hotel to try and get help.'

'How are you going to get there?'

'If I can find where Anna has put Johnson's car, I shall use that. If not, I shall cross the river and take the short cut over the moors. I want you to remain here under cover until I get back.'

'But suppose Daggers, or Kurt, intercepts you?'

'I shall have to take that chance.'

'Are you going to leave Anna Pryde to take her chance?'

'I don't want to, but there's nothing else we can do. I shall never forgive myself, Robert, that I failed to call in the police right from the start.'

'But you had no evidence. You said so yourself.'

'My duty was to report my suspicions, unfounded or otherwise, to the proper authorities. But I thought I knew better. At my age, too. And this is the result. Two men murdered already. Anna Pryde in the power of a homicidal maniac. Your life and mine spared by a miracle. And that's not the end of it.

'In this weather, with the telephone lines cut, the police can't get here for hours. In the meantime, God only knows what may happen. Daggers is probably looking for us now. Kurt, when he has settled his differences with that creature of his, will take any risk to get those cursed jewels.'

'There's the Frenchwoman too,' said Robert. 'Obviously she's after the jewels as well.'

'Probably she is.'

Mr. Cork spoke almost absent-mindedly. He was thinking back, flogging his tired brain to recall the details of the encounter with Kurt.

'Have you ever heard of these Pongratz jewels?' he asked.

'Of course. Everybody has. There was a terrific hullabaloo about them immediately after the war, about the same time that they discovered that cave stuffed with art treasures in the American zone. The boffins of Mil. Gov. were swanning round all over the Continent looking for them. There was even an army order about it. It was the time when that Commission . . . what was it called?'

'The Macmillan Commission?'

'Something like that. The time when they were trying to recover all the treasures which the Nazis had looted to return them to their proper owners. Paintings, museum pieces, historical rarities, and all that sort of stuff. The Pongratz jewels were among the things they were hunting for. They were the heirlooms of some princelings in the Balkans who were bumped off by the Nazis. I remember reading all about it in the *Sunday Pictorial*, or somewhere like that.'

'But they never found where the jewels were hidden,' said Mr. Cork reflectively.

'Blamed it on the Nazis. And all the time this fellow Daggers had scooped the lot.'

'Clever man,' said Mr. Cork. 'A brave one too. How he shot his way out with that loot in the middle of a Commando raid, and got it home, must be one of the stories of the war. But he did it somehow. He got the stuff out, certain that the Nazis would be blamed for its disappearance, and presumably hid it up here.'

180

'But why do that?'

'He was a fisherman, Robert, and a jeweller. He called himself a jeweller's dealer on his policy. It didn't mean anything to me at the time, but now it's plain that it was Daggers' knowledge of jewellery that enabled him to identify the Pongratz collection for what it was, and later, to break it up and dispose of it, bit by bit, in a way that the stones wouldn't be recognized. Hence all the journeys he made to the Continent: hence the jeweller's workbench in his house; hence the money he had, and the mystery with which he surrounded his life.'

'Hence too the disabling of the car with a jeweller's saw,' Robert added. 'But how does the fishing part fit in?'

'I was coming to that. And listen carefully to what I'm saying, because we don't know what may happen to either of us in the next few hours. I want you to know what I've guessed of this remarkable crime story so that, if necessary you can tell it to the police.

'When Daggers had got the jewels to this country, it was obviously essential for him to hide them in a safe place; a place where they'd never be suspected, a place which he could always go to to draw on his hoard without arousing suspicion. I'm sure now that the place he chose was the bed of this river. As a fisherman, Daggers knew that there are secret places in the rocky bottom of rivers, underwater cavities in the rocks, where you can hide something more effectively than in any hole in the ground. With a rod in his hand, and the right to fish, it was inconceivable that anyone would suspect his real business. He chose this· lonely river in this lonely part of Sutherland. He came once or twice a year to draw what he needed from his cache. And, by a million to one chance, this fellow Kurt traced him down. How he did it, we don't know. But I suspect that he was in the German army and saw the actual raid in which the jewels were looted. He himself boasted that he was present when Daggers stole them.

'But, even when he realized that Kurt was after him, Daggers was confident. He determined to throw him completely off the scent by arranging to have himself officially drowned; drowned in the very river, perhaps in the very pool, where he had hidden his treasure. Why did he pick this particular place? Because, to commit the murder that he planned, to create the alibi that he needed, he could most easily use the place already carefully picked for his other purpose. How he organized the murder, how he brought his unknown victim secretly to Edendale, is still unsolved. But his plan succeeded admirably.

'Daggers would be safe to-day except that he had fallen in love with Anna. And he was no more prepared to part with Anna than with the Pongratz jewels. So he made that will, and took out the accident insurance, to keep Anna in reserve until it was safe for him to reappear with a new identity. He was convinced that he would conquer Anna ultimately for himself. He believed, like many other people, that money can buy anything. And he had the wealth. But Anna, like most other women, didn't run true to Daggers' idea of her. With feminine perverseness, she turned down £25,000. And then, unknowingly, Anna and ourselves led Daggers' enemies, convinced of his death, to the very place where Daggers is lying out and the Pongratz jewels are hidden.

'Daggers, who intended to disappear long ago, is drawn back by Anna's coming and fear for his treasure, to the Black Brae. After watching us to-day, after the discovery that he had killed one of Kurt's gang in mistake for us, he was desperately anxious. So he took the risk of sending a message to Anna, asking her to come to him secretly and alone. He wanted to measure up the opposition.'

'Where does the Frenchwoman fit?'

'It's still anybody's guess. The fact that she was raking about in the Black Brae this afternoon suggests that she knows about the jewels. It may be that she's an old accomplice of Daggers. It may be that she was the woman before Anna. Whatever she is, she's dangerous too.'

'Nice people,' said Robert laconically.

Mr. Cork got to his feet.

'I'm going to leave you now, Robert.'

'Aren't you taking the rifle?'

'I can't even load the wretched thing. Anyhow, I've lost my glasses.'

Robert grinned.

'In case anything happens to me,' Mr. Cork went on, 'it's important you should know my intended movements. My plan, if I can't find Johnson's car, is to cross the river at the Black Brae and follow the sheep track to Edendale. When I get there, I shall come back with what help I can raise to this point. So don't leave here unless you have to to keep out of trouble. Is that clear?'

'Quite clear.'

'And look after that head.'

'I will.'

Mr. Cork gave a parting wave of his hand.

'Good luck, sir.'

'And to you, my boy.'

Robert watched him until he was out of sight. Then he acted quickly. He picked up the rifle and, with practised hand, pressed the clip of five cartridges into the magazine. Next, he plunged his head into the burn to refresh himself.

Finally, in flat contravention of orders, he got to his feet and followed Mr. Cork.

After the unexpected deliverance from Kurt, and Daggers, Mr. Cork had helped Robert out of the wrecked car. There was nothing they could do for Snatcher. Snatcher was dead. The essential thing was to put the greatest possible distance between themselves and Daggers. Keeping off the road, they had followed the watercourse of a burn into a narrow cutting, overgrown with rank bracken, where they could take cover while they rested and considered the next move.

Robert never had the slightest intention of obeying Mr. Cork's instructions to stay put. He knew that Mr. Cork was in far worse shape than he was. But he also knew his boss well enough not to argue. Luckily, he had handed over the rifle on his own initiative. Now, Robert had a double purpose. First, he meant to keep Mr. Cork under his eye until he arrived safely at the hanging bridge over the pool of the Black Brae. Subsequently, he had another engagement.

Skirting along the hillside, Robert kept Mr. Cork in view. It wasn't difficult to spot him. Mr. Cork was too weary to think of concealment. He plodded along bravely in the centre of the road. When he took a corner, Robert pushed forward to another point on the hillside. If anyone interfered with the G.M. now, he was in no doubt what he would do. He would shoot to kill; and damn the consequences.

But Mr. Cork went on unscathed. When he came opposite the Black Brae he turned down towards the river. Robert, two hundred yards behind him on the hill slope, watched him until he disappeared. At last, with a breath of relief, he hooked the sling of the rifle over his shoulder and headed towards Wully Sutherland's hut.

That was the place where, according to Snatcher, Anna had kept her rendezvous with Daggers. Clearly, it was the first covert to draw. As the hut came into view, Robert dropped to his knees.

The only windows were in the front and they were shuttered up. If Daggers had a spy hole, it was either overlooking the river or the road up the glen. He decided to make his approach from the back of the building.

When he reached the hut, he already felt certain that his quarry had flown. But he needed to be sure that Mr. Cork, down in the Black Brae, wasn't overlooked as they were this morning.

Feeling his way round the woodwork for an entrance, his feet yielded underneath him. Bending down to throw aside a covering of turf and laid bracken over a sheep hurdle, he exposed a sort of enlarged rat-hole under the wall. Dropping on his knees, he bobbed into a damp pop-hole, under the timbers, into the musty single-roomed croft. The room, evil-smelling and damp, was empty except for a stove in one wall, a few trusses of straw, a lighted candle-end stuck in a bottle and some empty cigarette packets thrown about on the stone-flagged floor.

Robert went across the room and pulled out a plug of straw from a spy-hole in the timbers. As he expected, it gave a clear view of the Black Brae. Daggers, and perhaps Anna, had been there earlier in the evening. But Robert had called too late. His only hope now was Snatcher's croft somewhere on the other side of Cnoc Craggie.

In the grey light of early morning, the flooded burns glittered like burnished copper. The fronds of bracken, lining the banks, were sticky and heavy with rain. The peat hags were swollen like leeches with blood red water. The storm, drawing all the bright colours out of the hills, had washed the landscape till it was all drab sepias, olive greens, and the reds of rotting vegetation. The silver birches, fighting for a living among the outcrop rock, bent and creaked in the wind like rows of dead men on a gibbet. Robert, as he climbed Cnoc Craggie for the second time, reflected that at last he realized what Shakespeare meant when he set the scene on a blasted heath. Nothing was missing except the nameless morons to carry the bier and sound the roll of muffled drums.

It was probably the effect of two cracks on the head in one day, but he felt as melancholy as a character in a Shakespearean tragedy and as optimistic as the hero of a Russian play. He was also tired and cold and hungry. It was extraordinary, he thought to himself, how reminiscent his mood was of the start of those early morning attacks in the war. The same sense of unreality, the same cold feeling of indifference, the same disbelief in danger. But, in the war, there was always a group of other chaps with whom to share the experience. Now he was alone.

Warming up with the exertion of climbing the hill, he planned his future moves. He recalled that, when he had stalked the man in the morning, he had not sighted Snatcher's hut from the crown of the hill. Probably the croft lay in a fold further south. Robert determined to work round the top of Cnoc Craggie till he could find, as he must do, a track to the croft.

By sheer force of wartime habit, he spied out the hill carefully, and, on the southern slopes, discovered what he was looking for; a well-trodden track winding down through skeleton woodland to a field gate.

Snatcher's croft—it could be none other—was built into a shelf in the hill at a point where two streams joined with a larger stream, itself a tributary of the Edendale on the other side of Cnoc Craggie. The croft was so well concealed that, even when he was within fifty yards of it, Robert would never have suspected a human habitation but for the presence of the newly-wakened chickens scratching in the hungry soil between the rocks that were scattered everywhere on the slope; rocks lying about as if the biggest rock garden in the world had gone to seed.

The croft was the typical two-roomed, stone-tiled hut of the Highlands, with a centre door, windows on either side and a lime-washed face. Robert noticed that there was very little smoke wreathing from the chimney. Obviously the fire had not been made up. Keeping a wary eye on the easily-excitable chickens, he slipped up to the first window and peered in.

The room, a sort of kitchen sitting-room, was empty.

The pieces of a fishing rod stood in one corner and Robert thought he recognized a deer's hide laid out as a carpet on the stone-flagged floor. There was a stove, glowing dimly, in the outside wall.

Easing the rifle strap off his shoulder, he went to the other window. But, when he rubbed the mist off the pane with his fingers, that room, too, was deserted. An iron bedstead, with a tousled blanket, stood in one corner. Across the room, in another corner, was a straw-stuffed palliasse, where a second person had apparently been sleeping. But, now, the place was vacant.

Robert felt sick with weariness and disappointment. Daggers wasn't there either. He went round the back of the croft through a turf track between the building and a chicken house, along the fringe of the birchwood which led to the top of the hill. He calculated that it was the quickest way back to the river. If he was going to find Anna, it was essential to pick the shortest route over the ground to the place where it was most likely she had parked the car. Robert recalled that, in the strain of driving under the muzzle of Snatcher's pistol, he had completely failed to notice where she had put it. He must find out now. But, as the thought struck him, he slipped the rifle off his shoulder.

Anna, as large as life, was standing among the rocks in front of him.

'Don't move,' she shouted. 'Whatever you do, don't move. He's up there on the hill and he's got a rifle.'

Twelve

ANNA was working her way down the steep hill towards him, dancing from one rocky platform to another, picking her footing among the crags, choosing her path with the agility of a mountain hare. At intervals, she stopped to shout incoherent warnings.

Robert brought his rifle to the ready, rolled over the wing of the safety catch and, with the sharpened instinct of the hunter and the hunted, stood his ground and searched the broken surface of the hill above him. After the first surprise of seeing her, he never glanced at Anna at all. Somewhere among the rocks a few hundred yards above him, perhaps nearer, Daggers was looking for him. But Robert, wise in the experience of living dangerously, almost without conscious reasoning, realized that he was a difficult target. The light, in the early dawn, was still vague and deceptive. On one side, he had the birchwoods to confuse his outline. Behind him, his figure was obscured by the merging colours and the mixed shapes of the glen.

But, if his opponent made a revealing movement, he had the advantage that he himself was looking east into the dawn sky. A streak of yellow light silhouetted the ragged line of the hill top. Looking upwards, he was studying a landscape drawn against the clouds and defined in the clear detail of a scissor-cut.

He had checked his first instinct, on hearing Anna's warning, to drop to cover. If he had done that, his own sudden movement might well have been sufficient for his opponent to get a bead on him. He remembered the beasts he had shot—and the men too—who had betrayed themselves by a quick movement in a moment of panic. Anyhow, the risk of standing was worth taking. He calculated that, if he could tempt Daggers to shoot first and reveal his position, he might offer a chance for a snap shot as he raised his head; and raise his head he must, to get a clear aim down the hill.

Fieldcraft apart, Robert had the confidence of his own ability with a rifle. He felt in his bones that this was the sort of duel he was qualified to win. Without taking his eye off the hill, he called to Anna:

'Don't come any closer. Stay exactly where you are.'

'He means to kill you.'

'I know he does. He's had one good try already. But, this time, the odds are even.'

'Where is he?' he went on, still scanning the hillside. 'Tell me roughly where to look for him.'

'You haven't a chance, Robert. He's made up his mind to get you.'

'Calm yourself down, and answer my question. Where is he? No, don't point, you silly idiot.'

Robert's shout was too late. The crack of a rifle cut through the glen and echoed back with a thump from the surrounding hills. He heard the whine of a ricochet bouncing off the rocks behind him, but he had marked the flash of the discharge. His man was lying on the face of a ragged shelf of outcrop granite towards the top of the hill, about two hundred yards above him and to the left. Swinging his own rifle like a shotgun, while the report from Daggers' bullet was still echoing behind him, Robert pulled the trigger at the same instant that the butt touched his shoulder.

'Damn . . . high,' he said to himself. As he said it, he flopped forward and flattened into the ground. Daggers' second shot, accurate but a fraction late, cut the air harmlessly above his head.

'Are you all right?' Anna shouted.

'He couldn't hit a haystack,' Robert shouted back over the palm of his hand. 'But you'd better take cover yourself.'

'He's not after me,' Anna called back.

'Sure of that?'

'Quite sure.'

'Then stay on your feet and do my spotting for me. And, this time, don't point. Is he in the same place?'

'No, I think he's moving.'

'Downhill?'

'I can't see very well. Listen, I must talk to you. I can't tell you all of it now. But he's mad.'

'Is that what you've run down the hill to tell me.'

'He doesn't know what he's doing. He's even raving that you and Mr. Cork know about something he's hidden in the river.'

'He's quite right. We do.'

'Then it's true.'

'He's not all that mad. Why on earth did you put yourself in his hands, Anna?'

'Why couldn't you keep your own hands out of it? I told you what would happen.'

'You mean you knew he was mad all along?'

'Wasn't it obvious? He's not responsible for his own actions. He's a sick man.'

'Funny sort of fellow to fall in love with.'

She didn't answer.

'Are you still there, Anna? I'm sorry about that last remark. I only said it because I'm potty about you myself. I'd like to pop up and say so officially but, if I do, that basket will take a crack at me. Hi, there, where are you?'

He peered over the rock he was using for cover. Anna had vanished. A bullet chipped the stone a few inches from the side of his head. He ducked again hastily.

'If you're at all interested, Anna,' he called into the blue, 'he missed.'

'You needn't shout any more. I'm just beside you.'

Her voice carried to him from behind another rock on his right. He still couldn't see her.

'Better not come any closer. This fellow's such a poor shot, he might hit you in mistake for me.'

'Don't underestimate him, Robert.'

'I'm not likely to. I ought to tell you that he nearly succeeded in murdering us a little while ago.'

'I know. Is Mr. Cork all right?'

'Just about. But how the devil did you find out?'

'I was with him when the car crashed. We heard the pistol shot. When he went after you, I followed him. I thought you were dead, Robert.'

'Were you sorry?'

'Yes, sorry for everything. Who were those men?'

'Kurt and his sparring partner.'

'So it was him.'

'We thought we'd had it.'

'I got hold of his rifle and spoilt his aim.'

'I wondered why he'd missed.'

'You shouldn't have come here.'

'I thought you might need help.'

'I told you I didn't want it.'

'I can't make you out, Anna.'

192

'I don't expect you to.'

'Well, you needn't worry any more. So far as Gabriel Daggers is concerned, this is the reckoning.'

'I wish you wouldn't talk like that. He's dangerous. Terribly dangerous.'

'That's what you keep on saying. I know he's a murderer. I've got very personal reasons for remembering it. But I'm tired of hearing what a formidable fellow he's supposed to be. All I can say is that, so far, he's shown himself to be a very average shot. Gabriel Daggers has had it, Anna. Can you see him now?'

'No, he's out of sight again.'

'All right, keep your eyes open and hold your ground. I can manage Daggers. I'm going to work up hill towards him. If you sight him again, try to give me a signal.'

'Do you want to kill too?'

'What do you think? If I'd shot up to my usual form, if he hadn't hit me over the head with a spanner, I'd have stopped him the first time.'

'You said just now that you . . . liked me, didn't you? Do you mean it?'

'Of course I do, Anna. Why not?'

'If you mean what you say, don't try to kill Gabriel.'

'Well, I'll be . . .'

Robert rolled on to his side in surprise and peered through the rocks for a sight of her. But she was well hidden, and this time he remembered to keep his head down.

'Did I hear you straight?' he called. 'Are you seriously suggesting that I should give this fellow a chance to make a getaway?'

'You know what Mr. Cork said. Leave it to the police. It's their job. Not yours.'

'The way you talk he might almost be a friend of the family's. I can't understand you, Anna. What do you want me to do? Run away from him?'

'Yes, you can do that easily enough. Go and warn Mr. Cork. I'll stay here and he'll think you're still with me among the rocks.'

'What happens to you?'

'I can look after myself. And I want to keep an eye on him. It's all right. Do as I say. If he goes on like this, he's bound to be caught in the end. Please, Robert!'

'All right. But I haven't the same confidence in your Gabriel as you appear to have yourself. So I'm not going to leave you to his doubtful mercies. But I'll make you a promise if you want it. I won't kill him unless I have to. Nevertheless, I suppose you'll have no objection to my winging him. By the way, do you know if he has any spare cartridges?'

'I haven't seen any. Why?'

'Presumably, he's got five in the clip. And three have gone already. Don't look my way. I'm about to give Gabriel Daggers a lesson in stalking. And in shooting too.'

Zig-zagging among the rocks, he started to worm his way up the steep slope of the hill. It was easy country for stalking by comparison with the open ground he had had to cover earlier. But if he was to keep his promise to Anna, he realized that he must get very close to his man to be absolutely certain of a shot that would cripple without killing. Furthermore, the extra hazard made his own task more chancy. But the chance was worth taking. It was worth it if only for the satisfaction it would give him to prick this blighter's reputation, once and for all, under Anna's own nose. She seemed to be besotted with the idea of Daggers' invincibility. She talked of him, with a sort of wide-eyed wonder, as if he were one of those characters in a strip cartoon. She was so exasperatingly sure that this fellow could kill him; kill him out of hand, as if he, Robert, were a barnyard fowl only fit to have his neck wrung. She even suggested that he ought to run away from the fellow.

Very well, she should see for herself where Daggers got off. Up till now, Robert reflected, he had hardly given an impressive performance, either as a marksman or a superman. Admittedly, as Mr. Cork said, it was pretty smart work to carry off that loot under the eyes of the enemy in the thick of a Commando raid. But nothing that Daggers had done subsequently seemed particularly decorative. He had murdered some poor devil in rather sordid circumstances. He had laid a treacherous trap by messing about with the Bentley. He had ambushed Mr. Cork and himself. And he had succeeded in making poor Anna's life a misery by pestering her with his attentions.

Anna, of all people. Robert felt angry and confused.

What funny creatures women were. If she believed Daggers was mad, as she said, why the devil had she put up with him? And why make a song and dance to save him from a well-deserved bullet in his guts? No doubt, she had her reasons. But, like many men in love for the first time, Robert felt that women were very difficult to understand.

He had now worked up hill to the level where he had first seen Anna and to the left of the place where he guessed she was now lying. He wanted to be well clear of her in case he invited another bullet, but thought it wiser to pinpoint her position before going any further. He now had a better view of the rocky slopes below him and, before long, worked his way to an overhanging crag which gave him a view of Anna crouched in a rocky cleft about fifty yards down the hill. Presumably Daggers could see her too, her mackintosh belted carelessly, her dark hair blowing in the wind and setting off the pallor of her face. She looked at once desirable and strangely remote and unreal.

'Don't look at me, Anna,' he shouted, 'I just want to tell you that I love you—I wanted to say it before but I couldn't make it—and then I want to know if you can tell me the next instalment of Superman. Where is he now?'

So Robert was past reasoning too. He was carrying on as if this was a game of cowboys and Indians. He was baiting Gabriel into some irreparable action.

In the name of pity, why couldn't they have left him to her? When she got that crumpled note, soiled by Snatcher's greasy fingers, asking so anxiously to see her, she knew that, left to herself, she could persuade him to leave this cursed place. She had received so many notes from him in that familiar jagged handwriting, notes scribbled on the back of ivory cards bedded deep in baskets of roses. And she had learnt to read his mood.

Even if he hadn't sent the message, she had meant to go in search of him. It was cowardly, a silly hysterical decision made in the panic of the moment, to have admitted as much as she had to Mr. Cork. Right from the beginning, she should have recognized that Gabriel, alive or dead, was her own terrible responsibility.

Murderer he might be. But, after all that had happened between them, it was impossible to associate him with murder. Gabriel wasn't a murderer in the sense that people ordinarily used the word. He was ill. When she broke it off with him in one of those explosive scenes which came so often between them, she ought to have realized that the outcome would be something like this. She knew him so well, his brooding moods, his violent outbursts and his strange unbalanced mind.

Poor Gabriel . . .

It was typical of him, when he met her in that awful storm, to apologize that he hadn't brought her any flowers. He seemed to have no realization, even then, of his mortal danger. He kept on saying that he was dead and that the other man, the man who was drowned in the river, was a ghost too. All he seemed anxious about was Kurt and something which he said was hidden in the river. He thought that that was what they were looking for in the morning.

But, when she reassured him, he was more like his old self. What was it he said? He said he would disappear into the sea like the salmon and come back like the salmon into the stream of her life again. By this time, she might have got him out of harm's way. At worst, he would have been put in the hands of the doctors. But now . . .

Why couldn't they have left her alone with him? Gabriel promised that Snatcher was watching them; that, if they came out after her, Snatcher would keep them away. But it had come to this.

Biting her lip with strain, looking blankly into the dawn sky, Anna prayed for inspiration. Somehow, even at this late hour, she must keep Gabriel and Robert apart. She had to save both of them from themselves.

'Anna,' Robert called out more urgently. 'Are you all right? Don't get in a panic. I'll fix him. But, for God's sake, give me a clue where he is.'

'I'm not sure where he is now,' she called back. 'Last

time I saw him, he was climbing up the hill, away to the left. Right over there, away from you.'

'Okeydoke,' said Robert cheerfully.

But, as he moved off in the direction indicated, he was bothered.

'Funny business,' he muttered to himself. 'I'd have expected him to come my way if he's serious.'

He snaked faster along the broken ground. If Daggers, contrary to all expectation and Anna's opinion of him, was trying to make a bolt for it after all, he'd have to overtake him. He might even have decided to head for the Black Brae. If he did that, Robert could only hope that Mr. Cork was either out of the way or had heard the exchange of shots over the hill. It would at least give him fair warning that the game might move in his direction.

Robert was now nearly out of shouting distance from Anna. He could see her on the slopes below him and, for a moment, he wondered whether to risk a last call to her before going on. But Anna herself anticipated him. She was signalling with lowered arms, clearly indicating that he must move still further to her left. To the left.

He did as he was told, skirting the crown of the hill and searching every likely hiding-place in the ground for his opponent; and, as he did so, he grew increasingly disconcerted. First of all, he knew that he was covering the ground fast, almost dangerously so. He was already well to the left of Daggers' original firing point and, at a rough calculation, he was downstream of the pool at the Black Brae. If Daggers planned a retreat to the Black Brae, why was he making his way beyond it? What possible advantage could there be to Daggers in drawing away from the ground in this strange fashion? He was reducing his chances of killing Robert, and of making his own getaway. The more he thought about it, the less he liked it. Either Daggers was much closer than he realized, or he was backing away aimlessly into the roadless hills.

He crawled on until he found a rock with a fractured opening sliced down the middle. Spying through it carefully, he could see no sign of movement. Raising himself on his arms, he peered cautiously over the top. If Daggers was there, he didn't accept the offer of a shot. Robert, with a confidence that was now near certainty, circled round to the other side of the stone and looked back over the ground he had already covered.

The pock-marked and rock-pimpled hill was laid out below him, with all its now familiar features. There was Snatcher's hut, hugging the slope. There was the birchwood, there the shelf of rock from which Daggers had made his first two shots. But Anna had gone. She had left her original position, and she was nowhere to be seen in the landscape. And of Daggers there was no sign.

Robert raised the barrel of his rifle in the air and pulled the trigger. As the report reverberated through the hills, he saw his opponent's head and shoulders pop up and down, like a target in a shooting gallery, high on the hill and five hundred yards at least to the right of him. The sickly suspicion dawned on Robert that perhaps Daggers too had been taking signals from Anna; that she had deliberately misled them both in an attempt to keep them apart. So she still believed that Robert was no match for him. Cursing all women, he tightened his grip on his rifle.

At that range, Daggers had made no attempt to fire. That seemed to confirm that he had no ammunition to spare. What he would do now was to close the gap as quickly as he could. But so far his tactics suggested that he was a canny fighter. It wasn't likely that he'd give a chance for the mere sake of making ground. And he'd probably expect Robert to do the same.

Robert thought quickly. It was long odds on Daggers wasting one of his last two cartridges on a long range shot at a moving target. It was likely that he'd be much too busily engaged sweating over the wet ground to lift his head until he was fairly sure that he had closed the range to a reasonable distance.

Robert sprang to his feet, his rifle at the trail and, doubling himself up, made a fifty yard rush. He rested just long enough to nurse his head and regain his breath; then he jumped forward again. He covered about two hundred yards without incident. Daggers, he reckoned, would now be approaching him along approximately the same contour of the hill. Lying along a shelf of rock, he recovered his wind and muscle control, and waited.

Daggers moved more quickly over the ground than Robert expected. He saw him first, the dark hump of his back, creeping forward just a little below him at about seventy-five yards range. It was a plumb easy shot, but Robert, in spite of the way that Anna had misled him, meant to keep his promise. A bullet through Daggers' lungs would kill him. He was content to wait until his man delivered himself utterly into his hand.

But, surprisingly, while he was watching for his opponent round a peat hag a little below the shelf of rock on which he was lying, he stiffened at the sound of a pebble falling above him, almost on the cap of the hill itself. He was certain that Daggers hadn't sighted him. But, accidentally, Daggers had got him at a tactical disadvantage. A hump-backed bank of peat, over the top of the shelf where Robert had positioned himself, blocked his vision. Cursing his luck, he slipped off the edge of the shelf and, hugging the ground, got behind a boulder which gave him reasonable cover and an opportunity to raise his gun up hill.

It wasn't an ideal position: but he got there just in time. A movement enabled him to mark his opponent a mere ten yards away. Daggers crouched behind a large rock stuck into the turf like a nut in the icing of a cake. He didn't offer a shot. But Robert reckoned he must be looking for him in the wrong direction. It was as satisfactory as beating an old stag to the wind. The risk of closing the range had been justified.

'Your number's up, Daggers,' he shouted.

Daggers swung round in surprise. He raised his rifle and put a wild shot in Robert's direction. For a moment Robert saw his outline.

'That's four bullets,' he shouted, as Daggers bobbed behind the rock again. 'Only one left, I think. You'll have to do better than that, you know.'

He watched, mind and muscle taut for a betraying movement. He saw the barrel of Daggers' rifle slide cautiously round the side of the rock. The butt of the rifle tightened against his own shoulder. He took up the first pressure on the trigger and, holding his breath to steady his aim, fired. Immediately, Daggers half rose to his feet and returned the shot. The bullet whizzed harmlessly over Robert's shoulder.

'Five,' he yelled triumphantly.

Ejecting the spent cartridge from his own rifle, and closing the bolt on another round, he rose to his knees for the settling shot. Even if Daggers had a pistol, he had him now. But, as he lifted the rifle to his shoulder, a weight landed on his back and he was thrown sideways. The rifle wrenched out of his hands, and, rolling helplessly, he came down heavily to the ground.

Anna, her arms wound round his shoulders, hung on desperately.

'Run, Gabriel,' she shouted. 'Run while you can. I can't hold him much longer.'

Daggers rose from behind the rock. He glanced at the two struggling figures. Then, without a word, he turned and ran towards the crown of the hill.

Robert, recovering himself, broke away from Anna's clawing hold. He saw Daggers running and looked wildly about him for the rifle; but Anna remembered it, too. In a moment she was on to it. Lifting it with both hands over her head, she dashed it down the hill.

Daggers was already well clear. Together, they saw him reach the crest and, without a backward glance, start down the far slopes of Cnoc Craggie.

Thirteen

MR. CORK dragged his legs through the sopping bracken to the river bank. He was glad to be off the road. There was no sign of Johnson's car—Anna must have left it further down the river—and he preferred the prospect of a seven mile walk over the moors to another encounter with Daggers or Kurt. He was relieved to have come as far as he had without incident and he would feel happier still when he had put the Black Brae behind him. Once across the bridge over the salmon leap, he could feel reasonably safe. Within a couple of hours, he could be back with help for Robert and, if they could find her, Anna as well. After that, his responsibility was ended.

There was a chance, of course, that Kurt had been sufficiently unnerved by what had happened to make a run for it; or he might have been thrown off the car, and himself injured, by his terrified accomplice. But it seemed unlikely. Mr. Cork had an uncomfortable feeling that Kurt couldn't be written off so easily. It was more probable that the wretched Fred would regret his faintheartedness.

Daggers, who disappeared so surprisingly after the shooting, might have gone to ground. But it was difficult to believe it. Daggers' first objective, now that his cache was discovered, would be to move his treasure. And there seemed little doubt that the hiding-place was somewhere in the pool of the Black Brae. Mr. Cork approached it again with sinking heart. But it was the only place within miles where there was a footbridge. And one glance at the river showed that there was no hope, after the cloud-burst in the night, of fording the stream lower down.

In a few hours, the flow of water had swelled from a gentle crystal-clear current to an angry peat-coloured flood. Boils of yellow foam swirled in the eddies. A dead sheep, swollen-bellied, floated in the current. The banks were choked with broken timber and rubbish carried downstream in the spate. The water level had risen about four feet in twelve hours. It was the bridge, or nothing.

As he approached the red rocks enclosing the pool, he looked behind into the hills. Nothing moved, except the rabbits and the sea-birds, in the morning stillness of the glen. Only a heron, swinging lazily up the river, welcomed him with a hoarse squawk. Watching the bird, he stumbled. When he recovered himself, he looked down to find what it was that had tripped him. Lying at his feet among the bracken was a bicycle. He was not alone.

Only sheer desperation could have persuaded Mr. Cork to attempt the crossing of the hanging bridge over the Edendale. Strung loosely across the abyss of the salmon leap, it was a frail cobweb, sticky with the mist which steamed up from the white water and swaying like a ham-mock over the jagged rocks below. As he clutched the single wire strand provided as a hand-hold and stepped tentatively on to the reeling foot-boards, he swallowed giddily. But he didn't turn back.

Phoebe would never believe it, but he meant to get across. He had told Robert that that was what he intended to do. And the fact that the Frenchwoman was obviously nearby made it more than ever necessary to get the ordeal over quickly.

He seized the wire cable in both hands and launched himself crabwise over the watery pit. As he moved, the narrow foot-planks bounced and twisted. The wire cable, cutting into his palms, swung playfully under his weight. His feet slipped on the greasy wood. And he was enveloped in the cold spray thrown off the rocks by the fall.

In spite of himself, he looked down. It was only for a fraction of a second that he peeped into the boiling mess tumbling and pitting and mushrooming under his feet. But it was enough. His stomach heaved and his legs turned to water. His courage seeped out of him. And he realized, with awful certainty, that he could neither go forward nor move back. He hung pitifully on the holding wire like a trapped fly.

Madame Breuvart, baulked from crossing the river by the paralysed figure swaying in the loop of the bridge, made up her mind quickly. She couldn't leave him there. It was necessary, even at the cost of showing herself, to get him out of her way. And she was curious, anxiously so, to learn what it was that had brought Mr. Cork, once again, to the Black Brae.

Balancing herself lightly, she swayed out to him as casually as a cat on a roof-top. Then, wrapping her left arm firmly round his waist, she used her hand to ease his white-knuckled grip on the cable. He gaped at her, in his agony, in dazed astonishment.

'You're quite all right,' she said over the rush of water. 'Let go that right hand and put your arm on my shoulder. There's nothing to worry about.'

Mr. Cork did as he was told. Hearing her steady voice, and feeling her solid shoulder under his grip, the control came back into his legs. Unreasoningly, he felt safe again. He followed her, with the stumbling confidence of a blind man, to the bank. Then he collapsed.

'I'll get you some cognac,' she said.

Presently, she returned with a flask. He supposed she carried it in the gear on her bike.

'This will do you good.'

He nodded gratefully. The neat spirit made him cough but it glowed inside him bravely. He felt rather better.

'Thank you,' he said. 'You saved my life.'

'I wanted to cross the bridge myself. You were in the way.'

'I was foolish to make the attempt. I'm afraid I haven't the head for that sort of thing.'

'Then why did you do it?'

'I was running away.'

'Who from? What has happened?'

'Daggers has tried to murder us. Two people have been shot; one of them killed by Kurt. And the young man you saw with me this morning has been injured.'

Mr. Cork helped himself tremblingly to a cigarette. The Frenchwoman's eyes narrowed. She scanned the hills behind them.

'Where is Daggers now?'

'Over there somewhere.'

'And the Boche?'

'Which Boche?'

'Kurt.'

'I hope he's out of the way; but I doubt it.'

She peered again into the hills.

'You must go away from here immediately,' she said.

'That was my purpose. I was going to Edendale to get help. But I don't think I can make it now.'

'You must,' said Madame Breuvart, impatiently.

'I shall never get across that bridge.'

'I'll help you. Come quickly.'

She took his hand to drag him to his feet.

'No, it's no good,' he said. 'I know when I'm beaten. You must leave me here.'

He put his hand wearily to his head.

'You must go to Edendale for me. Tell them what's happened and . . .'

'It's impossible.'

For the first time Madame Breuvart seemed excited.

'Why impossible?'

'Because I say so. You must go. You must go immediately. You can't stay here.'

'And you?'

'I will follow you.'

She was becoming more agitated.

'What's the matter, Madame Breuvart?'

Her obvious anxiety to get rid of him roused Mr. Cork to assert himself again.

'Why can't you leave me here?'

'You are in terrible danger.'

'Is there no danger for you?'

She didn't answer.

'What do you know about these Pongratz jewels?' he asked suddenly.

Her face hardened. Tired as he was, Mr. Cork saw the change in her.

'Suppose you tell me the truth,' he said. 'You know Daggers, although you denied it the last time we met. You know Kurt. And you know about these jewels. What else but the jewels were you looking for yesterday? What are you up to at the Black Brae now?'

'What are you doing here yourself?' she asked, defensively.

'Exposing a murderer.'

'You come from the police?'

'I am going to them. They'll ask you a lot of embarrassing questions.'

'What have I got to fear? I had nothing to do with it. Johnnie wasn't even my husband.'

'Who was Johnnie?'

She stared at him incredulously.

'You didn't know?'

'How should I?'

'You tricked me.'

'I should forget that pistol if I were you,' said Mr. Cork, watching her. 'It'll only get you into trouble. I should forget the Pongratz jewels, too. You won't get away with them now: too many people share the secret. As for the suggestion that I tricked you, you tricked yourself. The best thing you can do, in your own interests, is to make a clean breast of it. Who was Johnnie?'

In her damp clothes, with her hair in dripping rats-tails, Madame Breuvart looked like a naiad of the angry river. She stood hesitating between a curse and a confession.

'What will the police do?'

'If you're not an accomplice of Daggers or Kurt and providing you don't try to steal the Pongratz jewels, nothing.'

'Why should I trust you?' she asked, suspiciously.

'That's for you to judge.'

'Will you help me?'

'You saved my life just now.'

'What do you want to know?'

208

'Who was Johnnie?'

'He was a British soldier.'

'What else?'

'He was the man who was murdered here by Daggers,' she said, in a low voice.

'What was he to you?'

'I loved him.'

'Had you known him long?'

'Since the raid.'

'What raid?' Mr. Cork studied her face with sharpened interest. 'Was it the Commando raid in which Daggers looted the jewels?'

She looked at him apprehensively.

'You're only telling me the other half of something I know already. Daggers stole the jewels in a raid on the French coast. Was this the same raid?'

'Yes.'

'Did Johnnie know the jewels had been stolen?'

'They did it together.'

'What happened to Johnnie?'

'He was left for dead on the beaches. I saved him from the Boches.'

'And Daggers?'

'Daggers got away.'

As if in echo to the sound of the name, the hills answered back with a distant report. Almost at once, another report, like a second syllable, followed. The Frenchwoman, slumped and sullen while Mr. Cork questioned her, became alert.

'Rifle fire,' she said.

'Where does it come from?'

'Over the hill beyond the hut. Listen, they're shooting again. You must go.'

'Why must I go?' said Mr. Cork, obstinately. 'Are you expecting somebody?'

'Maybe.'

'Is it the man you've been looking for since Johnnie was murdered?'

'Why don't you go while there's still time?'

'I want to persuade you, if I can, to change your mind.'

'You're wasting your time, and risking your life.'

'Those jewels are no good to you.'

'Nor, much longer, to him,' she said, gazing into the hills.

'What you're planning to do won't solve anything. Why don't you leave it to the police?'

'I am doing what Johnnie would have wished,' said Madame Breuvart. 'Do you still want to stay here?'

'Yes.'

She shrugged fatalistically.

'Then you had better get under cover,' she said.

How long it was that he had watched, and waited, he couldn't remember. Sheltering under the rocks, his perceptions blunted by weariness and his feeling dulled by horror, he was almost past caring. Shot by shot, he listened in a puzzled way to the duel on the hill. Somewhere near, he knew that Madame Breuvart was looking for vengeance.

But his limbs were immeasurably heavy. He was cold and stiff and light-headed. And he was at first only mildly interested when he noticed the black spot of a man running down the face of Cnoc Craggie towards the Black Brae.

Flailing his arms to keep his balance, taking the descent in long swinging strides, Gabriel Daggers plunged recklessly towards the drain-hole of the Black Brae. As he followed his feet in wild arcs down the hillside, his mind was racing with desperate calculations. With every jarring leap, the hammer thumping inside his head urged him to fiercer effort. He, who had never made a mistake, was suddenly struggling in a whirlpool of inexplicable challenge.

What had gone wrong? What, in the name of reason, had gone wrong? Nothing before that he had planned had failed. He was cleverer than they were, subtler in strategy, bolder in action. Yet now, when he had most brilliantly achieved the most daring exploit of all, the pawns in the game were incomprehensibly defying him. He was dead; and they wouldn't believe it. He had them in his power; and they wouldn't go down. The very bullets in his rifle had turned against him. And Anna, the one person he trusted, had betrayed him.

That was it. It was Anna's fault. The mistake he had made was to share himself with anybody; even Anna. It was Anna, like a bag of aniseed, who had put the German and his gang on the trail again. It was Anna who had disturbed his aim when he could have wiped out the whole hornet's nest of them. He hated her.

She had never really loved him. She had sacrificed herself—that was the lick-spittle phrase that people used— she had sacrificed herself because she was sorry for him. He would almost have preferred the bullet to the look of pity she had darted at him, just now on the hill, over that fellow's back. Damn her pity. Her pity and everybody else's. He could do without it. If there was any pity about, it was he, and nobody else, who was going to do the pitying.

He needed neither their sympathy nor their company. He had something more valuable to concern himself with.

With the Pongratz jewels in his pocket, he could afford to laugh at the lot of them. Let them bring the police. What could they prove against him? These people could say he was alive, but what evidence could they produce in support? The law said he was dead. First they had to lay hands on him, and then they had to discover who it was they had hooked out of the river. But they wouldn't find him and they couldn't explain away that body in the Black Brae. He'd set them a poser there all right.

The more he thought about it, the more his spirits rallied. The German would hang for shooting Snatcher. The others would have to explain, as best they could, the two cars piled up in the glen. And he himself would disappear like a shadow in the trackless wilderness of the hills.

As he ran towards the Black Brae, his pulse began to beat excitedly and he was possessed by the rising pressure of returning self-confidence. All he had to do now was to collect the jewels from their hiding-place. With the river in flood, it was going to be difficult. But the job must be done, and done quickly. He had to get deep into the hills before the arrival of the police. He also had to make the most of his start on the fellow who had tried to shoot it out with him. It was a pity that he wasn't armed. But the chance was one he had to take.

As he leapt on to the road, he gazed down arrogantly at the silver ribbon of the Edendale. He estimated that, if the rain held off, the spate would have spent itself by the following morning. But he couldn't wait. He had to rely on his own strength, and knowledge of the water, to move the box in the cavity under the racing salmon leap at the Black Brae.

He walked up the bank, studying the current and the

water level with the experienced eye of the angler. He followed the same well-trodden track that Colonel Johnson had followed behind the big fish that led him to the corpse. He stood looking at the pool at the same spot where Mr. Cork had watched Madame Breuvart. Then, creeping along the shelving rocks, he lay down in exactly the same place where, earlier, Madame Breuvart had been at work with the gaff.

Leaning down, he thrust his arm under the edge of the waterfall into the still water below. The current, even at the side, pulled strongly against his arm. But, straining himself, Daggers was able to run his fingers lovingly over the underwater rocks, like a cracksman feeling the combination of the locks on a safe. He couldn't reach the cavity he was feeling for. Standing up, he threw off his hat and scarf, coat and shirt, and stripped himself to the waist. Then he lay down again and, knuckling his legs firmly round a crag on the brink, he bent his whole torso into the current. With one hand he got a grip on a rock under the fall, with the other he reached into the hole where he had hidden the Pongratz jewels.

Mr. Cork, hidden by the rocks at the side of the pool, looked at the man of whom he had heard so much with quickening interest. Seeing him there, stripped to the waist, struggling with the angry river, he seemed at first sight almost ineffective. Then he saw his eyes. He remembered how Anna had talked of them. Deep-set and heavy-lashed, Daggers had eyes like coiled snakes. The flash in them was hypnotic and venomous. He was mad, stark mad.

Mr. Cork, watching him with fascination, waited to see what he would bring up from the bottom of the river. He noticed that Daggers had a struggle to pull himself clear. The muscles in his back rippled with effort, and, when he twisted himself free of the fall, he doubled up for a moment, breathing hard from the exertion, shaking his head and blowing to clear his nose and ears of water. It was apparent that the effort in the current had been almost too much for him. But, almost at once, he ducked down again and, with a heave, pulled a greenish-looking, rusty box out of the river.

It looked like a small deed box. It was bound with twists of wire and, as Daggers lifted it clear of the river, it dripped leakily with water.

In his curiosity, Mr. Cork became careless. He leant right over the rock where he had hidden himself to get a better view. And Daggers spotted him. With half-lidded eyes, he sprang to his feet. Mr. Cork saw his shoulder blades twitch and his jaw muscles working. He said nothing. But, with fierce agility, he jumped up the face of the rock from the river level and made straight to the place where Mr. Cork was hiding at the mouth of the hanging bridge. When he was within ten yards, he suddenly stopped and looked about him suspiciously.

'You're quite right,' said Mr. Cork. 'You've walked straight into a trap.'

Daggers backed a few paces and watched Mr. Cork slyly.

'You can't trap me,' he said.

'Where's Anna Pryde?'

'What's that to you?'

'She's the only person who's likely to help you now.'

'I don't want her help.'

He moved back until he was standing on the huge rock overlooking the pool.

'You can't save the Pongratz jewels,' went on Mr. Cork, inexorably. 'The game's up, Daggers.'

'Don't call me Daggers.'

'Are you still pretending to yourself you're dead?'

'Who are you?'

'The man you tried to murder.'

'What do you want?'

'Are you thinking of trying to bribe me?'

'Why have you interfered with me?'

'Because you tried to cheat my company out of £25,000.'

Daggers laughed. With legs astraddle, and hands on his hips, he was almost enjoying himself. It might be a trap but this fellow amused him. He smiled haughtily, and Mr. Cork watched him from behind the rock with growing interest.

'How can you prove that I'm alive?'

'It may only be necessary to identify the dead.'

Daggers' eyes narrowed.

'I suppose you know that a gang of ruffians is after you? It was the threat from them, I imagine, that made it necessary for you to disappear?'

'What's that to you?'

'To me, nothing. But, for you, it must be alarming to know that they're on the track again.'

Daggers continued to watch Mr. Cork carefully, but his steady gaze in return never faltered.

'Have you anything else to say to me?'

'Yes, I have. Who is the Frenchwoman who shares your interest in this pool?'

'I don't know who you mean.'

'Pity. I had hoped you would enlighten me.'

'Why?'

'Because she's standing behind you now, with a pistol levelled at your back.'

At Mr. Cork's warning, Daggers half swung round to

face the challenge from behind. But Madame Breuvart, after her catlike advance through the bracken, jumped forward and jabbed the barrel of her automatic into the small of his naked back. He stiffened. But he didn't put up his hands.

'Who are you?' said Daggers, coldly.

'Johnnie's girl.'

'But I told him . . .'

Madame Breuvart punched the barrel of the automatic into his back, leaving a red circular weal in the white skin.

'You told him that nobody must know of your meeting here on the Black Brae. That's right, isn't it?'

Madame Breuvart raised her husky voice in anger.

'You thought Johnnie himself wouldn't dare to talk because he wanted the world to go on thinking he was killed and because he wanted to collect his fair share of the loot he helped you to get. But he told me. When he came here to collect his half of the Pongratz jewels, which you promised, it was me he confided in. I loved him and he loved me. And you murdered him, your wartime comrade, here in cold blood on the Black Brae.'

With the point of the pistol, she turned him until he was standing on the edge of the rock looking into the swirling waters of the pool.

'What are you going to do?' said Daggers.

'Kill you, as you killed Johnnie.'

Mr. Cork, half rising to his feet, gave a cry to check her. But the cry died on his lips. As Madame Breuvart took up the pressure on the trigger, Daggers jumped.

For a moment, he seemed to hang in the air over the river. Then, scarcely making a splash in the restless current he was buried in the Black Brae. The last they saw of him, he was bobbing helplessly in the race below the fall.

Fourteen

ROBERT and Anna had nothing to say to each other. As they followed Daggers down the hill, each of them pretended that the other wasn't there. Utterly divided in purpose, speechlessly out of sympathy, they yet shared a common fear and a common objective. Anna believed that, in spite of Robert, she might still save Daggers: Robert, in spite of Anna, was determined to prevent him from making further mischief. They dogged each other's footsteps with resentment and they behaved with the flushed indifference of mutual misunderstanding and pricked pride.

Daggers had a long start on them. They saw him crossing the road to the river as they gained the windswept crown of the hill. When he vanished from view, they watched and listened. But there was no sound except the distant whisper of the river and no movement showed in the circle of rocks round the Black Brae.

Robert concluded that Mr. Cork had got across and was on his way to Edendale. Anna wondered whether Daggers would make for the car which she had hidden in the birchwoods lower down the glen. Both of them were planning to rid themselves of each other's unwelcome attentions.

'Stop,' said Robert, suddenly.

It was the first word they had exchanged since Daggers

had made his escape. With a glance of disapproval, Anna went straight on.

'Get down.'

This time, the anxious command in his voice checked her. When she looked back, Robert was already on his knees, pointing warningly up the glen. Moving over the rough ground of the river bank, above the Black Brae, somebody was coming downstream.

'Who is it?'

'I can't tell yet. But if it's who I think it is, we need to be careful.'

Holding his hands over his eyes to concentrate his vision, Robert studied the man carefully.

'Well,' said Anna, restlessly, 'can you identify him now?'

For a moment, he didn't reply. Then he slithered down the slope close to Anna's side.

'As I thought,' he muttered. 'It's Kurt.'

'Alone?'

'Yes, there's no sign of the other fellow. He was pricked with a bullet and Kurt's probably got rid of him somehow. But he's come back himself, just as old Cork thought he would.'

'What does he want?'

'That's a long story. But he means business. What's more, he's armed: or he was when he killed Snatcher.'

'Where's Mr. Cork?' asked Anna.

'I hope to God he's safely on his way to Edendale by this time. What I'm wondering is what we ought to do ourselves.'

'What you do is your own business,' said Anna. 'I'm going on to the Black Brae.'

She half rose to her feet, but Robert pulled her down fiercely.

'Stay where you are, you silly little idiot. Do you want to get yourself killed as well?'

'Let me go, damn you, let me go.'

'I won't let you go. He's not worth it.'

Robert threw a leg over her back and getting his hands on her shoulders pinned her firmly to the ground.

'You'll stay here,' he said, 'until we've seen what happens. I've had enough of you, young woman. From now on, whether you like it or not, I'm taking charge.'

Anna lay there sobbing as Kurt moved relentlessly along the river bank towards the Black Brae.

Mr. Cork and Madame Breuvart knelt together on the flat rock at the foot of the salmon leap peering into the rusty box which Daggers had dragged out of the river. It was a small box, covered with streamy green weed like dead man's hair. When they untwisted the wire which had been used to lash it up, the lid hinged open stiffly. Inside, bedded in rust, discoloured by contact with the water, was the tarnished treasure of the Black Brae.

Mr. Cork stirred up the stuff in the palm of his hand; pearls rotted off the string, rings with empty claws, gold trinkets sticky with green stuff, discoloured stones, broken bracelets, blackened crosses, coronets and pendants; a porridge of jewels and precious metals in a cheap tin box half-filled with stale river water.

Mr. Cork turned it over idly. Idly, he wondered to himself what the premium would be to insure it. Then he remembered the price which so many people had paid for the jewels' possession. He forced down the lid of the box.

'Well, are you satisfied now?' he asked the Frenchwoman. 'What are you going to tell the police?'

'About you? There's nothing to tell. You didn't shoot.'

'He deserved to die.'

'I suppose he did. It depends whether or not one believes in vengeance.'

'Don't you?'

'I can never make up my mind. Just now, I wanted to save his life. But, if I were in your shoes, I might have felt differently. Tell me,' he said, tapping the box, 'how did these things find their way to a village on the French coast?'

'I don't know. Somebody was caught trying to smuggle them overseas in a fishing boat. He was shot. Others were shot, too. When the Commandos raided Avranches, they had them in the District Commandant's house. Johnnie and Daggers broke in, and got them. Fleischmann was one of the few they didn't kill.'

'Who was Fleischmann?'

'Kurt.'

'And who was the man who was killed in the car? The one you recognized?'

'He was another who was in our village.'

'A German soldier?'

'He came later, after the raid. He was sent to find out if we were hiding any of the British.'

'But he didn't find Johnnie. How did you manage it?'

'I hid him in a hay loft. They operated on him there by the light of pocket torches. When he was better, we disguised him as a Frenchman. We were married.'

'But you said he wasn't your husband?'

'We married only to deceive the Boches. He had a wife in England. But I loved him, Monsieur.'

'And, after the war, you stayed together?'

'We were very happy, so we kept our secret. Johnnie,

so far as England was concerned, was dead, killed in action. We had a farm and a cider orchard and some money in the bank. But he wasn't satisfied with that.'

'He wanted the Pongratz jewels?'

'He couldn't forget them. He was always talking of going to England, finding Daggers and collecting his share. I didn't want him to go. It was dangerous that anybody should recognize him again. But his mind was made up. And I yielded.

'He had a French name and a French passport. He dressed and talked like a Frenchman. It seemed so safe. Johnnie believed that Daggers had only left him behind because he was sure he was dead. "He will be pleased to see me again," he said.'

'How did he trace Daggers after all those years?'

'He had it all lined up. He said he would find him by making enquiries in the fishing shops.'

'How do you know all this? Did you see Johnnie after he saw Daggers?'

'He came home the first time. He said that Daggers had promised him his share and that we should both be rich. But we had to wait. He was to come to Scotland on June 28th.'

'When was the first visit?'

'February.'

'The same month that Daggers took out the insurance.'

'I don't understand,' said Madame Breuvart.

'It doesn't matter. What was Daggers' plan for Johnnie?'

'He was to visit London as a tourist, hire a car to drive himself, and come here to Edendale. Daggers made a map to show him the rendezvous.'

'Do you remember where it was?'

'It was here on the Black Brae, Monsieur.'

'And Johnnie told you about it. So, when he failed to come home, you wondered what had happened to him?'

'I came to London. I telephoned the hotel at Edendale to enquire for Gabriel Daggers. They told me he was drowned on June 28th in the river, the same day that Johnnie was to have met him. So I booked a room at the hotel and came here.'

'How did you confirm your suspicions?'

'It was you.'

'When you held me up with your pistol?'

'I was frightened. I didn't know who you were. You might have been Daggers himself.'

'You didn't look frightened. And your anxiety for Johnnie didn't prevent you fishing for the jewels.'

'I didn't want the jewels. I wanted to be sure that Johnnie told the truth. I thought perhaps it might be an invention and that Johnnie had gone back to his old wife again.'

'But you had seen Kurt in the hotel? Wasn't that evidence enough?'

'It warned me to be on my guard.'

'Do you think Kurt recognized you?'

'I don't know.'

'He's after these jewels, too.'

'Of course.'

'He may come back. I want you to help me hide this box again.'

'Where?'

'It doesn't matter, as long as we both know where it is.'

Kurt, bruised by his fall from the car, limped along painfully. He would have to settle later with that cowardly swine who had run out on him when he had the Pongratz jewels virtually in his pocket at last. The only course now was to get another car and make a race for it to the Continent before they got after him for the shooting. But, as he hobbled down the river bank, his leering optimism never quite deserted him. There was a chance, just a chance, that he might catch up with Cork again. He was already up to his neck in trouble and, if he could have the satisfaction of settling with him, the risk he took wouldn't be any greater than the mortal risk he faced already.

When he heard the sound of voices below the wall of rock which divided him from the river, his first thought was that it might be the police. His hand closed over the butt of his pistol and he strained his ears to hear what was being said. But the noise of the river submerged the sense of the conversation.

He advanced, step by step, until he arrived at the brink. Then he looked down on the kneeling figures of Madame Breuvart and Mr. Cork. Between them he saw the weedy box. Closed it might be but, with leaping spirits, he knew for a certainty what it contained.

In his exhilaration, he almost crowed with glee. Two white faces turned up in alarm. Kurt swung his pistol at them merrily.

'So you didn't know what had happened to the Pongratz jewels?' he jeered. 'You thought you had fooled Kurt. You hoped he was dead, like Daggers. But Kurt has come back.'

Mr. Cork got shakily to his feet. The Frenchwoman squatted back watching Kurt's twisted eyes; looking for a chance, if he would give one, to bring her own pistol to bear.

'Hand up that box,' said Kurt.

'So that you can shoot us without the risk of losing it?'

'You are wasting time.'

'No, I'm not. You've got a pistol in your hand and I don't doubt you have every intention of using it. But we've got the jewels. You can't shoot both of us at once. If you fire, we shall at least make sure that this box you want so badly goes with us into the river.'

As Mr. Cork made his last desperate throw, he saw that something was happening to Kurt. His mouth was opening in surprise and he was staring, like a man who sees a ghost, at Mr. Cork's feet. As his attention wandered, Madame Breuvart seized the advantage she had waited for. Her hand dropped and she fired from her coat pocket.

The shot was wide, and it was also unnecessary. Kurt, with his deathly grin, suddenly turned away and stumbled excitedly downstream, hunting the water with his pointed pistol.

He had indeed seen a ghost. While Mr. Cork was talking two hands rose out of the river. Closing on the box, they lifted the Pongratz jewels back into the Black Brae.

When Daggers leapt, he recognized that he was taking a desperate chance. No swimmer, however powerful, could expect to hold his own in the angry turmoil of flood. But better the hope of survival in the river than standing on the bank, like a clay pipe set up in a shooting range, waiting for the killing shot. Besides, he knew the ways of the Edendale.

Jumping big to clear the sharp rocks, sticking up like broken teeth around the rim of the pool, he threw himself deliberately into the heaviest water; not merely because it was deeper, and therefore safer from the height he was falling, but because the strength of the current there offered a possible outlet for escape.

The main pressure of water, from the salmon leap at the

mouth of the Black Brae to the tail, followed a rough semi-circle formed by a deep cleft in the rock in the river-bed. The curve of the run extended in an arc from the top of the pool over to the opposite side of the river and then round again through a narrow gully which thrust the head of water directly into the bank. There the run exhausted itself in a deep and foamy hole under the rocks before it spilt over and thinned down in the shallow rapids below.

Daggers had the idea that if he could survive the battering of the current, keep a hold on his consciousness while he was tumbled through the gauntlet of the spate, he might recover control as he was swirled under the bank at the tail of the pool.

As he stiffened to meet the boiling cauldron of water, the breath was punched out of his lungs and the river wrapped round him like a thick brown blanket. Working his limbs fiercely, he fought to free himself from the smothering pressure that enclosed him. But the current tossed and rolled him and held him helpless in its cold embrace.

He felt himself dragged across the river. He winced with pain as he was bashed into the jaw of rocks on the opposite bank. Then he noticed the steadily increasing pressure as he was sucked underwater into the tail of the run. His consciousness was slipping fast when he felt his back rubbing gently against a flat plate of submerged rock. Forcing his legs to work, he kicked his way to the surface and breathed again. The current, pushing into his chest, pinned him to the safety of the bank. Not for the first time in his life, Daggers had achieved the nearly impossible.

Edging slowly out of the current, he worked his way upstream again into a V-shaped piece of slack water between the pull of the stream and the bank. He paddled until he could find a footing. Then, leaning against the mud with his head sticking out of a berg of yellow foam which had collected there, he rested and recollected himself.

They hadn't got him yet. By God, they hadn't. Even Johnnie couldn't do what he had done. Johnnie was tough but, when it came to a choice, he wouldn't face the Black Brae. So Johnnie died. But not Gabriel Daggers. The river, cruel as it was, was his friend. Those people standing on the bank had the evidence of their own eyes now that he was drowned. When everything seemed lost, he had almost achieved his purpose again.

Who could have guessed that Johnnie, with so much to hide, would have blabbed to a woman? And yet, what Johnnie had done was no more than he had done himself. He, too, had allowed himself to be bewitched and betrayed. Anna was responsible for all this. Whatever she argued, she was responsible. He could never forget that.

But, for the moment, he had to think of himself. He couldn't stay where he was. He was beginning to feel cold and stiff and it was essential to get on the move again. He wondered whether he should risk floating down the river under the bank to the burn of Baile an Or, and making his way into the hills from there. He rejected the plan as impracticable. The pull of the current, with the river in flood, would almost certainly sweep him into the Devil's Staircase; and, once there, he hadn't a chance. His best hope was to cross the river through the rapids to the opposite bank. It would be difficult and he had to take the chance that he might be seen. But, if they believed he was drowned, they wouldn't be looking for him. It was much more probable that they'd be making for the road in search of assistance. When the hue and cry was over, he could come back for the jewels.

He had become so confident in his ownership of the Pongratz jewels that, in the struggle for his own survival, he had forgotten for the moment that he had left the box on the edge of the river. As he recalled what had happened, the hammering started again in his head. The adrenalin pumped into his bloodstream, and he was gripped with a crazy urge to recover what he had so nearly lost. He couldn't give up the Pongratz jewels. Without them, he might just as well drown. With them, the world was his whipping-top.

Clawing the muddy bank with his fingers, hauling himself through the current with slimy armholds on the rocks, he worked his way laboriously upstream again. Avoiding the main thrust of the current, he was able now to control his movement in the deep water which eddied and pooled under the bank. The undertow dragged him dangerously. But, after years of fishing the river, he knew every hold and every snag. He found a footing on underwater shelves and a grip round the boulders.

Deafened by the sound of the waterfall, his ears blocked with water, he couldn't hear what was happening on the bank. Neither could he find a change of foothold to enable him to raise his head. The best he could do was to run his fingers enquiringly over the plate of rock above him. Almost at once, he touched the box. Raising both his hands he pulled it down with him into the river.

There, like a hunted otter in his holt, he waited. He heard the shot which he was sure was meant for him. Then, hugging the box, he let go of the bank and allowed himself to be tumbled down the river again.

He was feeling for bottom. When he touched it, the current was so fierce that, at first, he was unable to control himself. But the river, as it widened into the rapids, thinned down till the larger boulders stuck out of the water. Daggers snagged himself, like a piece of broken timber, in the triangular throat of a run.

Clutching the Pongratz jewels to his naked ribs, he pushed himself clear and, fighting for a footing, plunged across stream to the next rocky haven. The boulders slipped under his feet. The sharp-edged stones brought him down. But, bruised and cut and breathless, he stumbled on.

Halfway across, the river deepened and he was carried again by the current. For a time, with one arm wound round the jewels, he could make no progress. But a salmon, disturbed in its lie, gave a plunging splash within a few feet of him. The sudden explosion in the water inspired him to renewed effort. It was enough to get him across. His feet found a foothold in the bottom again and, tearing his nails on the rocks, he gripped at the tangle of roots in the bank and pulled himself clear of the water.

Kurt, standing on the opposite side of the river, shot Daggers in the back at the moment he exposed himself. The bullet hit him in the right shoulder. His arm dropped uselessly and, as he slipped back into the river, the box with the Pongratz jewels rolled out of his nerveless grasp. It bounced on the clay bank. Bursting open, a rainbow shower of bright stones and coloured metals tumbled like gravel into the white turmoil of the river. The box floated for a moment. Then it turned over and sank a few yards beyond the place where Daggers was lying slumped in the water.

Kurt fired at him again and then again. But the impact of the water turned the bullets. At last, when he pulled the trigger, the pistol in his hand gave a useless click. He loaded another clip of cartridges but, when he looked for Daggers again, he was no longer in the same place. It was Kurt's turn to cross the river.

If he thought of Mr. Cork and the Frenchwoman he gave no sign of it. He went straight to the hanging bridge. As he swayed across the river, Mr. Cork put his hand on Madame Breuvart's wrist and pushed the muzzle of her own pistol into the ground.

'Not now,' he said.

Crouching under the cover of the rocks, they watched Kurt limping down the other side of the river towards the place where Daggers had disappeared. They watched so anxiously that they didn't notice that, behind them, Anna, with Robert at her side, was also running towards the Black Brae.

While the bullets whipped the water all around him, Daggers lay still. As soon as the shooting stopped, he wriggled clear of the bank and allowed himself to bump inertly downstream. He was numb with cold and the dripping red hole in his shoulder pulled him down. But the stream was sluggish under the clay bank and he was checked in his downward drift by a dam of debris which had gathered in a hollow undermined in the bank. With his good arm, he dragged himself half clear of the water. There he lay, shivering with cold and weakness, and watching with his beady eyes the racing brown river.

He was trying, even now, to focus the opposition. He had had one momentary glimpse of his new opponent as the bullet struck him. There was something about the man that was vaguely familiar. But he couldn't place him. It was so difficult to remember things when his body was chilled and his shoulder so excruciatingly painful. He felt he ought to remember, but his mind was fogged and bewildered. It seemed that there was no end to the list of his enemies. But he would show them. Wounded as he was, he'd beat them yet.

Stirring himself stiffly in the water, he looked upstream. He sighted Kurt crossing the bridge. So that was it. They were coming hunting for him. He strained his ears over the sound of the river for a movement or a vibration on the grass bank above his head.

Staunching the blood from the wound in his shoulder with his cheek, biting his lip with pain, he hoped against hope they wouldn't keep him waiting too long. And, at last, he discerned the sound he was listening for. Somebody was hunting the ground above him.

Grasping a root for a handle, he drew up his legs and dug his heels into the soft clay below water. Next, pressing his back into the bank, he straightened his legs until he was standing in a crouching position under the shelf of the river wall. He waited for a moment, listening. Then, satisfied from the vibration that the enquiring footsteps had halted immediately over his head, he made a half turn of his shoulders and twisted his left arm over the ledge of the bank. Uncoiling himself, he sprang upwards.

Kurt was standing, as Daggers had calculated, immediately above him on the brink of the grass bank. He had estimated accurately where Daggers was hiding. But he was unable to spot him over the top of the overhanging edge. Daggers' attack, when it came, completely surprised him.

He rose out of the river like an apparition. His naked torso was discoloured by the clay and rubbish he had collected worming his way up the bank. The blood from his shoulder streaked down his ribs. He was marked with the red weals and bruises of his battering in the river. His black hair hung about him like water-weed and there was an inhuman glint in his eyes.

His left hand closed round Kurt's ankle like a steel trap and, with a violent muscular effort, he gave a twist of his wrist which tumbled Kurt into the water with him. Kurt, with a pistol in his hand, never had the ghost of a chance to use it. He dropped the pistol while, making an arc in the air, he instinctively opened his hands to meet the water.

Daggers never released the grip on his ankle. He held him as if he was tailing a fish while Kurt floundered and plunged downstream of him in the pull of the current. But it couldn't last long. There was a light of triumph in Daggers' eyes, and a look of recognition, too, as he identified his opponent: but the strain was telling on him. Kurt was a big man, fourteen stone at least to Daggers' eleven. Kurt was fresh and unwounded and, when he recovered from the first surprise of attack and the shock of immersion, Daggers couldn't prevent him from twisting on to his back and pulling himself towards the cover of the bank. As he did so, Kurt kicked fiercely. Daggers, for all his fanatical resolve, could hold on no longer.

He released his grip and reeled backwards. But, while Kurt was still struggling for a footing in the mud, Daggers let himself go with the current. Closing with him again, he wrapped his arm round his opponent's neck. Kurt tried to hold him off with a short arm punch to the groin, but Daggers was dragging on his neck like a dead weight and the tuft of weeds which was all Kurt could find to grab hold of, started to break away from the bank. He was slipping.

As he made a last effort to free himself, the two of them were carried clear of the side, out into the river and into the rush of rough water. As Kurt went under, with Daggers like a human anchor on his neck, he felt for his knife. Dragging it from his pocket, he managed to tear it open. Then, desperately, he plunged it again and again into Daggers' body. He could feel him moving under the repeated blows, but the strangling grip never yielded. He felt his lungs tightening and a thunderous noise in his ears. Then, suddenly, the awful grip slackened and slid away from his neck.

Kurt struggled to the surface to find himself in a race of white-flecked, mist-covered water. He saw the broken rocks ahead, but was powerless to protect his body from the repeated blows or the whip-lash of the current as it tossed him through a narrow gully of rock, down a staircase of boiling falls, lined with granite spikes. He was unconscious before his body rolled into the last of the rock-pans of the Devil's Staircase and over the brink into the waterfall of the Manse Pool.

There, the drowned body of Kurt rested, held loosely under the hang of the fall and viewed suspiciously by the salmon, waiting in ragged ranks for their turn to battle upstream on the last stages of their journey from the sea.

Gabriel Daggers was dying. But, mortally wounded as he was, he was still fighting for survival. The force of the current had warned him that they were being carried into the neck of the murderous race that funnelled into the Manse Pool. Releasing his armhold, he had kicked himself to the surface and, as he was carried downstream, he hugged one of the pyramids of rock that stood like sentries at the gates of a watery Hades. There he hung, marooned in the troubled water, his life blood seeping with the current down to the sea.

Anna saw him first. With a sudden cry, she stood still on the bank pointing at the dark head and the white sinewy arm clutching the rock above the white water leading to the fall.

'Gabriel!' she shouted.

Daggers gave no sign of consciousness. Then the head moved and a look of imploring recognition came into his eyes. His arm, wrapped round the rock, began to slip. At the same moment, Anna, standing upstream of him, slipped over the edge of the bank and plunged into the river.

'Hold on,' she shouted. 'I'm coming.'

With a ghastly grin, Daggers saw what was happening. His hold tightened and, somehow, he checked himself from slipping further.

Anna was making it. The current was carrying her down but her limbs were working at sprint speed and she moved in a steady diagonal across the river. She grabbed the rock on which Daggers was hanging and threw her other arm around his neck. But she couldn't hold him. He had made his final effort. As his arm slipped clear, he managed to close his hand in hers.

From the bank, they watched her hold his weight for a second or two. Then they saw a look of terror on her face. She was losing her own hold on the rock and Daggers was pulling her down with him.

Madame Breuvart ran downstream and, throwing herself on to her face, reached out to catch hold of her as she swept past. Mr. Cork shouted at Robert across the river. The only chance was to pray she might survive the Devil's Staircase and that they could intercept her lower down.

Wrenching off his coat, Robert raced downstream. He had a momentary glimpse of Anna in the gully. Then he slid down on his back to the point where the Devil's

Staircase joined the Manse Pool. He went straight on into the water at the edge of the fall, hardly knowing what he was doing, but trusting wildly in fortune. The water at the edge was fairly quiet. His feet settled firmly on the bottom in not more than four feet of water. If he could grab Anna as she was carried through, there was a chance he could hold her.

He saw her, still struggling in Daggers' death grip, as the two bodies came to the hang of the fall. As they toppled over, Robert leant forward and seized her arm. The pull was too fierce. He went with them into the deep water, but he kept his hold on Anna. Ignoring where the current was taking them, he worked about until he found the dead man's hand in hers. He forced open the fingers. And, as his lungs were bursting, he felt her drifting free. But he could do no more.

He came to lying on his back, with Montague Cork leaning over him, watching him with solemn eyes. He blinked.

'Is Anna all right?' he said.

'Madame Breuvart is giving her first aid now. She says she'll be all right.'

'Did you have much trouble getting us out?'

'No, you both drifted inshore where we were able to drag you out quite easily. But it was a near thing, Robert.'

'Is that bastard Daggers really dead at last?'

'I think so, God help him.'

'Then everything's O.K.?'

'Yes, Robert. It's all over.'

Robert smiled.

'Looks as if we'll have to pay that insurance after all, sir.'

Then he felt himself going to sleep again.

Fifteen

THE date was Saturday, July 30th, eight days after Daggers' death, thirty days after the procurator-fiscal had officially noted the recovery of his body from the Black Brae. As that bewildered official remarked, when he attended the Estuary Hotel to conduct his later enquiries into the startling series of fatalities at Edendale: in the case of Daggers, the man was now undeniably deceased and, fortunately it was therefore only necessary to alter the dates on the existing records. And he passed on, wearily, to review the evidence in the cases of the four other people who had perished violently between approximately the 28th ult. and the 26th inst. in the vicinity of the pool known as the Black Brae.

Representatives of the Allied Control Commission in Germany concerned with the recovery of the Pongratz jewels; motor engineers required to give expert evidence and to superintend the recovery of Mr. Cork's Bentley; officials of the Anchor Office in Edinburgh; the press, the police, the lawyers and the specialists all converged on Edendale and gathered, like wasps round a jampot, in Mr. Mackenzie's Estuary Hotel. They slept two and three to a bedroom, they dossed on sofas, and parked themselves out on every croft and cottage where there was an iron bedstead to spare. The single track road up the glen was never free of cars, reversing and manœuvring to pass each other on the journey between Edendale and the outside world. The bracken round the Black Brae was trodden flat by an invasion of experts with cameras and tape measures, and all the scientific paraphernalia of a modern police enquiry. Mr. Mackenzie, at the hotel, had never coined so much money and the inhabitants of Edendale, watching all the comings and goings from the bridge, were so diverted that there was no salmon-poaching in the district for almost an entire week.

Anna was taken away to the cottage hospital at Dornoch. Robert, after forty-eight hours in bed, insisted that he was fit again and stood by his boss during the ordeal of making statements and answering questions. Madame Breuvart, faithfully protected by Mr. Cork, returned to France. Fred Bowley was picked up by the police on the road to London. And, at last, the official enquiries were concluded.

The last page of evidence had been taken. The swarm of officials and journalists had dispersed with the remaining bottles of Mr. Mackenzie's special quota of whisky safely tucked away under their belts. And, finally, as if to restore an atmosphere of homely reality to Edendale, after the macabre adventure of the Black Brae, Mrs. Montague Cork had arrived unexpectedly from London, with another car and fresh supplies of clean warm underclothes, to resume charge of her devoted husband.

Secretly pleased though he was, Mr. Cork pretended that Phoebe had no business to come to Edendale. But Phoebe told him firmly not to talk a lot of nonsense. She had read what had been going on in the papers. It was evident that Mr. Cork, never mind Anna and Robert, hadn't been properly looked after.

With the intuition of thirty years of married life, she told her husband that he had been smoking more than was good for him, drinking things which didn't agree with him, and failing to take proper care of his health. Mr. Cork demurred happily.

Phoebe put flowers in the bare sitting-room; saw to it that the hotel staff put hot water bottles into damp beds; pottered off to Dornoch to make sure that Anna was well looked after; brought up Dr. McCluskie to the hotel to treat Robert; found out where Mr. Mackenzie could get fresh vegetables for the hotel in place of the usual diet of mashed swedes; and became the friend and confidante of everybody from Jock, the hall porter, to Lt.-Colonel Adrian de Crecy Johnson. Plump and affectionate, everybody liked Phoebe.

It was Colonel Johnson's suggestion that, before they went south again, Mr. Montague Cork should take a day's fishing on the headwater loch. The river which, as a consequence of the cloudburst, had been a torrent only a week before, had now dwindled, as quickly as it rose, to a sluggish trickle. The water was thin. The stones on the bottom were green with flannelweed. And the fish, said Johnson, were too sick to look at a fly. There was no chance of a salmon from the river until a freshet brought it into ply again. But Colonel Johnson was optimistic of the chances in the loch. The spate of a week ago, he calculated, must have brought a lot of new fish up the river into the headwater. And, when he put his head out of Mr. Cork's sitting-room window immediately after breakfast on the morning of July 30th, he gave it as his opinion that the wind and weather conditions were satisfactory.

Mr. Cork, reading *The Times* of three days earlier, said

that he didn't like loch-fishing. He objected to sitting in a rowing-boat all day. And his own experience of loch-fishing was that it was either so glassy calm that it was a waste of time to fish because the salmon could see you as plainly as if they were looking through a mirror, or alternatively, it was so damned windy that, when you tried to cast a fly, the line whipped back in your face and you were lucky if the hook didn't jerk your ear off. Mr. Cork told Colonel Johnson that he wouldn't go to the loch. He'd wait for his fishing, he said, until he arrived on Speyside for the remaining period of his holiday.

But it emerged that Phoebe had already had the picnic-basket packed; that Robert had been sent to get the car out of the garage; and that, without consultation with Mr. Cork, everything had been organized for the trip up the river. Mr. Cork, realizing that he was the victim of one of Phoebe's conspiracies, gathered together his fishing tackle and did as Phoebe disposed. Anyhow, it was a change for Robert.

'Why can't I go and see her?' he asked Mr. Cork, as he drove the new American car up the moorland road to the loch.

'Keep your mind on the driving, Robert,' said Mr. Cork.

'Doesn't Anna want to see me?'

'Anna's been very ill, Robert,' said Phoebe.

'What's that got to do with it?'

'Everything,' said Phoebe.

'I can't see it.'

'Listen,' Mr. Cork intervened. 'Take the advice of an old man. I think it's very improbable that a famous and beautiful ballerina, chased as she must be by half the eligible young men in London, is likely to be interested in a feckless and penniless insurance clerk.'

'She fell for Daggers,' said Robert sullenly.

'Yes, and in consequence she's had a very horrible experience. That's another reason why you should keep out of the way.'

'Leave her alone for just a little while,' said Phoebe, patting Robert's shoulder. 'Wait till she asks to see you.'

'Suppose she never does?'

'If that happens, she's not worth worrying about,' said Phoebe firmly.

'Anyhow,' said Mr. Cork, 'what you should be thinking about is your job.'

Robert felt more depressed than ever. But he thought it seemed the moment to be intelligent, if he could, about the insurance business.

'Will we have to pay out on Daggers' life insurance? You can't get away from it that he's dead now.'

'It's highly questionable, Shipley, that the underwriters can be called upon to pay a claim on an insurance policy which it can be proved was taken out with the intention to defraud, even though the insured's intentions worked out differently from the way he expected. As a matter of public policy, it would be improper that people should benefit, even indirectly, from a piece of villainy. And, if the matter went to arbitration, it's my conviction that the Law Lords would find in our favour. But the matter won't go to arbitration.'

'You mean because Anna doesn't want the money?'

'So she says. But we'll have to pay out something on this.'

'To Anna?'

'No, Robert, to you.'

'What do you mean, sir?'

'He's going to give you a lump sum as a reward for

239

what you've done towards clearing up this business,' said Phoebe.

'I was about to say, before Phoebe butted in, that it is my intention to recommend to my fellow directors . . .'

'Oh, shut up, Monty,' said Phoebe. 'Robert understands.'

'I want to say, sir . . .' said Robert, struggling to express himself, 'I want to say . . .'

'Say it another time,' said Mr. Cork. 'You know where you are. This is the hairpin bend we're coming to before the bridge over the burn. We're back on the Black Brae.'

The memory of what had happened along that stretch of landscape was too poignant and too real for comment. Mr. Cork realized that, in his inner thoughts, the real reason he hadn't wanted to go to the loch was because he didn't want to look on the Black Brae again. Phoebe, sensitive to her husband's mood, asked no questions. But Robert, exhilarated by Mr. Cork's promise, was stirred with curiosity as he looked again at the desolate place where they had all lived so violently, and come so very near to death.

'Looking back on it all,' Robert said, 'one thing I still can't understand is how Daggers managed to kill his man and make his getaway as he did.'

'It was only possible,' said Mr. Cork, 'because Daggers was so confident that, having once got his victim here, he would be undisturbed. We know, from our own experience how deserted this glen is.'

'But what happened?' said Robert.

'Nobody will ever know exactly,' said Mr. Cork, 'but it must have happened something like this. When Johnnie got here, by arrangement, in a hired car, Daggers was waiting for him. He gave his victim a friendly welcome and led him down to the Black Brae. Once there, Daggers got behind him, which wouldn't have been difficult because the man was unsuspecting, and brained him with a blow, probably with his metal gaff.

'After that, Daggers stripped off his victim's clothes and his own. He dressed the murdered man in his own gear and, hauling him into the water, spiked his body on the poacher's hooks at the bottom of the pool. Remember, he was a powerful swimmer and the water at that time, according to Johnson's diary, was low; nearly as low as it is now.

'Once he'd got rid of the body, Daggers put on his victim's clothes and had a last look round to make sure that no incriminating evidence was left behind. He found his rod which, after stripping off line to suggest that he'd been drowned playing a fish, he plunged into the bottom of the pool. Next, he had to get rid of his fishing bag. The fishing bag was lightly weighted and he couldn't make it sink. So, finally, he loaded it with stones to make sure it remained on the bottom. As we know, the weighting of the fishing bag was one of Daggers' mistakes.

'Once he'd changed his clothes and got rid of the body, the remainder of his plan was easily carried out. He'd already provided that they wouldn't miss him at the hotel. He simply climbed into his victim's car and drove it back to London.'

'What happened to the car?'

'It was returned to the hirers in the ordinary way. And, of course, they suspected nothing. From their viewpoint, there was nothing to suspect. The car was properly used, paid for and returned.'

'What about the mysterious figure that Colonel Johnson saw, or thought he saw, when he found the body? Was that Daggers?'

'We shall never know who that was for certain. It must have been either Daggers or Snatcher. Presumably, Daggers wanted to make sure that the plan had succeeded.'

'And it very nearly did, didn't it?' said Robert. 'The wonder is that he was ever caught.'

'Not really,' Mr. Cork went on. 'Admittedly, it was bad luck for him that Madame Breuvart got on to his track. He couldn't have anticipated that. But the weakness in his whole plan was that he couldn't bring himself to part with Anna. It was the will, and the insurance policy, that distressed Anna into talking and, in consequence put us on the scent. Even then, Daggers might have fooled us but for the fact that he was drawn back to the Black Brae. They say that a murderer always returns to the scene of his crime. It was true of Daggers all right. And by that time, a pack of wolves were on his trail. He was doomed from that moment when he couldn't resist having one last look at Anna in the theatre. It was characteristic of his particular form of arrogant insanity. If he couldn't resist that, how much less could he resist the temptation to follow Anna to Edendale and to keep an eye on his precious jewels.'

'In some ways, he was an attractive devil, wasn't he?'

'You noticed that?'

'He was a good fighter.'

'Daggers, like you too, Robert, was one of the products of a world war. In you, war confirmed your good qualities. In Daggers, it had the opposite effect. He found out that he was more courageous, more ruthless, more cunning in battle than the men around him. He rejoiced in the dangers of war and the lawlessness of it. The chance that put the Pongratz jewels in his possession was, for Daggers, the unhappiest chance of all. It confirmed him in his opinion of himself. With the spiritual superiority he believed he had, he now had the material advantage over his fellows too. He dedicated himself to the possession of material power: the Pongratz jewels and, yes, poor Anna too, because I'm certain that, in Daggers' mind, Anna was identified as nothing more nor less than a piece of beautiful jewellery. She was something he owned, like the Pongratz jewels. And he meant to keep both.

'When the German gang threatened possession of the jewels, and Johnnie, whom he thought dead, turned up to collect his share, Daggers got the idea of disappearing; of throwing one lot of dangerous enemies off his track by substituting the body of another in the Black Brae. And, while he was doing that, he planned to hold Anna against the future by taking out an insurance on his life.'

'That was his real mistake,' said Phoebe. 'When he did that, he brought you into it, dear.'

Mr. Cork looked over his shoulder at Phoebe, sitting in the back of the car, and smiled.

'What have we got for lunch?' he said.

Mr. Cork was lazily fishing the deep waters of the loch. The wind, gently ruffling the surface, as Colonel Johnson had promised, was blowing up the glen from Edendale. Robert, amidships in the rowing-boat, leant on the oars, controlling the drift. Phoebe sat in the bow, quietly knitting. Mr. Cork, perched on a revolving stool in the stern, cast his fly and allowed the confection of feathers to twist and glitter invitingly a few inches under the surface of the water. After each cast, he pulled in line through the rings, working the fly through the water and back towards the boat.

Mr. Cork had little faith in the chuck-and-change-it conditions of lake fishing. He could never believe that there was much hope of a salmon finding his tiny fly in such a vast expanse of open water. He knew the salmon were there. Most of the fish that came up the river Edendale spawned in the gravel beds of the loch. But it was so much easier finding them in the river. In loch-fishing, you never knew where the fish were lodged.

Nevertheless, Mr. Cork didn't mind very much to-day whether he caught a fish or not. Phoebe was with him. There was a good lunch waiting under the stern seat— bound to be good if Phoebe had organized it—and the loch was in a serene and lovely mood.

The loch was situated in a narrow basin on a plateau at the top of the glen. At the tail of it, sluice gates contained the headwater and controlled the flow into the river. At the neck, the sheet of water thinned to a point, like a silver arrow-head aimed towards the blood red heart of the hills beyond.

The banks of the loch were lined with rushes, where moorhens bobbed and the mallard quacked their orders to well-disciplined convoys of flappers. In the shallows, a group of shaggy-haired Highland cattle stood knee-deep in the water and, chewing the cud, looked at the rowing-boat with the indifference of content. Overhead, a kestrel hovered. Far away, at the other end of the loch, a salmon made a tempting splash as he leapt clear out of the loch.

Mr. Cork looked across at the fish hopefully. As a consequence, he failed to notice the fish rising, at that moment, to his own fly. Phoebe saw the swirl in the water and gave a startled exclamation. But Mr. Cork knew nothing about it until his rod jumped madly to life in his hands. The fish, as it turned down with the fly in its jaws, had hooked itself. Mr. Cork raised his rod point just in time to give his reel a free run for the first rush.

'He's a whacker,' he said excitedly.

'Now keep quite calm, Monty dear,' said Phoebe evenly. 'You haven't got him yet.'

'Of course I haven't got him,' said Mr. Cork cantankerously. 'Don't be silly, Phoebe. I'm simply saying he's a whacker. Quick, Robert, row like hell. He's coming back to us.'

Mr. Cork raced his reel to take up the slack which the fish had given in his second rush. Robert, pulling at the boat, tried to draw away from the fish.

'I'm afraid he's underneath us, Mr. Cork. Take it slowly.'

As Mr. Cork wound in the last of the slack, and felt again for his fish, the line scraped the bottom of the boat.

'I'll keep on rowing backwards,' said Robert. 'And don't nag at him. If we're careful, he might lie doggo.'

'Don't give me orders, Robert. I can manage the fish all right. Row, man, row.'

'Now don't get over-excited, Monty. You know what you are. You're impatient.'

'Of course I'm impatient,' said Mr. Cork. 'So would you be. If I didn't get excited, I wouldn't come fishing.'

The boat was now clear of the line and Mr. Cork increased the play of the rod. The line started to move in the water.

'He's off again,' shouted Mr. Cork.

But he needn't have spoken. The reel whizzed in his hand and the line was carried off across the loch. Mr. Cork saw with apprehension that the reel had run out to the backing.

'He's making for the reeds,' said Robert. 'If he gets in there, we've had it.'

'If you'd only keep on rowing, Robert, and stop talking, we might turn him. Look, he's turning now.'

'Oh, heaven,' said Mr. Cork, winding madly at his reel, 'this excitement's killing me.'

The mad chase round the loch went on till Mr. Cork's arms were aching and Robert was sweating with his efforts to keep the heavy old boat moving with the fish. But, at last, under the steady pressure of Mr. Cork's powerful split-cane rod, the salmon was answering the turn of the reel. As Mr. Cork slowly wound in, the fish permitted himself to be led quietly by the nose.

'Now's the time you must be careful, Monty.'

'I know that, Phoebe. Let me fish my own fish. And don't flourish your knitting about. That's just the sort of thing that upsets a salmon.'

'Look out,' said Robert. 'Here he comes.'

Mr. Cork brought the fish within ten feet of the boat. The top of the gut cast showed out of the water. And they all leaned over to get a first look at him. But the salmon who, up till now, had fought dourly under the surface, decided to show himself. At the disturbing spectacle of the black shadow of the boat so near him the water, he made a rush for the surface and, with a lash of his tail, jumped clear out of the water. Whether Mr. Cork dropped his rod point in sheer surprise at the size of the fish, or whether his angler's instinct stood him in good stead at that unforgiving moment in his fishing career, is a question which he himself has never settled. Whenever he retells the story, which is very often, he claims that he saw the jump coming.

It's true that if the salmon had been able to lay his full weight on the slender gut cast, Mr. Cork would have broken immediately. But, to Mr. Cork's lasting credit, it is also true that Mr. Cork wasn't broken. When the salmon made his next rush, he was still firmly hooked.

Before the fish jumped, Mr. Cork had been in a state of uncontrolled excitement. When he actually saw the girth of it and the length of it, he could no longer speak. He just gulped and, with an intensity which brought the sweat to his brow, he hung on to his rod.

'I think he'll be ready for the gaff soon,' said Robert. 'Do you want me to take him?'

Mr. Cork could only nod.

The fish was now swirling round in tired circles in front of the boat. They could see him quite plainly and he was having difficulty in keeping an even keel. Robert drew out the telescopic gaff and leant with it over the side of the boat, watching. Once he thought the fish was near enough to make the killing stroke. But, at the sight of Robert's white face hanging over the side of the boat, the salmon, game fighter that he was, made another rush. But it was nearly his last effort. Rolling on his side on the surface the great fish floated in towards the boat. Robert, in his anxiety, made an unsteady stroke with the gaff. The fish gave a plunging roll and, for one unspeakable moment, it looked as if he was away. But Mr. Cork still had him on. In grim silence, he brought the fish to the boat again and, easing the pressure on the rod, let him slip towards Robert. There was no doubt this time. He laid the gaff over the thick of the great hog-back and, with a steady lift, heaved the fish into the boat.

Phoebe clapped her hands and cried for joy. Robert grinned inanely. Mr. Cork, with glassy eye and trembling limbs, collapsed into the bottom of the boat and felt in his hip pocket for a Passing Cloud. He lit the cigarette shakily. Then he sat on his stool filling his eyes with the salmon of his lifetime and of most other fishermen's lifetimes too.

'Let's get him ashore,' he said at last. 'I shan't be able to relax until we've got him ashore.'

Robert rowed the boat to the bank with long and powerful strokes. The bow hit the jetty with a satisfactory thump. Phoebe and Mr. Cork stepped ashore. And then, reverently, Robert brought in the great fish and laid it on the turf.

'Have we got the scale with us?' he asked Phoebe.

'It only goes up to fifty pounds,' said Phoebe.

'It can't be more than fifty pounds,' said Mr. Cork in a whisper.

Robert took the brass scale and hung the salmon on the hook. With a sharp jolt, the button was pulled to the maximum. They all looked at it with wondering eyes.

'He's a good deal more than fifty pounds,' said Robert. 'We shall have to wait till we get back to the hotel to weigh him properly.'

But Mr. Cork wasn't listening. He was looking at the salmon.

'There's only one salmon in the river as big as that one,' he said. 'Do you realize what we've done? We've killed old Johnson's fish.'

Appendix

MONOGRAPH BY LT.-COL. ADRIAN DE CRECY JOHNSON (RTD.) ON A SPECIMEN FISH WITH SOME ADDITIONAL NOTES ON THE LIFE CYCLE OF THE ATLANTIC SALMON:

THE most notable fish of the season 1949, which was otherwise uneventful, on the River Edendale, Sutherland, N.B., was the capture by Mr. Montague Cork, a visiting angler, of a cock-fish of 57 lb. 3 oz. Taken by fair fishing, on a Hardy-tied No. 7 L.W. Blue Charm, this is the biggest fish which has been killed on the Edendale within living memory and probably the best summer fish taken in the British Isles for many years. Every angler will wish to extend his hearty congratulations to Mr. Cork. Every angler too will wish to learn the fullest and most accurate details; the more so, in view of certain misleading rumours which have gained currency as a consequence of the inevitable public interest in this remarkable catch.

Mr. Montague Cork has entrusted to the author of this paper, an angler with some thirty years experience on the Edendale, the responsibility for putting forward facts which, both from an ichthyological and angling viewpoint, command the most careful consideration.

It is well known that the salmon which normally run up from the sea in our northernmost rivers during the summer are mostly of small size; in a total of 2,972 fish to the author's own rod in 29 seasons, the average for the Edendale is 5 lb. 7½ oz. A fish of 20 lb. after the spring run, is exceptional; a fish of 57 lb. is without precedent on the Edendale although, from time to time, late summer fish in excess of 50 lb. have been taken in favoured rivers such as the Wye, the Aberdeenshire Dee and Tweed. It is credibly reported that, several years ago, a cock-fish of 61 lb. was taken in the nets off the Kincardine coast. But a fish of 50 lb., or over, anywhere in the British Isles, is a rarity.

The capture of this notable specimen on the Edendale raises, once again, the urgent necessity of setting up a scientific commission, with full Government backing, to solve that strange aspect of salmon behaviour known as 'divided return'; to enquire into ways and means of improving the condition of our salmon rivers; and to analyse the possibilities of developing the supply of the most valuable source of food in our inland waters.

It is characteristic of the cult of the mediocre, which is such a regrettable feature of our times, that, while science has spared neither money nor energy in studying the social behaviour of the Common Eel, the noblest fish that inhabits our rivers has been officially disregarded and its life habit studied scarcely at all. Of the mysterious sea-existence of the salmon, ichthyologists have scarcely any information. The science of scale-reading, the exact method by which we are now able to calculate the life cycle of individual fish, dates broadly from the work which was undertaken, at the beginning of the century, to interpret the scales not of the salmon but of the almost inedible Cod.

To the reader, who may be unfamiliar with modern methods of scale-reading, suffice it to say that, under the microscope, any single scale from a salmon reveals a system of ridges, not unlike the markings which are revealed in the severed trunk of a tree: ridges which, to an expert, disclose the growth-rate and various other particulars of the fish's career.

As a consequence of the scale-readings, undertaken by the author of this paper, it may be stated with accuracy that the 57 lb. 3 oz. fish, taken by Mr. Montague Cork in the head-water loch at Edendale on Saturday, July 30th, was hatched from the egg in the early spring of 1942. The close core of rings in the centre of the scale, marking the period of the fish's life cycle when growth was slowest, shows that this fish passed three years in the river in the phase from alevin, to parr, to smolt.

The alevin, it may be necessary to explain, is the name given to the infant salmon during the fifty days after hatching when it subsists on its umbilical sack. The parr-life of the fish extends from the fry stage through the two to four years when it feeds in the river, living much in the manner of a small trout, and having a trout-like appearance. Finally, the term smolt is used to describe the young salmon of between four and a half and six inches in length, when the fish puts on its silver going-away dress and shoals into the sea.

What happens during the sea life of the salmon—where it journeys to, what it feeds on, and what determines the varying periods of time before different fish feel the instinctive urge to return to the river of their birth—is still a mystery. It is presumably unnecessary to remind the reader that not the least remarkable fact about the salmon is that the fish normally returns to spawn from its sojourn in the sea to the actual river, and perhaps to the actual gravel bed, where it was incubated from the egg. But the principle of 'divided returns,' which arouses so much discussion among ichthyologists, is perhaps, less widely recognized. The subject is of special interest in a paper concerned, as it is, with the consideration of a specimen fish.

When the smolts, in their silver sea-dress, leave the fresh water for the salt, they are approximately of level size. When they return to the river to spawn, the size of the adult fish is determined partly by the quality of the diet on the ocean feeding-banks, but mostly, by the length of time which the fish have remained at sea. Once in fresh water again, the adult salmon fasts and it survives during the months in fresh water on its reserves of fat. Why, in a period when the fish is starving itself, it takes the angler's fly is another interesting and controversial question, but one which is not the concern of this particular paper.

The salmon feed in the sea for a period varying from a year—in exceptional cases, even less than a year—to four years or even five. A fish that returns to fresh water to spawn after little more than a year in the sea, is commonly known as a grilse and weighs between 2 lbs. and 10 lbs. Fish which remain at sea longer than a year before the first spawning are described as salmon or 'fish' and may weigh anything from 10 lbs. to

60 lbs. according to the length of their absence. The scale readings of the 57 lb. fish, caught this year on the Edendale, indicate that he went to sea in the summer of 1945 and returned to the river on approximately July 1st, 1949. For a reason, which is still unexplained, this particular fish chose to remain in the salt, and he was longer coming to sexual maturity than the majority of his species. He also returned to fresh-water at a time of year which is favoured by the smaller fish who have remained a shorter period in the ocean.

Generally speaking, there are three main runs of salmon each season which vary in importance and month from river to river. The spring run, which begins as early as January, brings up the larger fish. From June to August, the smaller fish, including the grilse, arrive with what is called the summer run. Finally, there is also a lesser run in the autumn of both small and large fish. It may therefore be concluded that the 57 lb. salmon, taken from the loch at Edendale, was an exceptionally early-running late summer or autumn fish.

Various theories are put forward to account for the mystery of 'divided return' which results in the very considerable variation in size between salmon. One theory, which the author is unable to subscribe to, is that like breeds like; that the progeny of a grilse, for example, are, like the parents, one-year-at-sea fish. But that theory makes no allowance for the fact that salmon, of different sea-ages, commonly mate to-gether. Another theory is that the salmon's period at sea may be determined by the accident of the distance that the fish has to travel in its search for feeding-banks, or in the pursuit of the herring which, it is suspected, plays an important part of the salmon's sea diet. Whichever theory is correct, the system of 'divided returns' is nature's remarkable provision for the preservation of the salmon species.

Since the spawning urge of any one generation of salmon is spread over seasons and years, the survival of the family is assured. If the grilse in the spring run of one particular season are destroyed by the perils of the sea or the river is so low that they sicken and die and fail to reach the spawning beds, other shoals of fish of the same year's hatching are waiting to replace them in the following months and years.

The natural provision is all the more necessary because the majority of salmon never recover from the exhaustion of their first spawning. In the spring, the pincer-jawed slimy and sluggish fish, known as kelts, which have spent themselves during the winter, try to work their way down the river back to the sea. But the proportion of salmon after spawning, as we know from the jagged absorption lines which show in the scale-readings, which survive to come back to the river again as 'mended fish' is very small indeed. The 57 lb. fish, taken in the Edendale this season, was a maiden.

The scale readings of this specimen fish indicate that, after three years as a parr, there was no check in development. We may therefore assume that, during four years' sea life, this fish enjoyed exceptional feeding conditions. The cast, presented to the author by Mr. Montague Cork, is of a magnificent cock salmon, deep in the girth, heavy in the shoulder, and only slightly coloured by four weeks in the river. The colouration, which is the spawning dress of the salmon, increases the longer the fish remains in fresh water. A clean-run fish, with the sea lice on him, is usually bright silver in coat. Later, the silver of the cock fish changes to an iridescent pink or purple. Finally, the pink on the flanks darkens to dirty red; in the case of the females to a muddy-black and yellow. But, fortunately, this cock fish was taken before he was seriously tarnished, and before he had suffered any appreciable loss of weight.

The reader will have noted that the writer states authoritatively that this fish entered the Estuary at Edendale, as nearly as may be calculated, on July 1st. In the interests of piscatorial history, it is now necessary to correct certain misapprehensions which appear to have been popularly accepted and which are as painful to Mr. Montague Cork as they are defamatory to the author of this paper.

The approximate date of the fish's arrival in the river can be attested personally by the writer because as early as Monday, July 4th, he laid first claim to the fish's capture by hooking it himself eleven miles upstream from the Estuary in the run below the Manse Pool in the Edendale known locally as 'The Aisle.'

The infamous suggestion that the author of this paper is

mistaken in claiming that this was the identical fish afterwards killed by Mr. Cork, containing as it does the implication that the aforementioned may be lacking in experience as an angler and in sportsmanship as a gentleman, is a slander which is both monstrous and unfounded.

It may be stated categorically that the fish which the author hooked in The Aisle on July 4th and the fish which Mr. Cork hooked in the Loch on July 30th was the same. It is clear that, in the welcome spate following the cloudburst on the night of July 25th, after a long period of abnormally low water, the fish was able to clear the leap at the Black Brae and make the ascent to the spawning-beds in the headwater where he was subsequently taken. But, apart from the known habit of salmon and the undeniable fact that no fish as large as this one had been seen in the Edendale in the life of the oldest inhabitant, it can be proved by independent witnesses that the writer immediately identified Mr. Cork's fish the moment he saw it, by the betraying scar of a seal bite on its shoulder.

It happened that when the writer first saw the fish on the stone slab where it had been laid out for examination in the hall of the Estuary Hotel, Edendale, the seal-mark was hidden. On being asked whether, in his expert opinion, this was the same fish which had been previously hooked, the writer immediately referred to the seal mark which he had particularly observed when he was playing the fish the first time and of which he had recorded a note in his fishing diary. When the salmon was turned over, in the presence of half-a-dozen independent witnesses, the seal mark was revealed in the exact position indicated. It is to be sincerely hoped that this statement of the true facts will put an end to further dispute and discourage idle gossip which has been occasioned, no doubt, largely in consequence of an unhealthy public interest in matters which are outside the scope of a piscatorial paper.

Touching strictly on a piscatorial note it is proper to affirm that, but for an obstacle which snagged the writer's line at a moment when the salmon was perceptibly tiring, the writer himself would certainly have killed the fish on the first encounter. In that event, it might have scaled nearer 58 lb. than 57 lb., it then being so soon after the fish had ceased feeding in the sea. It must further be admitted that Mr. Montague Cork, unlike the author, had the good fortune to hook this great fish in open water at a time when he was accompanied by a person able to use a gaff. Obviously, these circumstances materially assisted Mr. Cork's chances; but that, in no way detracts from his skill as an angler or diminishes the good wishes of the undersigned.

Adrian de C. Johnson (Lt.-Col., Rtd.)

Littlemead,
  Salop.

About the Author

Macdonald Hastings
(1909–1982)

Every bit as adventurous as his counterpart Montague Cork, author Macdonald Hastings loved fishing and hunting, owned famously uncontrollable hunting dogs, and once had himself cast upon a desert island for six weeks with just a knife and some fishing gear to prove that he could survive. He did, just barely.

Renown British journalist, broadcaster, and writer Hastings became well-known to American audiences during World War II, when he broadcast the "London Letter" weekly for the American service of the BBC. In later years he visited the United States regularly to write and make television programs. His Cork series was translated into six languages and filmed for British television.